WHAT READERS
ARE SAYING

"Jam-packed with titillating romance and thrilling suspense, *Unraveled* will leave you hot and bothered and begging for more."
—Jane Alvey Harris, author of the My Myth Trilogy

"K.D. Polk spins a compelling story of love and love gone wrong, as a girl with a troubled past tries to navigate an uncertain future."
—*USA Today* bestselling author of *I Do (But I Don't)*, Cara Lockwood

ALSO BY K.D. POLK

The Candle Wick Series

Unraveled

Untangled (coming soon)

UNRAVELED

THE CANDLE WICK SERIES
BOOK 1

K.D. POLK

Davis Lane Publishing

ACKNOWLEDGMENTS

To the most amazing editor on the planet—Cara Lockwood. Thank you for the years of advice and support. You've championed me the whole way!

To those select friends who read the first and second and third drafts—thank you for your feedback and taking a sincere interest in my work.

To my sister—for an author there always seem to be plenty of words to express an idea or an emotion, to convey thoughts or gratitude. For me, there are no words. You are everything.

CHAPTER ONE

I can't stop thinking. I have one of those brains that never shuts off. Even when I'm dead tired from a long-ass day at work and have gotten groceries, picked up the dry cleaning, and cooked myself dinner, when I lay down in bed, my brain keeps going. I think about all the things I didn't have time to do and all the things I should have done but forgot.

My brain ran into overdrive as I walked down Madison Avenue on my way to work. I thought about how this November seemed colder than usual. The air felt too still and frozen like it could break and shatter like glass. Steam billowed up from potholes like frosty geysers. Even with hundreds of people crowding and surging through the streets of New York, a stillness lingered. I was distracted by the cold and my overstuffed briefcase, which dug into my shoulder, making it ache. I held my cell phone in one hand and balanced a coffee and bagel in the other.

My brain was always churning with thoughts and I was a pretty good multitasker. I could think of all kinds of things at once and still pay attention to what was in front of me. For some reason, however, this particular November day, I was blindsided by a fire hydrant. By blindsided, I mean I bumped my knee into the metal rim—hard, and went tumbling onto the sidewalk. My coffee flew from my hand and my briefcase spilled open like a gutted fish. Pages and pages of paper floated through the air like errant snowflakes and into the wet gutters of New York. And as is the typical behavior of

Yanks, no one stopped to help. I rubbed my knee through my torn pantyhose and raised to all fours. I scrambled up the papers nearest to me, cussing the whole while, and stuffed them unceremoniously back into my briefcase. The lid of my coffee had fallen off and my bagel landed next to the curb like a discarded tire.

"Shit!" I swore in frustration as my knee began to throb.

"That sucks," some annoying passerby commented, but he didn't stop to help—he only offered his unnecessary and thoroughly irritating remark and kept moving. It was going to be one of *those* days.

I reached for the last of my papers and my dignity. And that's when I suddenly stopped short. I saw his hands first. They were unusually large and masculine with short, well-manicured nails. His knuckles were red with cold but his skin was smooth and tanned. They were the kind of hands that begged to be held, caressed. His veins pulsed with their lifeblood, a roadmap of soft lines and beats. They clenched with strength as they were placed on my upper arms and he lifted me almost effortlessly to my feet.

"I hope you didn't want that coffee."

Oh good. A comedian. I mashed my hair back as I stood, trying to collect myself as best I could and raised my eyes to funny guy. I opened my mouth to give a witty retort but the air seemed to get stuck in my throat.

"Are you all right? You took a nasty fall. I saw you from across the street."

The fact that he'd risked life and limb dodging yellow cabs and impatient commuters to get to me struck me in the gut. Or maybe it was the color in his eyes. One eye was brown while the other was hazel, each framed under thick dark lashes. I was immediately taken and I froze like I'd fallen under some sort of hypnotic trance where suddenly time and space seemed to no longer exist. I was bound. I realized my mouth was gaping open, the frozen air clouding in front of me as I took quick, heated breaths.

"I'm fine. Thank you," I said in a clipped tone. It sounded much shorter than I'd intended. I was suddenly very embarrassed over my clumsiness.

"Your knee is bleeding." He pointed and knelt in front of me. Those strong hands brushed the area around my cut. One hand held me steady on the back of the knee. The other made tiny circles with the thumb around the rip in my hose. "It doesn't look too bad but you'll need to put something on it," he said, rising to his full height. He loomed over me.

"Thank you," I breathed, almost inaudibly. *What was wrong with me?*

The man fished three dollars out of his jeans back pocket and turned, scurrying to a coffee cart half a block away. I stood there watching him as people rushed by me, bumping into me and cursing under their breath as I impeded the flow of foot traffic on the sidewalk. I was rooted to the earth like gravity as I watched him purchase something and begin walking toward me. He came back and handed me a steaming cup of coffee. I took it awkwardly, my cold-numbed fingers fumbling with a sudden lack of fine motor skills.

"I put in two sugars and a cream. I don't know how you take it. I hope your day gets better."

He tugged the high collar of his black pea coat around his neck and swiftly jogged to the other side of the street. My eyes followed him and he gave a polite wave when he reached the other side. Still in a slight daze, I was scarcely mindful enough to raise my coffee cup in his direction and acknowledge his kindness. He disappeared into the throng of New Yorkers and I finally gathered my wits about me. I did a quick search of the ground to make sure I'd collected all my wayward papers and continued down Madison. I carefully sipped the piping hot coffee. It was perfect—only because he'd made it, I was sure.

Fortunately, I was only a block and a half away from my office at Design 22 because my knee really begin to hurt. It seemed to have a rhythm and pulse all its own. By the time I reached the fifteen-foot glass front door of the studio, I practically hobbled in. I pushed on the glass and the door swiveled open as I shuffled in. A half-moon shaped, steel desk, bordered with large silver rivets, sat in the center of the lobby and I smiled at the receptionist sitting there.

Rebekah had her headset on and she returned the smile as I approached her.

"Good morning, Becks," I offered with much more cheerfulness than I felt.

"Morning, Sloane. You're bleeding. You okay?"

I winced as I remembered the pain. "Yep. Thanks."

I'd barely rounded the other side of the glass partition that separated the lobby from the rest of the offices before I ran into my coworker, Tucker. He frowned at me.

"You look like shit, Sloane," he began.

I sighed. "Thanks, Tuck. And good morning to you, too."

Tucker Stevenson draped a lazy arm around my shoulders. "I only meant that you are perfection every day but today you look a little… worse for wear, shall we say?"

"I tripped over a fire hydrant and scraped my knee."

Tucker's full mouth made the shape of an "O" as he grimaced. "Ouch. Let me see."

He followed me into my office and sat me down in an armchair in my small lounge area. He dropped to his knees and surveyed the damage. "That's a pretty decent cut. It's still bleeding. I'll find some antiseptic and bandages. Better take these off." He pulled at my pantyhose.

I thought I heard a bit of flirtation in his voice as he made his last remark, but I obeyed as he strolled out. Limping over to my desk, I sank into my office chair, unzipped my ankle boots and kicked them off. I shrugged out of my coat and hung it on the back of the chair. Carefully, rolling down my pantyhose, I tossed the ruined nylons in the trash. As I waited for Tucker to return, I checked my voicemail and booted up my computer. I had several emails that needed my immediate attention and an impatient sounding voicemail from one of my major clients, Dallas Braithwaite. But then Dallas always sounded impatient and a little frantic. Everything was a matter of urgency with him—even things that were clearly not. But he spent hundreds of thousands of dollars every year with Design 22 and it was part of my job as a fashion buyer to keep him placated. I reached for my phone but returned it to the cradle as Tucker walked in. He knelt in front of me again.

"Exactly how does one trip over a hydrant again?" he teased.

I rolled my eyes. "I wasn't watching where I was going. My briefcase exploded onto the street."

"And I bet no one stopped to help."

I bit my lower lip as colorful hazel and brown eyes flashed before me. "Actually, a very nice man stopped."

Tucker stretched my leg out and dabbed the cut with a cotton ball doused in alcohol. I winced.

"Sorry. You're lucky you don't need stitches." He rubbed the back of my leg with his other hand. His hand glided slowly underneath my pencil skirt and gripped my thigh. I gasped in surprise but not shock.

"Are you looking for something?" I asked wryly.

"Have I ever told you what incredible legs you have?"

I looked down into his handsome face. He was almost too handsome—like something out of a high end fashion magazine or straight off a runway. His square jaw gave way to a prominent cleft chin, a determined pink mouth, a straight nose and high, chiseled cheekbones. His dark green eyes bore holes straight through me and he flashed that wicked smile I knew all too well.

"Yes. I believe I've heard that before."

Tucker threw away the bloody cotton ball and retrieved another clean one. He held it firmly against my cut. "Do you ever miss what we had?"

I blinked rapidly. "Sometimes. But I'm with Reid now so…"

"Ah yes," he started as if he didn't remember I was dating him. "How is Reid?"

"We're great," I lied.

"Great. Now back to you and me."

I laughed at his arrogance and blatant disrespect for my relationship.

"Seriously. We had a good thing going on."

When the gauze was securely fastened, I stood and walked around to the other side of my desk. "We had sex going on. Not a relationship."

"Exactly. A *good* thing going on."

I flushed brightly as I reluctantly began to reminisce about the way Tucker's hands felt on my skin, his smell, and his undeniable skill in the bedroom.

"The color in your cheeks makes me think you remember, too," he said, strolling over to me.

"I also remember you inviting Stewart into the bedroom with us."

Tucker bit his lower lip enticingly and I actually felt my stomach clench. He was so devastatingly attractive and sexy I could hardly stand it at times.

"I seem to recall you didn't mind that either."

I blushed again as I remembered our threesome. "But it's not something I wanted to get used to. I need monogamy, not a bisexual lover. That was a one-time thing. Why are we even talking about this? You and I agreed that the sex thing was over and we'd be friends with no weirdness between us. And this conversation is getting weird."

He held up his hands. "You're right. It's just that sometimes when I'm close to you like this—," He leaned in to me, "—I have a hard time resisting you. But I'll mind my manners."

"Thank you. And thanks for taking care of my knee."

"Maybe you and Reid can join Stewart and me for dinner some time," he suggested casually.

I laughed. "Most awkward dinner party ever."

Tucker shrugged his broad shoulders. "Consider it. I'll see you later."

He sauntered out of the room, his perfectly cut black suit hugging his wide shoulders and his well-tailored pants showing off a tight ass and muscular legs. He was every woman's dream—including mine occasionally.

I closed my eyes briefly and tried to erase my memory of Tucker's seductive everything. But even his scent lingered in the air—that masculine smell of heat and soap and virility. It was intoxicating.

I walked back around to my chair, picked up my handset again, and replayed Dallas' message before I returned his call. I pulled up the corresponding spreadsheets on my computer because I knew he'd ask me for them and dialed his number. He answered, his voice laced with the same hint of irritation that seemed to always be there. *Was this guy ever pleased with anything?*

"Good morning, Dallas. I got your message."

"Where are the numbers for this month?" he barked.

I rolled my eyes again. He knew I was on top of it—I always was. He was frustrating on so many levels.

"I emailed you the inventory numbers last week but I've just sent them again. I'm reworking the figures on the budget and I'll get those to you within the hour and once you've approved it, I'll make the final purchasing decision and send the catalog to you as well for approval. Anything else?"

His satisfied grunt was enough for me and I smirked. It would be too much to expect a thank you.

"I've got big news," he started.

I sat back in my chair and rolled a pen absently between my fingers. "Do tell."

"I've decided to open another store. Upper East Side is doing so well I thought it wise to move forward with expanding."

It was great news for me—and more work. "That's terrific. Have you decided on a location?"

"My realtor is out now scouting locations in Chelsea, but I think I've decided on the space I want."

I grinned. "Prime real estate. Frenzy should do well there."

"That's exactly what I was thinking. I want you to handle that store, too, when we get up and running. You in?"

"Completely."

"Excellent. I'll let you know when we've decided on a final location. If you don't mind, I'd like to have you come out and look at the property."

"I'd love to. Let me know when."

"I'm close to a decision. It could be as soon as tomorrow. I'll be in touch."

Dallas hung up the phone and I couldn't hide the smile on my face. I was the fashion buyer for Dallas' first boutique store, Frenzy, and it was doing remarkably well. So well that he was going to open another store and wanted me to purchase the collection. I was singlehandedly in charge of deciding what to buy for his men and women's clothing line, including accessories and shoes. It was a dream job for me. I'd always loved fashion and being in this industry was more than I could have ever hoped for. Not only did I get to look at beautiful clothes all day but the success or failure of a store was completely on my shoulders. I loved the challenge that presented and knowing Frenzy was doing well because of decisions I'd made, amazed and excited me. Another store meant more business for me and more revenue for Design 22.

Design 22 was made up of the most creative and talented people I'd ever met. We had designers, financial wizards, and sketch artists. There were seamstresses and business consultants, buyers and realtors. Our small company was a haven of brilliant people who possessed a myriad of abilities. It was like working in a hospital full of the brightest neurosurgeons and cardiothoracic physicians; the walls of Design 22 held the finest the fashion industry had to offer. We sewed and mended, designed, fashioned and clothed the patrons of New York City. The garments sketched and sewn in our building clad thousands of people in the city; they were walking billboards proudly displaying months of our hard work. We not only represented Frenzy but three dozen other boutique stores and were on the verge of landing a huge department store deal.

Our company was growing leaps and bounds because of an unmatched, talented, synergetic crew of individuals. To know I was a part of this team filled me with pride. Three years ago, we started with only twenty-two employees and now we'd grown to forty people. Our staff was big enough to get the job done and yet, small enough that they felt more like family than coworkers. It was that familial cohesiveness that led me to Tucker.

I was taken with him almost immediately. He was more than just attractive. He was talented and imaginative. He sketched numerous clothing designs for men and women that many of our clients flocked to and with good reason. His clothing was well made, fashionable, bright, and moderately priced. Tucker was constantly watching the ever-changing styles and keeping his finger on the pulse of new trends. He had a knack, an instinct that can't be taught. It was in his blood and I fell for his intuitiveness and ingenuity. Hard. I understood clothes. I had an eye for this business, but I'd also learned a great deal working with Tucker over the past three years. Our love of fabrics and patterns and textiles brought us together in a way many other people wouldn't understand. It was the love of creating we had so heavily in common. I was in awe of his vision. He was my male counterpart, my other half in this crazy fashion world. He kept my world from tilting and spinning out of control. He kept *me*, at times, from spinning out of control.

When Tucker first approached me romantically two years ago, I was flattered. Every single woman in our office wanted a piece of him. He was our eye candy, our breathtakingly beautiful relief when the day got to be too much or we were exhausted from work. And I was *more* than attracted to him. He carried himself in a way that made me instantly want to follow. He took charge, commanded attention in a room, wore his confidence like this season's winter coat. After a few weeks of steamy flirtation I found myself in his home, in his life, in his bed. We were good together. Really good together. But after about twelve months, he and I came to an end. I didn't mind that Tuck was bisexual until it interfered in *our* relationship. In retrospect, I was an idiot to think his bisexuality wouldn't be a factor. I was a serial monogamist. I'd seen my mother bed one too many men who weren't my father and I swore I'd never be like her. Her extramarital affairs scarred me, broke our family, and I vowed never to come second to anyone or anything.

Tucker and I managed to remain friends for which I was grateful. I couldn't imagine working here without him—without being able to tap into his creative mind and watch his wheels spin as he designed the next big thing. His artistry was captivating and I wanted to be a part of his rise to the top.

Outside of Tuck's talent, he was also fun to be around. He was easy to get along with and I looked forward to seeing him at work every day. Our current relationship ran on amicability and mutual respect. He was one of my closest friends.

My computer dinged, alerting me to a new email, and shook me out of my extended daydream. Tucker's scent had nearly left the room now, only a hint of him remained. It was still just enough to make me bite my lower lip in former longing for one of his kisses. I couldn't deny my attraction to him. I knew we'd never work—we were better as friends. Besides, I was dating Reid now and he and I were happy. Sort of. We could probably be happier if I'd just...

I couldn't think about it anymore. I had work to do. I checked my emails and began to calculate the new figures to send to Dallas.

CHAPTER TWO

"I knew it was a mistake giving you a key," I moaned as I walked into my brownstone on East 68th Street later that day. I kicked off my ankle boots, took off my coat, and placed it on the nearby coat rack.

My younger brother sat up from the couch, a crumpled bag of potato chips resting on his stomach. The TV was blaring and he flashed me his winning smile, which always seemed to dissipate my frustrations.

"What happened to your leg?" he asked.

"Fire hydrant."

He nodded as if it were an everyday occurrence.

"Did you have a good day? Help design yet more clothes for the elite and upper class?"

I pushed him on the shoulder playfully. "You may want to try this thing called work like I do. I have no doubt you'd find it quite rewarding."

Dane hit the remote on the TV and it blinked off. "I have a job as a full time student."

I rolled my eyes. "And two stupid roommates who let you live rent free."

"Jane and Hilary are not stupid. I can't help they've fallen under the spell that is me. Besides, I contribute to the household in other ways."

I made a gagging sound. "I don't want to know. What are you

doing here anyway?"

"One of my professors was sick today. No class. I thought I'd come and visit you before I went home."

"And eat up all my food?" I asked, reaching for the empty chip bag. "How kind of you."

Dane laughed and again my irritation lightened. He'd had the same effect on me since we were kids. His laugh and smile brightened up my most dreary days. I wasn't particularly having a dreary day, I didn't think, but I did feel a bit off.

"Janie and Hil don't like to keep beer in the house, but you're always stocked."

"How are your classes going?"

"Really well. I think I may have a knack for this stuff after all."

I rolled my eyes again and plopped down on the couch next to him. "Of course you do. You wouldn't have been accepted to Columbia if you weren't an amazing artist. Your portfolio was incredible. They're lucky to have you."

"I'll overlook your sibling biases and assume you're right. Did you ever think we'd be here? Me, a student at Columbia, and you, a graduate of Pratt? Considering the home we came from?"

I bit the inside of my cheek, an annoying habit I had whenever *home* was mentioned or anything associated with it. "We're survivors. And we're talented. We worked hard for everything we have. Some harder than others." I kidded.

Dane stood and stretched his tall, lanky frame. His army green T-shirt pulled across his flat chest. "Once I graduate and have my paintings at the Met, you'll eat your words."

"I look forward to the day, little brother."

"Speaking of home, what's the plan for Thanksgiving?"

"Do we *have* plans?"

"I assume Dad will want us to come visit. Have you talked to Mom?"

I brushed chip crumbs off the couch. "Why would I? And will you vacuum your mess before you leave?"

"Sure, sure. Mom's not doing so great. Just wanted to know if you'd talked to her."

"Nope. And I don't plan on it. Listen, Reid's coming over for dinner tonight. I've got to figure out what to cook."

Dane grabbed his black leather jacket from the back of the couch and tugged it on. "You two still going strong?"

"We're still going. *Strong* remains to be seen."

"You're not sabotaging another good relationship are you?"

I narrowed my eyes at him. He was always so quick to assume I was getting ready to detonate my life at any given moment. "No, I'm not. Reid is great. He's perfect in fact."

"Then what's the problem SloMax?"

"I hate that nickname and you know it. Nothing's wrong. And if there is, I'm sure it's me and not him."

"Oh, I don't doubt that." He smirked, zipping his jacket. He tied a gray and white scarf loosely around his neck. He looked like a young model off the cover of Seventeen. He was handsome and lean with penetrating green eyes and a curly mop of brown hair. He had that sexy tousled hair women love. It was annoying to walk down the street with him and see teenagers nearly swoon to death over his youthful good looks.

"You should really consider talking to someone about your mother issues," he continued. "I'll even go with you if you want."

"If I need counseling, *you* need it just as badly. We grew up in the same dysfunction. However, that has nothing to do with me and Reid. We're just feeling our way through things. Now, if you'll kindly make your way toward the front door…"

"I actually have been thinking about talking to someone," he admitted quietly.

I glanced at him and his lips were pressed into a serious, thin line. He wasn't kidding. "Really?"

He nodded. "I think it would do me good. Both of us good. You'll think about it?"

"Sure," I lied again. I didn't want to think about our family history anymore.

"And about Mom—you really should reach out to her. I've done my time. It's your turn."

Dane leaned in and kissed my cheek before he opened the door.

"Hey, what about the vacuuming?" I hollered.

"Next time, sis. Promise. Love you."

I sighed and smiled reluctantly. "Love you, too."

I closed the door behind him and surveyed my home. He'd left two empty beer bottles on the glass coffee table, a half-eaten bag of gummy worms, and a can of spray cheese dripped in pasteurized yellow blobs onto crumbled crackers. I only kept junk food on hand for him. I shook my head, ran my hand through my bobbed hair and went to the kitchen to grab the trash can.

"Sloane Maxwell," Reid greeted me three hours later as he entered the brownstone.

Why did he feel it necessary to call me by my entire name? Maddening.

"Hi, Reid. Come in."

He kissed me briefly on the mouth as he passed me.

"Something smells terrific in here. Besides you, I mean."

I faked a smile. "I cooked salmon with steamed veggies and fixed a salad."

"Very healthy. I appreciate that."

Reid was a health nut and constantly worried about his physique. He was well put together, I had to admit. He worked out five days a week and I often appreciated his commitment to the gym. His stamina was definitely something I admired—in the gym and in bed. Compatibility in the bedroom had never been an issue.

He was also dazzling to behold. He had cobalt eyes that peered out from behind his rimless frames. I'd always been a sucker for men in glasses. His light brown hair was kept short and close cut and he always smelled delicious.

Reid owned a small accounting firm in the financial district. His father had given him the business when Reid turned twenty-one and he'd been at the helm ever since, turning the small firm into a flourishing business. A small part of me was bitter that Reid had practically walked into a career—had been handed a future when I'd had to work so hard and had to overcome so much. My parents didn't have a family business to turn over to me. Dane and I had both gone to work at the age of fifteen in order to have any kind of money and save for the things we wanted. I knew I was supposed to feel better about my achievements having earned them instead of having them handed to me. But it'd be nice to catch a break every once in a while.

"Hey, beautiful. What are you thinking about?" he interrupted.

I gave my head a quick toss, my eyebrow-length bangs swishing to the side. "Work."

"Did you have an interesting day?"

"Not particularly. But my work load is starting to pick up again. One of my clients is opening another store and he wants me to oversee it. I'll be working longer hours again."

Reid leaned back in his chair and crossed his arms over his chest. "Does that mean I'll see even less of you than I already do?"

"We have a couple of big deals on the table that are going to keep me pretty busy. I'm just giving you a heads up about what's coming down the pipes."

"You didn't answer the question."

I took two plates down from the frosted glass cabinet. "I'll purchase most of the same collection for the new store as the one in Manhattan. But I'll add some new pieces as well. And that means I'll be out researching the trends in Chelsea. So, yeah, I guess I'll be a bit busier than normal over the coming weeks."

"Can we talk about the elephant in the room?"

I looked around flippantly. "Is there one?"

He smirked. "Don't be coy. Something's been up with you lately and I'd like to know what it is."

I poured a light raspberry vinaigrette on the salad, gave it a quick toss, and dished some onto our plates. "I don't know what you mean."

"So you don't feel the distance between us? Have I done something to upset you?"

"Not at all."

"Then what is it, Sloane? Because for weeks now you've been giving me the cold shoulder and I don't know why. I thought you were just distracted because of work, but now I think it's more. Please talk to me."

The sincerity in his voice was almost enough to break me down. But truthfully, I didn't know what my problem was. I couldn't put a finger on my issues. What was I supposed to tell him? Secretly, I thought I was developing a severe case of commitment-phobia. Reid and I had been together six months. That was plenty of time to feel comfortable with someone, plenty of time to figure out common interests and dislikes. But things still felt off between us, stagnant. What I didn't know was, was it him or was it me?

I sneaked a bite of my broccoli cauliflower mix to buy myself some time. I chewed thoughtfully as I scooped up veggies into bowls and put salmon on our plates. I sat down at the table across from him and smiled. I even reached for his hand and I thought that was a nice touch.

"I'm sorry if you feel I've neglected you. I'm sorting through my own stuff and I don't mean to cut you out." I surprised myself by answering honestly.

"What stuff?" he pressed.

I shrugged. "I don't want to get into all of that." *Especially since I don't know what exactly those issues are,* I thought. "But I'll try and do better. I promise. I do care for you." And that was an honest answer, too.

He covered my hand with his and squeezed it tenderly. "Whatever you need from me I'm here for you. If you want to talk, if you don't want to talk, whatever. I'll be here. I want us to get to a better place. We have a good thing going."

That was the second time I'd heard that phrase today. "I appreciate that. Eat up."

"What are you doing for Thanksgiving?"

"Dane and I will probably go and see our dad. What about you?"

"Another typical Blackmore family event—complete with all the trimmings. Mom will cook tirelessly, my sisters will gush on and on about who they're dating this week, and me and my dad will plant ourselves in front of the TV watching the Giants."

I sighed wistfully. "Sounds perfect. Except for the Giants part. My dad and I are Cowboys fans."

He looked appalled. "You traitor! You were born and bred a New Yorker. You should be hanged for your treachery."

I laughed. "Don't hate the star, man. Don't hate the star."

Reid and I managed to have decent conversation over dinner. I listened to him discuss the plans for his firm, talk about redecorating his place, the flag football team he wanted to join, and his most recent conversations with his family. I blabbed on about my job and bragged about Dane's paintings and his boundless talent. When dinner was over, I was feeling better about the state of our relationship. We sat down on the couch with coffee and I was feeling much more optimistic. As I was growing comfortable in this new state of mild euphoria, it was no surprise his next words bowled me over and my euphoria wafted into the air and disappeared.

"I want to move in."

I felt like everything paused in that moment and I'd lost a few seconds of time. I rewound his comment in my head and tried to make sense of it.

"I know it's sudden," he continued, "but we've been dating for six months and I feel ready. I know things are not perfect between us now, but they could be. And I think if I moved in we could work on our issues together. Or you could move in with me if you want."

He was serious! He was actually serious!

"Reid, that's not a good idea. For so many reasons I can't even list them all."

"You're scared and I get that. But you don't have to be. Not with me."

I drank my coffee. The brew was overheating me. Or I was warming up from the inside out with anxiety and major reservations. I put my cup down. Maybe I wasn't a commitment phobe after all. Maybe Reid was just too clingy.

"I wouldn't even live with my own brother. I'm a loner in the most serious sense."

Reid smiled his dazzling white smile and his glasses reflected the pendant lights over the kitchen island. "And that's why you need me. Only *I* can help you through your perpetual loner phase. I've had many years of practice breaking people out of their shells and I welcome the idea of trying my technique on you."

I smiled back at him and then did what I do best. I cocked my head to the side feigning bashfulness—men find that charming. I blinked twice and leaned in next to him so he could inhale my scent—the one he loves so well. I licked my lips slowly and bit the lower one for only a second, just long enough to send color rushing to my mouth.

"I welcome the idea of your techniques, too," I teased and then his mouth was on mine.

His kiss was sweet at first and then quickly became hungry and insistent. I knew we'd no longer be discussing him moving in with me and the thousands of reasons it was a bad idea. Sex was a distraction to every man alive and I knew it. I exploited it—well. I abused the fact that they were led around by their balls, misused my wiles to thwart uncomfortable conversations and situations. It was so easy it seemed a shame not to use my talents. But Reid broke free prematurely, my spell on him lifted. I frowned.

"Promise me you'll think about it. Please. I know it could work. We'll *make* it work," he breathed against my neck.

I grabbed his face in between my hands and stared into his glorious blue eyes. "I will," I lied for the third time that day. "Now, no more talk please."

He grinned. "As you wish." He pushed his weight down on top of me, pressing me into the couch and there was no more discussion. Only the soft sighs and melodic moans of gratification.

My cell phone buzzed around my nightstand waking me from a satiated slumber and I glanced at the clock. It was nearly eleven. I picked up the phone and saw it was my dad was calling. I glanced over at Reid, still sleeping silently beside me, and tiptoed out of bed.

"Hello?" I whispered as I walked into the living room.

"Hi, angel. Did I wake you?" my dad's gruff voice asked.

I sat down on the couch in the dark and wrapped a throw blanket around my shoulders. "Yes. Are you okay?"

"I'm fine, honey. I was just thinking about you and thought I'd call. But if you're sleeping—" He trailed off.

I exhaled an expectant breath. "It's fine, Dad. I'm up."

"How are you?"

I smiled in the darkness. The light from a streetlamp outside slipped through the narrow slits in the blinds and cast fragmented shards of light across the wooden floors. I reached into the air and traced the light with my finger.

"I'm good. You're up late for an old man. You sure you're okay?"

My dad's chuckle rumbled deep in his throat. "Watch the old jokes. I'm starting to get sensitive about that. How's it going at work?"

"Really good. I've been busy but I'm loving every minute of it. How are you enjoying retirement?" A loud, drawn-out sigh sounded on the other end of the line and for some reason, it made me nervous.

"Retirement allows me too much time to think. But I've gotten to spend more time with your mom and that helps a lot. I miss you kids, though."

"We miss you, too."

"Have you talked to your brother?"

"Every day."

"Stupid question. How's he doing?"

"He's great. He's doing well in school and occasionally he actually looks for a job."

Dad laughed. "I'm glad you guys have each other in the city. It helps me sleep at night knowing you two are together watching out for one another."

"You could move back here, too, you know."

"What about your mother? I couldn't be that far from her."

"But we're your family," I argued childishly.

"Your mom is my family, too. You and Dane are grown with your own lives. Mom still needs me."

I desperately needed a change of subject. "We'll see you for Thanksgiving, right? Do you want me to bring anything?"

I could almost feel him shaking his head at me.

"Thanksgiving is the one holiday where I get to eat what I want all day long. So no, I don't want you bringing anything tofu related, nothing made with kale or sprouts or sprinkled with flaxseed. I'll also take a pass on your grass and wheat germ casserole this year."

I giggled. "It wouldn't hurt you to try something different every once in a while. And I didn't mean food. Florida is too far to travel with a casserole."

"Why don't you guys fly in on Tuesday or Wednesday and I'll pick you up at the airport? Mom won't be there—in case you were worried. The doctors won't give their consent. Not yet, anyway."

I gnawed on the inside of my cheek. "I've got an early day tomorrow, Dad."

"Of course, honey. I just wanted to check in. Sleep well. I love you."

"See you soon. Love you."

I disconnected the call and tossed my cell on the cushion beside me. Why did conversations with him always leave me feeling uneasy? I loved him; I thought my dad hung the moon—mostly, but his tireless dedication to my mother was exasperating. She didn't deserve that kind of devotion.

"Hey, Sloane. You okay?" Reid asked sleepily from behind me, leaning over the couch to kiss my cheek.

"Yep. My dad called. I didn't want to wake you."

"Is everything okay?"

I nodded.

"Then come back to bed. The sheets get cold without you beside me."

I grinned at that, took his outstretched hand, and let him lead me back to bed.

CHAPTER THREE

The next morning, I took a cab into Chelsea to meet Dallas and check out his new store front. Hailing a cab in the city is like being in a cage fight. You have to claw and shove, wrestle and grapple to be declared winner. Occasionally, you get knocked to the ground and the taxi departs with the last man standing. But I wouldn't have it any other way. I loved the energy, the force of nature that was New York. There's a perfect dynamism, an unending excitement and anticipation that something big could be just around the corner. The city was alive with possibility, primed for brilliance and potential. You could be anything you wanted in New York.

Dallas decided to move rather quickly on the location in Chelsea and he was meeting with his realtor to sign the papers. He'd asked me to tag along while he took care of the paperwork and give the place a once over. I was anxious to see the new store I'd be purchasing the new collection for and glad to be out of the office for an hour or so.

The day was bitterly cold, made even colder by the height of the buildings in the city towering over the earth and draping the sidewalk in grayness like a heavy cloth. Skyscrapers and apartment buildings choked out the sun and obstructed its warming rays. But when I glanced far up, there was a gorgeous patch of blue sky and cotton clouds reminding me the sun had not forsaken me. Although I couldn't feel its heat, I was aware of its existence and inexplicably I felt warmer.

I paced outside the empty store front and then walked up to the locked front door, cupping my hands and peering inside the desolate space. I could barely see through the windows, smudged with dirt and dust. What I did notice was how large the space was—easily twice as large as Dallas' first store. Broken ceiling tiles hung haphazardly exposing ducts and pink, fluffy insulation. Rubble covered the floors and built-in counters and wires shot out of the walls like electrical serpents, coiled and dangerous. I rubbed the arm of my coat across the glass door, dirtying my sleeve with a light film of dust, to get a better glimpse inside. I turned when I heard a car door slam behind me.

Dallas' glossy gray Volvo XC90 was at the curb and he exited, exuding authority. He was dressed for business in his suit and tie. His navy pants and blazer were familiar and I instantly recognized it as being a suit from the collection at Frenzy. Cut well, the suit hung masterfully, even on Dallas' short five-foot-seven frame. His navy and white tie had a sparkling gem fastened in the center. Had he asked me, I would have strongly encouraged him to forgo the tacky stud. But I was only his buyer, not his personal shopper.

A taller man exited from the passenger side dressed much more casually with no jacket or tie. He had a shock of red hair and a spattering of freckles across his nose.

"I can't believe you managed to get a parking space," I venerated.

"Morning, Sloane. This is my realtor, Lawrence Frost. Lawrence, Sloane."

I shook hands with Lawrence and he promptly handed me a hard hat. "You'll need this."

I took the hard yellow cap and turned it over in my hands distastefully. It clashed drastically with my outfit.

Dallas and Lawrence capped their heads with the protective gear and I reluctantly followed suit. I frowned at my reflection in the smudged glass of the store front. Lawrence took a key ring from his pocket and opened the front door.

Fusty, frigid air blasted us as we entered the store and I pulled the lapels of my baby pink, wool trench coat closer around my ears. I stepped over a broken tile and walked to the center of the large room. As I looked around, suddenly, I was seeing racks and racks of clothing. Shiny lights bounced off glossy floors and polished countertops and registers. The room smelled of perfume samples and designer shoes lined the back wall. Display arms held shimmering, dangling necklaces and oversized cocktail rings. I could easily envision the style of clothing that belonged in this store—something that captured the feel of the people in Chelsea. The space was perfect.

"I think this will do nicely." I shrugged nonchalantly, just in case Dallas was still in negotiations over the terms of the lease. I didn't want to tip his hand. "Is there a way to knock down the back partition to make space for fitting rooms?"

Lawrence nodded his fiery head. "Shouldn't be a problem." *He was a man of few words*, I thought absently.

"What's the square footage?" I wondered.

"Just under five thousand."

"There's still quite a bit of work that needs to happen before we get this place going," Dallas chimed in. "But the foot traffic around here and the proximity to the High Line and meatpacking district is unbeatable. I think Frenzy will be a welcome addition to the art galleries and restaurants in the area."

Dallas was obviously not concerned about revealing all his cards to Lawrence so I relaxed some. "I agree. I think this place is golden. You can do a lot in here and the front window is perfect for displays."

Dallas clasped his hands behind his back confidently and Lawrence had the unmistakable gleam of a promised commission check twinkling in his eyes. "I think we can knock through to add another window on the other side."

Lawrence nodded again. "I'll get the builders out here tomorrow if you're set."

"What's the tentative completion date?"

"Before Christmas, I'd guess. The builders will have a better idea when they come out and inspect."

"I want these electrical wires taken care of as soon as possible; they're a fire hazard," Dallas demanded. "And this wall…"

Dallas and Lawrence began walking the length of the room discussing Dallas' immediate concerns and other property lingo I didn't care to be a part of. I captured a few pictures of the space on my cell phone and took off my hard hat. I placed it on the counter and headed toward the door.

"Sloane? You leaving? I thought maybe I'd take you to grab some food. As a thank you for coming out."

That was decent of him. "No thanks, I have to get back to the office. But call me when everything's set and you're ready to go. I'm going to start work on some ideas I have for the store. Nice to meet you, Lawrence."

Lawrence bobbed his head in my general direction, evading any more laconic replies, and I gave a polite wave. I tucked my hands in my pocket and decided to take a leisurely stroll back toward the office instead of hailing a cab. Design 22 was roughly three miles away and I could walk back. I cherished the quiet time of solitary walks. Despite hundreds of people swarming the pavement, I could ignore the clamor of city life. I enjoyed the paradox of being alone and yet still surrounded by people. I could block out fire engine sirens and ambulances shrieking. I disregarded maladroit saxophone players on the street corner and the screeching tires of aggravated drivers. It took many years to learn to block out frenetic noises but I'd finally mastered it. It must have been something I'd learned in my youth—the ability to ignore the screams of yelling parents or dismiss the cries of a little brother. Yet another gift I possessed. The gift of blissful unawareness.

Abruptly, I decided not to walk back to work just yet but, instead, do some people watching in Chelsea. I walked a few blocks to a nearby coffee shop and entered—a warm, dark roast hitting the Spidey olfactory sense I had for coffee and whetting my taste buds for a cup of joe.

I chose a table by the giant, front glass window so I could stare outside and watch the people as they hustled by. I whipped out a pen and small notebook from my purse and jotted down the style of clothing people were wearing. This proved to be somewhat difficult because everyone was so bundled, but I took note of shoes, accessories and outerwear. *I can't believe I get paid to do this*, I thought with a grin before I was interrupted by a friendly waiter. I ordered a coffee and oatmeal and jotted down everything I saw from my glass fish bowl. It felt strangely voyeuristic and sneaky—like gawking through a key hole at your naked neighbors. But it helped me to get a feel, a true sense for what people were wearing. Chelsea was only a few miles from the Upper East Side, but there was a world of difference in this neighboring borough. The style was more hip and funky. Chelsea was the home of chunky jewelry and bold colors.

There was a vibrancy that hummed there—a street smart, vintage vibe that pulsated and throbbed with potency and life. Frenzy's collection would have to capture the essence of Chelsea—its whimsical spirit.

I flipped to a clean sheet of paper as a design for a shoe came to mind. I wasn't an artist like Dane by any means, but I could sketch just well enough to convey my ideas on paper. I would take my drawing back to Tuck and I knew he would appreciate my vision, improve upon it, and then craft some amazing shoe.

A pair of brown, Dalton wingtip lace-up Oxfords caught my attention outside the window. I recognized the shoe, not because I worked in fashion, but because I'd bought Dane the exact same pair. They'd cost me over four hundred dollars. But it was an incredible shoe. The man's back was to me and his dark jeans covered the beautifully detailed brogue perforations on the leather upper. A crime in itself. Those shoes were almost a work of art. As my eyes raised from his hem, the man turned and caught my gaze. I gulped in a huge gasp of air, sucking all the oxygen from the room. It was the brown-eyed/hazel-eyed man who'd bought me coffee yesterday. His brow creased as he realized he'd seen me before and then a half smile crept across his lips. I felt myself getting sucked in again. Drawn into another dimension where only he and I existed—some alternate universe where there were only hazel brown eyes. It was the most peculiar, significant feeling. But the connection was brusquely severed. I blinked and it was almost as if it hadn't happened. He was gone. Did I dream him? Was it my imagination? And if so, why was I conjuring up images of this stranger?

I wanted to ponder more over my apparition, but my phone blared from the confines of my purse and I answered distractedly.

"Sloane Maxwell. What are you up to?"

I groaned silently. "Hey, Reid. I'm doing some research for a client. What's up?"

"I wondered if you'd given our discussion last night any more thought."

"Not really. It's been less than twenty-four hours since you suggested it."

He laughed but it rang false in my ears. "Good point. I'm just anxious for your answer. When do you think you'll know?"

I already knew. "I told you I didn't think it was a good idea. I like living alone."

He sighed. "I really wish you'd give it some more thought. I know I'm right about this. I'm right about us. Trust me. I know what's good for you."

I frowned. "How would you know that?"

"Because I watch you. I notice everything you do and say. Isn't that what an attentive boyfriend does?"

Or a creepy one, I thought.

"I know what you need and I know what's good for you because what's good for you, is me."

Thankfully, my phone beeped, alerting me to the call waiting. I glanced at the number. It was a Florida area code.

"My other line is ringing. We'll talk later?"

"Sure, babe. I'll call you tonight."

Terrific. "Okay."

I hung up and clicked over.

"Miss Maxwell? This is Lucy from St. Mary's Medical Center," she purred over the line. She sounded more like a nighttime sex operator than a nurse.

"Yes?"

"The credit card we have on file for you for your mother's monthly care didn't process. Is there another card we can use?"

I grumbled. I'd completely forgotten to call them. "My wallet was stolen last month and I cancelled all my cards. I guess I forgot to call you and give you the new number."

"That's quite all right. I'll be more than happy to take it from you now."

I bet you would, I thought sorely. Another eighteen hundred of my hard earned dollars down the drain. I read the card number off to Lucy the sex kitten and replaced the credit card back in my new leather wallet.

"Do you need anything else from me?" I questioned.

"No, Miss Maxwell, that's all. Unless you'd like to speak to your mom. I believe I saw her only a few moments ago and she..."

"No, thank you," I interrupted. "Have a good day."

I promptly hung up and returned my attention back to my oatmeal and my pleasant morning people watching. I spent another hour in the coffee shop vaguely wondering about the people passing back and forth in front of the window. What were their lives like?

What did they all do for a living? Where were they headed on a crisp November day like this? I thought of everything else except my mother.

"Where've you been, gorgeous?" Tucker grinned as I walked past his office.

I unbuttoned my coat. Either the heat was on full blast in the office or I was having my usual reaction to Tucker's hotness.

"Dallas wanted me to check out his new location in Chelsea. Then I stopped and did some research."

"You've become his pet, have you?" he ribbed.

I smirked. "Green much?"

"Not even a bit. I've had you. And I plan on having you again."

I felt my face blast with a heat of color. I reached into my purse and drew out my notebook. "Look at this sketch."

Tucker took my notepad and glanced over my drawing. "I like it. I really like it."

He took the sharpened pencil he always had tucked behind his ear and began to draw. He turned the pad of paper toward me.

"What if we made the heel a little wider and added a leather strap here across the top? Or maybe even round the toe a bit?"

I watched in awe as Tucker's hand glided gracefully across the page—like a potter with his clay or Dane sweeping across his canvas with his brushes. He'd done exactly what I knew he'd do. He made my work better. In some ways I think he even made *me* better.

"I really love that," I breathed. I never tired watching him create.

Tucker rolled to his feet. "I'm going to take this to the design department and see what they think. You might be on to something."

"How close are we to getting the bid for Winston's?"

"Sandra is being tight lipped about it. We should hear soon, though. That department store gig will really put Design 22 on the map."

I nodded in agreement and crossed my fingers. "Here's hoping. Let me know what design says about my sketch."

"Will do. You're far more talented than you give yourself credit for. I've always seen it in you. Maybe soon you'll see it in yourself."

I released a soft sigh as Tucker dashed out of his office. His enthusiasm for his work was evident in everything he did. Even his exit from a room was full of life and energy.

I gave courteous nods to my coworkers as I made my way to my desk. I ambiguously noticed a few sneers from my female coworkers as I left Tucker's office. It was common knowledge he and I were good friends and even more tacit was the romantic relationship we'd shared. You can't work in an office our size and not notice the goings on of others. Not to mention all of our offices were behind walls of glass. Every move you made was viewed by someone. Our relationship had very literally been put on display for everyone to see. Sometimes, it felt like the entire office was holding its breath—waiting on us to kiss or embrace. An endless inhale. Fortunately, there hadn't been a nasty fallout between us. Our relationship ended cordially. And privately.

I turned on my computer and once it was rearing to go, I searched for two airline tickets to Florida. After a half hour search on every airline imaginable, and seriously considering bus tickets, I paid an extortionate amount for two seats on Wednesday afternoon. The airline industry should really be more closely monitored. People were getting utterly ripped off. But it was done. Tickets purchased. Thanksgiving plans set.

My personal email chimed with my flight confirmation details and as I read, I suddenly began to get fidgety. My pulse quickened and my hands became damp with sweat. It was as if I'd just finished an exhausting Aikido training class. My anxiety level spiked as I imagined travelling in two weeks to see my dad for the holiday. I wanted to see him, so why was I suddenly so completely overcome with dread? Or was it my recent conversation with Reid and the relentless talk about moving in together that had me on edge? I couldn't think straight. I was overwhelmed with a vertiginous sensation—as if I'd collapse any second. My brain raced and yet I thought of nothing. My mind was blank but occupied and I glanced around without really seeing anything. The tightness in my chest made me think I might be having a heart attack, but I wasn't sure. All I knew was that I was scared and desperately trying to control my erratic breathing and stop my brain from imagining the worst.

I wiped a palm across my sweaty brow and tried to close my eyes for a minute, but they gaped wide when I heard my office door swing softly open.

"The guys in design say your shoe has real potential. I knew you'd—" Tucker paused as he studied my pale face and then hurried toward me. "Sloane, what is it?"

I shook my head trying to find the words to explain. "I can't breathe," I mumbled.

I could just make out Tucker's worried expression as my vision blurred. I felt him near me; his breath mingled with my own. His hands were on my cheeks and then rubbing down my arms. Somewhere in the back of my brain I realized he was calm. Oddly calm.

"Sloane, listen to me. You have to breathe. Listen to the sound of my voice as I count and match your breaths with me."

I nodded, but I wasn't completely sure I understood. Noises in my head clanged and I couldn't silence it. Normally, I could shut out the racket, but these sounds dazed me—deafened me. Was I really that freaked out about my relationship with Reid?

"One... two..."

Tucker begin to speak to me soothingly and I took in a shallow breath with each number.

"Three... four... five..."

I felt myself slide and get lost in the timbre of his voice. His hands rubbed up and down my forearms lazily giving me a familiar sensation to concentrate on. By the time Tucker reached ten, I could hear my own thoughts again.

"Open your eyes."

I did and they focused in on his concerned green ones.

"Are you okay?"

"I think so."

"What happened?"

I shrugged. I was embarrassed and vaguely aware we were being watched through our transparent office walls.

"I'm not sure. All of a sudden I couldn't catch my breath. But then I focused on the sound of your voice and I was okay again. I thought I was having a heart attack." I tried to tease, but the joke fell flat.

"What set you off this time?"

I balked. "*This* time? Tuck, this has never happened before. I don't know what was wrong with me, but I feel much better now. How did you know what to do? You were so calm."

I saw Tucker's eyebrows snap together in confusion and he turned his head to the side like a curious puppy.

"I knew what to do," he said quietly, "because I've seen you like this before. Don't you remember?"

I was as offended as I could be for someone who'd almost passed out in her own office and I raised to my feet swiftly, feeling a recalcitrant surge. "What do you mean I've done this before? I've never felt that way in my life. But I'm better now so thank you."

"Sloane," he started again.

I was beginning to feel like a child he was trying to reason with.

"You *have* done this before and I was with you. You should really consider talking to someone about it or seeing a doctor. More importantly, why don't you remember?"

I stared at him blankly. If what he was saying was true, why *didn't* I remember? And what was wrong with me?

CHAPTER FOUR

"Angel!" Dad exclaimed. He scooped me up into a bear hug and crushed me against him as Dane and I exited the airport.

I sank into his hold cherishing the feel of being in my dad's arms. It was like I was five-years-old again and he was ridding me of the monster underneath the bed. There was such safety in his arms. I'd never felt that safe in any man's arms except his and I suspected I never would.

He kissed my cheek and his rough stubble tickled my face. He looked older to me—more aged around his eyes and it saddened me. I knew the reason for every frown line and crinkle on his beloved face. He put me down and engulfed Dane in a similar grasp of affection.

"Hi, son," he breathed against his neck.

"Hey, Dad."

"I'm so glad you two are here," he said, tears misting in his eyes. "It's been too long."

Dane slapped his shoulder hard. "We won't stay away so long next time. Right, SloMax?"

I wrinkled my nose at him. "No, we won't."

"Let's get your luggage in the car and head out."

The 82-degree West Palm Beach warmth was a welcome respite from the frigid cold of the city. It was balmy and humid and my hair stuck to my forehead like gum on a sidewalk. It lay plastered against my skin and I had to fish a headband out of my carryon.

The drive to dad's house was a scenic one. Palm trees lined the median on either side of the street and the ocean stretched out to touch the horizon. Numerous shops and hotels blurred past my window as we neared River Bend Boulevard. Brightly colored houses stood vividly against a cloudless, clear blue sky. The rainbow of homes lifted my spirits some.

I could appreciate the slower pace of life here. People strolled instead of scurried. Life ambled in Florida; it didn't hustle by unnoticed. It was a good place to gather your thoughts, find time to be alone and take in the scenery. It was the kind of town where you stopped and smelled the roses. I could never live here again.

My dad pulled his Chevy Tahoe into the brick driveway and I stepped out, shading my eyes against an unforgiving sun. His Mediterranean styled yellow house with the red Spanish tiles was just as I remembered. Overgrown white crepe myrtle bushes and hedges lined up underneath the front windows of the house and lofty palm trees dwarfed the small yard. It looked unkempt compared to the neighbors—not quite deserted but not quite lived in. Forlorn. Lonely. I wondered if my dad felt that way since Dane and I had moved. The thought made my eyes well with tears.

"You're not getting teary-eyed being back at the old homestead are you?" Dane teased me, tossing his arm around my shoulder.

"No. It's not that."

Dane pulled me close and kissed my hair. "We're home."

"This isn't our home."

"It was for a while. And it's where Dad is. Home is where he is."

I managed a winsome smile and looked at my brother. This kid was my whole world. He always had been. I wonder if he knew it. "Wherever you are is where my home is."

Dane's eyes darted across my face as if he were studying me or seeing me for the first time. He grabbed my hand in his and I followed him inside.

The air was thick inside the house and I slid open the white plantation blinds and cracked a window. A stream of sunlight pierced the room leaving a trail of floating dust in its broad shaft of light. I watched the dust particles float languidly, entirely too engrossed in my subject matter. I snapped out of my own head.

The living room was exactly as it was the last time I visited. The tattered, checkered couch I hated was shoved against a wall and stacks of outdated newspapers were piled on top of the end tables. A dying plant slouched lazily in its pot, its leaves brown and brittle. An outdated TV set sat on a metal stand with casters and foil wrapped around one antennae. It was as if time had stopped in this house. Perhaps time had stopped years ago when Dane and I left. Maybe even before that. I'd only spent three years in this house before I graduated high school and moved back to New York to attend Pratt Institute. But three years was more than enough time to make memories, for this house to birth painful ghosts and hold dirty secrets.

It was strange to be here. I didn't feel like myself. I felt like my former self—a rebellious teen, an angry person, a hellion to my poor father. This house made my guilt resurface, my pain anew. Regret and shame clawed out from the grave where I'd buried it—its skeletal fingers reaching out to take hold of me again. I should have considered staying in a hotel. I clamped down on the soft tissue on the inside of my mouth.

"You guys hungry? We can order pizza," Dad asked from the kitchen. "You still take pineapple on yours, Sloane?" I could hear him going through the routine of opening the fridge and rummaging through the empty cupboards before offering to buy pizza. It was as if he thought food would magically appear in the pantry. He probably hadn't even bought food for tomorrow.

"Yes. Dad? Do we need to go grocery shopping?"

He stuck his head around the corner and grinned. "Not this year. I went shopping earlier this week. We have everything we need for tomorrow."

I nodded in mock appreciation. "Well done."

"Why don't you both get settled in your room and I'll call in the pizza. We'll sit outside on the patio and catch up."

Dane grabbed our bags and we headed down the narrow hallway to his old room. My room had long been converted into an office slash game room slash den. It was filled to the brim with miscellaneous things my parents had collected over the years. Yearbooks and photo albums, old toys and clothes took up every available inch of carpet space.

"God! Look at this place. Nothing's been touched," Dane whispered as he swung open the door to his old bedroom.

"You know Dad's not going to change anything in here."

"I think he misses us more than he lets on. We should really make more of an effort to visit more."

"Or he could come to New York."

Dane put the bags on the floor. "He won't leave Mom and you know it."

I looked around the room. There were two twin beds covered in matching plaid comforters. Dane's old baseball pennants lined the wall and his gear and trophies from Little League sat on a bookshelf. A layer of dust covered everything and I couldn't believe I had to share a room with my little brother. It really was like stepping back in time.

I put my bag on the bed by the window, claiming my usual spot, and plopped down. I kicked off my boots and took a pair of shorts and flip flops out of my bag.

"Do you think we should hire someone to help Dad out around the house? Like a housekeeper or something?" Dane questioned as he changed into a white T-shirt.

By *we*, he meant me. "I don't think he'd go for it. I don't know how much time he really spends here anyway. He's at St. Mary's most of the time."

Dane tugged on a lightweight, orange and white striped knit beanie over his curly hair. He could toss on anything and make it look fashionable. He had effortless style. I liked to think that was my influence on him.

"You're probably right. I can't imagine being *that* dedicated to one woman. I'd go crazy."

I chuckled. "Of course you can't. You're twenty-three. No one your age is thinking about that kind of commitment."

"Not because of my age. Because I can't imagine loving anyone that much. So much that I'm blinded by all their flaws. Dad is a better man than I'll ever be."

"I don't think he's blinded by Mom's flaws. I just think he loves her in spite of them. And when you find the right girl, you'll understand that."

He shot me a lopsided grin. "You think so? Because as I recall, you let Dad have it pretty good for sticking by Mom's side all these years. Now you defend his decision to stay with her?"

"It's his choice, isn't it? Despite what I think."

"You think he should have divorced her?"

"Many, many years ago."

"Do you resent him because he didn't?"

I stood. I was tiring of this conversation. "Maybe. Can you shut the door so I can change?"

"You're the queen of avoidance. Do you know that?"

"One of my many gifts. Don't let the door hit you."

With a grunt, Dane closed the door behind him and I changed into my shorts and T-shirt. It felt good to be in casual clothes. It must be the small dose of Floridian blood in me. For the next four days, gone was the fashionista of New York. She'd been replaced with the girl-next-door of West Palm Beach. I heard my phone beep with a text. It was Tuck.

You okay?

I smiled. The forever concerned Tucker Stevenson. I replied back.

I'm fine. I'm in Florida visiting with my dad. Thanks for checking in.

Good. Some time away will do you good. You should talk to a doctor. Really, Sloane. I'm worried about you.

Don't be. I'm fine. I'll see you when I get back.

I look forward to it. Take care of yourself.

My fingers flew across the touchscreen.

Happy Thanksgiving!

Same to you.

I vaguely wondered if Tuck thought I was crazy. It wasn't the first time I'd had a meltdown, but nothing like what happened in my office. But I'd felt that same strange sensation many times before—the same foreboding, gripping fear and anxiety. I'd have to get a handle on my emotions. Work was not the place for a breakdown. Although I couldn't remember all of them, when I thought back to previous panic attacks, they all seemed to center around Reid.

When Reid and I were only two months into our budding relationship, he'd asked me if I wanted kids. I remembered having a hard time catching my breath. And four months in, he'd asked to meet my parents. That really sent me into a tailspin. Now, six months later, he wanted to move in together and I'd had my third panic attack. I was developing a definite pattern where he was concerned, but I didn't understand why. It had to be more than my moderate fear of commitment but I couldn't say for sure. Whatever it was, I had to get over it. My fears would prevent me from what I eventually wanted in a relationship—a loving husband and family someday.

I heard the doorbell ring in the living room and knew the pizza had arrived. The peal of the bell was promptly followed by my dad's jovial voice and I tossed dismal thoughts aside.

"Sloane! Come eat."

I couldn't help but grin. I'd heard that cattle call all my life.

My favorite part of the house was the backyard. The large covered porch backed up to a sparkling lake. Waterfront homes were coveted in Florida. I remembered sitting on that very patio as a teenager staring out at the water, plotting my escape, my future away from here.

Dad and Dane followed me outside carrying two pizzas, paper plates, napkins and three bottles of Heineken. We all sat down at the wooden picnic table underneath a sun faded blue umbrella. A breeze flittered across my face carrying with it the zesty scent of pepperoni and the briny smell of salt water from the nearby Atlantic. My dad popped the cap of his green bottle and raised it in the air.

"To my kids. I've missed you both and I'm glad you're here," he toasted.

Dane winked at me. We clanked our bottles and I took a swig of the cold, malty brew.

"Pass the pie." Dane laughed.

"How's school going? When can I expect to see your artwork in one of our museums?"

"Not for a while. I've got two years to go. But I've decided to apply for an internship at the Museum of Modern Art this spring and try and get some exposure that way."

I nearly choked on a chunk of pineapple. "You didn't tell me that."

"I only decided a few days ago."

"That's amazing."

"They'd be lucky to have you. I couldn't be prouder of you two, do you know that? You've gone out in the world and made something of yourselves." He paused and cleared his throat. "What about your love life?"

"Nonexistent," I kidded.

Dane shoved my shoulder lightheartedly. "Not totally. I'm not dating exclusively, but I go out. A lot."

"What about your roommates? Any connections there?" Dad pressed.

I swore I glimpsed a hint of pink on Dane's cheeks and I laughed out loud. I knew Dad was going to give him the third degree. Then I frowned. It was certainly my turn next.

"The girls are cool and we get along great. But we're all better as friends."

Dad leaned back knowingly, crossing his arms. "So you're telling me there's no romantic involvement at all? You live with two pretty girls and nothing?"

Dane licked his lips and shrugged. "I'm not saying nothing *ever* happened. And I can't promise nothing will ever happen again."

"That's what I thought. What about you and Reid? Things going good there?"

And there it was. My turn on the hot seat. "He asked me to move in with him."

"What?" Dane exclaimed. It was his turn to be surprised. "You didn't mention that."

"I told him no so there really wasn't anything to tell."

"You guys have been together for a while. Did you even consider his offer?" Dad asked. He had green eyes like Dane but his were paler—wiser. He saw through me.

"I'm not ready for that step yet. Things are good the way they are. I don't want to mess that up."

Dad nodded and raised his bottle to his lips. "I hope neither one of you have relationship fears based on what you saw your mom and me go through. *Our* relationship doesn't have to be *your* relationship. Don't hold back on love because of us."

I could tell his statement caught my brother off guard and we glanced at each other.

"If you learn anything from me," he continued, "learn that love is worth fighting for. When you can let someone see the best and worst of you and come out the other side—that's worth fighting for. That's what you both deserve."

Dane chugged back the rest of his beer and stuffed his remaining crust in his mouth. "This is too heavy for me," he garbled jokingly. "Some buddies of mine from high school heard I was in town and want to catch up at the beach. I'm going to go hang with them for a while. Dad, can I borrow your truck?"

Dad gestured toward the house. "The keys are on the counter."

"Thanks. I won't be gone long."

Dane jogged out and my dad stood to his feet. "You want another beer?"

I nodded greedily. I needed more alcohol. Pronto. I walked to the edge of the porch and onto the deck and stretched out on a plastic chaise. The sky was incredible. It was four distinct colors, each shade fading into the other. Pinks and blues, oranges and yellows melded into one and you couldn't tell where one color stopped and another began. I couldn't remember the last sunset I'd seen. Or if I'd *ever* seen one. I hated to admit I was often oblivious to my surroundings. I couldn't quiet my brain long enough to take note of anything else around me. My thoughts were always turning, churning, preoccupied.

Dad came back outside and handed me another beer. He sat on a chaise across from me, eyeing me in that patriarchal way of his. He wanted to talk about stuff I was positive I didn't want to discuss.

"What's on the menu for tomorrow?" I asked, purposefully avoiding eye contact.

He sighed. "Just the normal grub. Turkey, mashed potatoes, broccoli rice casserole, mac 'n cheese, rolls."

"Mmmm, sounds yummy. I'll get up early and help."

He nodded. I could feel his eyes on me. "Are you and Reid really okay?"

Here we go again. "Dad, what are you fishing for? Reid and I are fine. He's great. We're great."

"I'm not fishing for anything, angel. I haven't seen you in nearly two years and I want to know what's going on in your life."

"We talk all the time."

"But on the phone you're so closed off and in such a hurry to be rid of me."

My heart ached. "I'm not trying to be rid of you, Dad. I'm just busy."

"I get that. I do."

I swung my legs around and sat up to face him. "I like Reid a lot. He's funny and sweet and smart and we get along well together. He makes me happy. I just don't want him to move in. I'm not ready for that. Maybe one day that will be a possibility but not now."

"Okay. As long as you're doing it for the right reasons and not because you're scared."

"What are you talking about?" As soon as I asked the question I regretted it.

"Your mother and I did irreparable damage to you and Dane. I know we have. And I'm sorry. If I could turn back the hands of time I would."

I clenched my jaw. "Would you?"

He reached for my hand. "In a New York minute. The choices we made, the choices *I* made, took a toll on you and your brother I could have never imagined. I'm sorry, sweetheart."

I gave his hand a reassuring squeeze. I felt compelled to lesson his guilt even though I wasn't sure he deserved it. "Water under the bridge."

"Is it?"

"Dane and I are fine, can't you tell? We're smart, well-adjusted adults. We're doing well for ourselves. Let's leave the past in the past."

"I'd be persuaded to do that if I didn't think it still affected you both. How could it not? Every choice we made concerning you two was the wrong choice. There's no handbook on parenting, I'll tell you that much."

I peered up at him from under my lashes. I gave him my best doe-eyed expression. That look had gotten me out of trouble since I was a little girl. I was sure it still worked. He was a man after all.

"Well, you don't have to parent us any longer. And what's done is done. We only have a few days here, Dad. Let's make the most of it, okay?"

He kissed my knuckles. "You're right, of course. Water under the bridge. At least for this weekend."

I stood hastily. Watching the sun set would have to wait for another time. I needed another beer. "I'm going to go call Reid. All this talk about him has made me miss him," I lied with my best disarming smile.

"Sure. What do you say when Dane gets back we pop some popcorn and watch old movies like we use to?"

"You're on."

I couldn't get to the bedroom fast enough. I closed and locked the door and flung myself on the bed. I guzzled down my beer without breathing and reached for my phone. I checked some work emails and my weather app for New York. The forecast was predicting snow tomorrow. I moaned loudly. If I couldn't get back to the city because of crappy weather and was forced to stay in Palm Beach, I'd lose my mind. I knew I would. The very thought made me want to vomit. I couldn't do it. I said a silent prayer the snow would hold off until we were back. I didn't want to miss the first snow of the season and I didn't want to be trapped here because that's how I felt. Trapped. Trapped in this house, trapped in the past, imprisoned in my own thoughts and fears. How did I break free from that? How do you escape from your own mind? What reprieve is there?

The small room grew wonderfully dark as the sun set outside. I closed my eyes to block out any remaining light filtering in through the window. Eventually, I heard Dad's truck door slam and I knew Dane was back. Not long after his return, I smelled popcorn and heard the faint sound of laughter and the crackle from our ancient TV. The familiar song, "Don't You Forget About Me" by the Simple Minds, blared from the living room and I knew they were watching *The Breakfast Club*. I loved that movie. But I didn't move. I was fastened to the bed. The blackness embraced and comforted me. It was in the dark I found some solace and my mind began to quiet. And it was in the dark where I remained.

CHAPTER FIVE

Early the next morning, my cell rang loudly and unexpectedly and Dane groaned in the next bed. He put his pillow over his head and grunted loudly, then turned to glare at me.

"Sloane!"

I silenced the phone. "Sorry," I whispered. I answered and took the phone outside on the back patio. I curled up in the same plastic chaise. It was cool against my bare legs.

"Hi, Reid."

"Happy Thanksgiving, babe. Sorry to call so early."

"It's okay. I had to get up any way. Happy Thanksgiving to you."

"Maybe next year we'll spend the holiday together. What are your plans for the day?"

I ignored his first comment. "I'm just going to hang with the fam. What about you?"

"Same. Everyone's asleep right now and it's the only time I have some quiet when I come to my parent's house. I'm just trying to enjoy it before the insanity begins."

I smiled. "I get that."

"When do you come home?"

"Saturday. How's the weather holding up there?"

"No snow yet but the weather guy said it's on the way. I hope the weather doesn't detain you."

Reid gave voice to my same concern. "Me too."

"Can I pick you and Dane up from the airport? I'm anxious to see you."

I was surprisingly moved by the offer. If I just gave him half a chance, maybe I could be happy. He deserved that much; he'd only ever been kind to me.

"I'd like that. I'll email you my flight information."

"Great. I'll take you both to dinner. It'll give me a chance to get to know your brother better. I know how much he means to you."

I heard the hopefulness and eagerness in his voice. I realized I made him feel that way. I made him happy. He wanted to live with me and I was treating him as if he had the black plague. All he wanted was to be near me. No one had felt that way about me since Tucker. Except Reid didn't want to share me with anyone else. Perhaps I'd been too quick to write him off. I decided to give our relationship some serious thought.

"That sounds perfect. Dane never turns down a free meal. I look forward to it."

"Good. Enjoy spending time with your dad. I'll see you soon."

I hung up the phone and forwarded my flight information to Reid from my cell. I stared out over the dark lake as it changed into various hues of blue as the sun gradually rose above it. A white sandhill crane skimmed the top of the water stretching its gray tipped wings in graceful elegance. He dipped his red crowned head searching for a fish, I assumed, but came up empty beaked. He landed on a delicate stem of cattail and kept watch for his breakfast.

The morning was unbelievably peaceful. It was as if the entire world was asleep and I had a secret glimpse of the breaking of a new day—a rare view into a transitory moment. I realized this moment happens every day but I'd never seen it. Dreamily, I wondered how many other things I'd missed out on.

"The mornings can be cool," my dad interposed, stepping through the sliding glass doors and coming to drape a blanket over me. He leaned down to kiss the top of my head.

"Thanks."

"We missed you last night."

I bit my lower lip. "Sorry about that."

"The bedroom door was locked so I assumed you wanted to be alone."

I wrapped the blanket around me as if I could disappear inside its sheath. "I just had some things on my mind. I didn't mean to miss out on movie night."

"We didn't watch anything you haven't seen a dozen times before. I just want to know you're okay. You keep telling me you're fine and I want to believe you, angel, but every fatherly instinct I have is telling me otherwise. I know we decided yesterday not to dwell on the past, but I can't help thinking the past is the very problem. Because we haven't talked about it, and you haven't dealt with it, I think it's stifling our relationship. You're different when you're here. You're closed off."

"I don't know what else I can tell you. You don't believe I'm okay when I tell you I am so what can I do?"

He sat down across from me, his eyes too intense, too dark. "I talked to your brother last night and he seems to think it may help for you to speak to someone. For *both* of you to speak to someone. Professionally."

I sat up swiftly. "So what? What does he know about anything?"

"He knows you better than anyone. Do you deny that?"

I shook my head. *Why were we talking about this again?*

"And if he's concerned about you then I know there's good cause. Your childhood wasn't an easy one."

"I remember. I was there. I don't know how many more ways to say it. I have a good life now. I'm happy. And I don't want to keep talking about this. You'll just have to take my word on the fact that I'm fine."

"Then tell me Dane's wrong and I'll let it go."

"He's wrong."

His shoulders slumped with defeat. But I didn't know what else to do. He was causing problems where there were none.

"I'm going to shower and start on lunch."

My legs felt shaky and weak as I stood to leave. I was feeling overwhelmed again and betrayed by Dane. I didn't like that he was discussing me with our father behind my back. He had no right and there was nothing to tell anyway—at least nothing the three of us didn't already know.

I was pretty sure I'd used all the hot water in the house by the time I was done with my shower. When I was dressed and finally emerged from the bedroom, Dad and Dane were sitting in front of the TV watching a parade. Wordlessly, I walked past them.

"Can I help?" Dane offered.

"No, you've done enough," I snapped.

I plugged headphones into my cell phone and clicked on one of the many playlists I'd created. I stuffed my phone into the back pocket of my jeans and I washed and peeled potatoes to the beat of the music. I diced onions and chopped broccoli to the upbeat tempo of Pit Bull and the electrical guitar of Imagine Dragons. I washed and trussed a turkey to Coldplay and smashed sweet potatoes to Beyoncé. I had a front row seat to my own private concert. I created a whole world in that tiny kitchen where nothing else existed except me, food and music. I danced, I spun around, and I slid across the linoleum in my socks. I forced myself to think of nothing else but the task at hand.

I didn't know how much time had passed but I'd set the oven timer, put all the ingredients away, cleaned the kitchen, and set the dining room table before I appeared again. Dad and Dane looked up at me as if they were scared to speak. I couldn't stand the tension.

"The turkey will take another two hours and fifteen minutes before it's done. Does anyone want some breakfast?" I suggested. It was the only peace offering I could manage at the time.

Dad lifted up a box of doughnuts and Dane patted the empty space beside him on the couch. I tried to stifle a grin as I looked at their pale, contrite faces. I squeezed in between the two of them and grabbed a chocolate-covered doughnut from the box. Together in silence, we watched the Thanksgiving Day parade.

"Slo and I brought you some red," Dane announced as we were all seated around the dining table hours later.

Dad took the wine bottle from him and grabbed the corkscrew lying on the table. "Thanks. I wish your mother was here to see you two home and all of us sitting here."

I stifled a groan solely out of respect for my dad and the holiday we were trying to celebrate. "Let me open the wine, Dad. You carve."

I took the bottle from him and popped the cork. I filled everyone's glass as Dad carefully carved the juicy bird and placed the cut slices of meat on a platter. We helped ourselves and dished out generous helpings of macaroni and cheese and buttery mashed potatoes.

"Another toast," Dane started. "To family. It's the most important thing in the world and everything we do is out of love. Loving each other is how we make it work."

I knew it was his subtle attempt at an apology to me and I accepted. I never stayed angry with him long; I was incapable of doing so. "You're both very poetic this afternoon," I kidded. "Cheers."

"Cheers," they said in unison and we sipped the delicious wine.

Conversation flowed as easily and as quickly as the wine. I surprised the two men in my life with a sweet potato pie and when our bellies were full, we loafed on the couch and geared up for the Cowboys versus Redskins game. As long as I could remember the three of us watched the Thanksgiving Day football game together. My mother had never shown an interest in sports, so she left the three of us alone to scream, yell, and chant at the TV. It was the only tradition we had and subconsciously I think I held on tightly to it—clutched in my fist one of the few pleasant memories I could recall from my childhood.

We must have all dozed off after the Cowboys win because when I opened my eyes, I was leaning against my dad's shoulder and I had a terrible crick in my neck. Dane was next to me, snoring softly, his curls falling across his brow like it did when he was a boy. It was a serene sight; I hesitated to disrupt it. I rubbed my neck and massaged my stiff muscles causing Dad to stir beside me.

He yawned. "I didn't mean to fall asleep. Your lunch put us all in a food coma. It was delicious by the way."

"Thanks."

He grumbled as he rolled to his feet. "I'm going to go see your mother before it gets too late. Maybe take her a piece of pie. I don't presume you'd want to come with me?" He had only to glance at my face to know my answer. "No, I didn't think so. Let Dane sleep. If he wants to see Mom he can come with me tomorrow. So can you, if you change your mind."

I nodded. That wasn't going to happen and he knew it as well as I did.

"I'll be back soon."

I stood and stretched my back. "We'll try movie night again when you get back?"

"You got it."

My dad changed into a starched, blue button-down shirt and tucked it into his jeans before he left the house. He was in the hopeless habit of dressing up to visit my mother. She wouldn't notice he'd changed and even less likely to care. He told me once that he always wanted to be his best for her. I wished his efforts were reciprocated. Why wasn't she ever her best for him? It pained me to think of his love going unrequited. It had for many years. And yet he pressed on. He fought for their marriage, for their life together. His fight had nearly cost us everything and no victor declared—only defeat on both sides. What was the point of it all?

At some tender age I vowed to never live my life like my father. Even as a child I knew what I didn't want. My dad had been used, affronted, cuckolded. He stood by and watched while she wrecked their marriage, shredded it until it was unrecognizable. She'd taken lover after lover, used sex like a weapon against my father. She'd torn our family apart without a second thought and he, my dear father, watched her hurt us all time and time again. He tried to reason with her, tried to rationalize her behavior, made excuses for her instead of calling her to her face what she was. She was a whore. She was a tramp who wasn't worth our love or time or effort. But somehow he found a way to keep loving her. He treated her still as if she made the sun shine and the birds sing. As if the earth revolved around her. He certainly did. He moved when she moved. She pulled on him like the moon pulls the tide—she drew him in and then let him go—watched him drown in the depths of a churning sea. And she did it over and over again. It was a constant hurt, a relentless cycle he couldn't break from. I don't know that he even tried. He seemed content in the cycle, complacent. Unwittingly he gave her permission to keep mistreating him. All of us.

I bit my cheek hard until I scowled in pain. I tasted the wet, salty flavor of my own blood. My head started to pound with recollections of the past, anguish I'd tried for years to suppress and forget. It was impossible to do that in this house. That imprisoned sensation begin to skulk again, began to creep up from my toes and invade my sensibilities. I felt my scalp prickle, my heart hammer, my eyes sting with tears.

Rushing to the bedroom, I shut the door and wedged myself between the bed and the wall. I tucked my knees under my chin and wrapped my arms around myself. The ache in my chest was absorbing, all consuming. Why was the hold of the past so strong? Why wouldn't the past stay where I'd buried it? It was intent and determined to destroy me.

I buried my head in my knees. I wanted to disappear. I tried to make myself as small as possible, tried to slither beneath the worn, shaggy carpet, sink into the earth and become no more. Tears streamed down my cheeks in angry rolls. It was this house. I had to get out of this house. It held too many memories, too many demons that had never been exorcised. I rocked back and forth muttering to myself—incoherent rants of a lunatic. That's what I felt like. As if I was slowly losing my mind in this place. This house where I'd only spent three years and yet those years were soiled with destruction, marred by injuries and slights. Each day I'd spent here seemed longer than twenty-four hours. Each hour I'd spent in this house was a lifetime. I'd lived a thousand lifetimes during my time here. This house sucked the life from me—left me fearful, wheezing, gasping for air.

I heard the bedroom door groan open and I wanted to be invisible. And then I sensed Dane beside me. I wanted him to go away. *Please go away,* I begged. *You can't help me. No one can help me.*

He touched my arm and I flinched as if he'd burned me. He settled down beside me and my cries turned into obnoxious, jerky sobs. Strangely, this place I was in, this place I frequently inhabited was becoming more comfortable to me. It was familiar. I was Alice in the dark, looming rabbit hole. I'd fallen into another world and made it my home.

Dane didn't speak, but I felt his arm circle around my shoulders. He pulled me to him and I lost my fragile balance and rocked into his arms. I tried to shove away as my tears continued to fall but his strength was too much and I was weak. I let him hold me.

It might have been hours or merely minutes that we sat there together. My brother didn't speak and neither did I. There didn't seem anything *to* say—nothing that would make a difference to either of us. The silence was only disturbed by my sniffling and the rustle of my T-shirt as Dane rubbed my back. The back of my eyes hurt and I knew my face was puffy and tearstained. I lifted my head and wiped my palms roughly across my face and through my hair. I felt my mascara and eyeliner smear and I had a feeling my look was something akin to that of a wet raccoon. I stared at the wall in front of me and Dane shifted beside me. I bravely raised my eyes to his. Somewhere I realized I was afraid of what I might see there. His probing green gaze travelled across my face, seemingly dissecting me, taking me apart and trying to put me back together like a puzzle he couldn't solve. His enigmatic sister. A brief, half smile touched his lips and then he blinked like he was shaken from a dream. His eyes never left mine and I noted something there. I wasn't sure what it was. Pity? Acceptance? He reached out and tugged on the bottom of my earlobe—a habit he'd had since we were kids. I think it brought him solace in some way.

"Let's go home," he whispered and he stood to his feet pulling me up with him.

CHAPTER SIX

"You sure you don't want to come to dinner with me and Reid?" I asked my brother as he rolled my luggage to a stop at the curb. Taxis whizzed by us and horns blasted angrily as they weaved through the airport traffic. Sounds of home comforted me.

"No. Hilary wanted to pick me up. She said she needed to talk." He grinned and I smiled back. His grin was contagious.

"Is that right? Do you have any idea what she wants to talk to you about?" I prodded.

"No clue. But I'll fill you in on our mystery conversation as soon as I know more."

"You better. But if it involves sex, please leave out the details."

He wiggled his eyebrows up and down suggestively and clasped his hands together. "Please, let it be about sex," he prayed. "No, I don't think it's that. But a guy can hope."

"I thought you weren't interested in your roommates. Isn't that what you told Dad?"

Dane shrugged. "We've already crossed that threshold. All I'm saying is I wouldn't be opposed to crossing it again. She's a cool chick."

"Try and refrain from calling her or any woman a 'cool chick.' Have I taught you nothing?"

"Don't worry about me. I've got major game. Game you haven't even seen yet."

I rolled my eyes at his cavalier attitude about women and dating.

Apparently, I hadn't done a good enough job of teaching him about women and how to speak to them. I made a mental note to sit him down at some point and really educate him on the dos and don'ts of relationships. Who was I kidding? I could barely manage my own affairs.

A honking car pulled up next to me and I turned my attention to the red Ford Focus that had sidled up beside us. The passenger side window rolled down and Hilary waved from inside.

"Hi, Sloane. How are you?" she said in her girlish voice, leaning over the front seat. She was a striking girl with smooth brown skin and warm eyes and I could see how Dane had had a hard time resisting her.

"I'm good. Did you have a good Thanksgiving?"

She shrugged. "The usual. Mom and stepdad arguing and me gorging on pie to drown my sorrows."

I smirked. Someone else's dysfunction was peculiarly comforting to me.

Dane opened her back door and tossed his duffle bag in and then turned to me. He put his hands on my upper arms forcing me to look up at him.

"You're sure you're okay?" he started cautiously. "I'll cancel this thing with Hilary if you want to talk."

I narrowed my eyes. "What do you mean? Why wouldn't I be okay?"

He pursed his lips and narrowed his eyes back at me. He had that searching look in his eyes again. I was beginning not to like that look.

"Are you serious right now?"

"Completely."

"Slo, you had a major meltdown at Dad's. I know what being in that house is like for you. That's why I wanted to get you out of there. Are you honestly telling me you're fine now?"

"I honestly am," I snapped back, a little too harshly. "Please go. Reid will be here soon and Hilary's waiting."

"If you think we're not going to talk about this later, you're crazy."

I was starting to think maybe I was. "Fine. Later."

He climbed into the seat reluctantly, stuck his elbow out the window, and leaned forward. "I can still cancel tonight."

"No!" Hilary protested from the front seat and Dane flashed me a smile.

"Game," he mouthed with a smirk.

"Go."

"We'll talk soon."

"Can't wait."

Hilary's red car jutted off into traffic, merging seamlessly into the flow and disappearing amongst the masses. Thunderous plane engines roared overhead and as I glanced up I noticed how white the sky was. Low clouds almost touched the ground; I'd noticed it when we were flying in. There'd been zero visibility, which always freaked me out a little. But the air was crisp with the promise of snow. I could smell it. The air held a glacial tranquility, a still serenity that alerted all my senses snow was on the way.

I loved the first snow of the season. It coated the world in freshness, covered all its grimy flaws and imperfections and replaced it with soft, white renewal. It offered second chances and fresh perspectives, a seasonal rejuvenation. It transformed the city into something new and alive. It transformed me, too.

A white Lexus pulled up in the back of the line of yellow cabs and Reid exited, smiling broadly. He looked amazing. His hip-length black, wool coat was buttoned to the top and a cream scarf was wrapped around his neck like an ascot. His blue eyes sparkled behind his frames, a dramatic contrast from the white sky we were ensconced in. I was glad to see him. At least I was trying to convince myself I was.

He engulfed me in his strong arms and kissed me hard. I'm sure we resembled a scene from a romantic movie, but I didn't care. I kissed him back with the same urgency. And his smell. *God, his smell.* It made the hairs in my nose tingle. His scent was so manly. Reid was all man. There was no denying I was highly attracted to his good looks. Those cornflower blue eyes entranced me the moment I met him and despite my misgivings about our relationship, his blue gaze continued to seduce me.

"You were only gone a few days and I missed you that much," he breathed against my mouth.

I bit my lip. "It's good to be home."

"You cut your trip short. I wasn't expecting you until Saturday. I'm not complaining but is everything okay at home?"

"Everything's fine. I missed the city. And I missed you." That was mostly true. I promised myself I'd give our relationship a try and that's exactly what I was going to do.

"Where's Dane?"

"His roommate picked him up. They had some things to talk about."

"Sounds serious. You ready?"

I nodded and Reid grabbed my luggage and tossed it in the trunk of his car. I settled in beside him, the heat blowing from the vents warmed my face and tinted my cheeks. I rubbed my hands together to try and warm them. I'd forgotten to pack gloves. Reid grabbed my left hand and held it firmly in his and I immediately thawed.

"How was your holiday?" I started. I stared out the window as buildings crawled by unhurriedly. The traffic was a nightmare.

"It went off just like I said it would. Mom slaved at the oven and then complained about how much work she'd done. My dad and I watched football literally all day and my sisters gossiped about their boyfriends for hours. I know far more than I care to."

I giggled. His sisters weren't much younger than me and I remembered what it was like when the relationship was new and exciting. It was fun imagining your future with a new boyfriend, like when you practiced writing your first name with his last name. It was a shame the feeling never lasted.

"Have you met their boyfriends?"

"Ryan doesn't really have a boyfriend. She's just dating. But Lindsey has been seeing her guy for a while. I met him but I didn't get good vibes about him."

I whipped my head around. "What do you mean? What didn't you like?"

Reid wagged his head back and forth and his lips tightened into a thin line. "It was the way he spoke to her—like he owned her or had some weird claim or rights to her. He was possessive. I know she sees it as affection or desire, but I definitely see it as strange."

"Did you say anything to her?"

"No. But I talked to him."

"How'd that go?"

I felt Reid bristle beside me and his hand tightened on mine reflexively.

"I told him if he ever laid a hand on my sister I'd rip his head off.

I will end him."

I glanced at him to see if he was joking, but his face was a mask of concealed rage. Concealed rage was far worse than an angry outburst of rage. But I could see he was deadly serious and I knew firsthand still waters ran deep. I shuddered, despite myself.

He smiled suddenly and kissed my hand. "You cold? Let me warm you up."

He reached for the knob on the console and turned the heat up. And just like that, he was back to being composed, congenial Reid. My shoulders tensed.

"I hope you're hungry. I've been wanting to take you to this place for a while now."

"Starved," I mumbled, still uneasy about his violent tirade. "You weren't serious about what you said to Lindsey's boyfriend, right?" I ventured. "You just wanted to scare him?"

Reid glanced sideways at me and smiled again. I shivered. "Of course I wasn't serious. I just wanted to put the fear of God in him and I think I accomplished that."

I sighed but it wasn't one of relief.

The car pulled to a stop in the underground parking garage at The Bentley Hotel and I eyed Reid questionably.

"Don't worry. I didn't get us a room here. We're just having dinner."

I looked down at my dark denim skinny jeans, black boat neck sweater and ankle boots. "Am I underdressed?"

"You're perfect."

I was intrigued. I'd never been to The Bentley before. I placed my hand in Reid's as he extended it to help me out of the car. The glass building shot up into the sky but the top was misted in a foggy haze. Silver lettering was mounted to the gleaming steel overhang and a doorman swung open the glass door. We strode through the cozy lobby and to the bank of elevators and walked into a waiting car. Reid wrapped his arms around me and I sank back against his chest. He was like a furnace. He heated my back, my arms, my insides. There was no negating my physical attraction to him. I turned in his arms and lifted my eyes to his. He lowered his head and captured my mouth, his lips moving across mine impatiently. I leaned up on my toes and grabbed the hair at the nape of his neck, imprisoning him against me. He felt so good. He was reassuring and inviting—he was exactly what I needed after my trip to Florida. He was steady and dependable and easy. Everything Florida was not.

Thirty floors later, the elevator doors slid quietly open and I begrudgingly broke free from his hold. I blushed madly as another couple entered the car, obviously having caught us at the tail end of a steamy smooch. I snickered and ran my fingers through my short hair. Reid grabbed my hand again and we exited.

I was blown away as we entered Prime restaurant, which was situated on the rooftop of the hotel. Floor to ceiling windows rose miles above us, bathing the room in soft, muted light. The clouds had lifted some since our drive in from the airport and the 360-degree view from this height was astounding. In the distance lay the East River and the Queensboro Bridge bustling with traffic and spotted with bright yellow cabs. Hundreds of buildings and twinkling lights made for an impressive skyline as the sun began its descent. Glass globes hung unevenly from the ceiling throwing tiny beams of light across the gray carpet.

We were seated near the windows by a petite, blonde hostess and her surgically-enhanced chest. She placed a menu in front of me and I caught a brief glimpse of her plastic surgeon's handiwork. Her blouse was cut entirely too low. Then, perhaps, that's what the management intended. I wrinkled my nose.

"It's amazing, isn't it?" Reid asked.

I opened my mouth to protest angrily but as I followed his gaze, I realized he was talking about the view and not the hostess.

"It's incredible," I answered sheepishly. Shame on me.

"The entire menu is kosher. I haven't eaten here before but I read the reviews online."

I was mildly impressed he'd done his research before bringing me here. It was thoughtful and in the spirit of giving us a chance, I'd remember to tell him so. I went straight to the wine menu and ordered a bottle of Merlot from a passing waiter. I perused the dinner menu and contemplated ordering sushi before eventually deciding on the Alaskan halibut and Reid, the pan roasted chicken and a side of grilled eggplant. My stomach growled with displeasure. I belatedly realized I hadn't eaten anything all day except pretzels and juice on the plane. Dane and I sat in the airport for hours waiting on standby before the airline put us on a late afternoon Friday flight. I'd been too anxious to eat. All I could think about was getting home and now my stomach was grumbling at my lack of consideration for its needs.

We gave our orders to an overeager waiter and he rushed to the kitchen with his pad and pen, nearly tripping over his feet in haste. My cell vibrated on the table next to me and I glanced at the screen, reading the text message. A quick smile flitted across my face.

"Who's that?" Reid asked before he took a swig of his wine.

"My colleague, Tucker."

You catching some rays in West Palm?

Nope. I'm back.

Early isn't it?

I wasn't in the mood for an inquisition.

"Didn't you tell me once you use to date a guy named Tucker? Surely, you don't know more than one," Reid assumed dryly.

"He's one in the same."

I wasn't feeling well. Needed to get back.

You okay now?

Better than ever. I'm at dinner with Reid. Talk later?

You bet.

"So you guys talk outside of work, obviously. Are you good friends?"

"He's one of my closest friends."

Reid rolled the stem of his wine glass between his thumb and index finger, the ruby red liquid swirling in the glass. "I wasn't aware."

I shrugged nonchalantly. "I never thought to mention it."

"Do you have a lot of guy friends?"

"I'm friends with most of the guys I work with. And I have some guy friends from college. Why? Does it bother you?"

Reid clenched his jaw and I watched his face harden like stone. "No. Not at all."

I licked my lips distractedly. "Work would be really awkward if Tucker and I hadn't remained friends afterward."

"I guess it would have."

Time for a change of subject. I reached for his hand and gave it a reassuring squeeze. I tilted my head to the side and leaned in close. "You have nothing to worry about. You know that, right?"

I felt him relax. "I know."

"You don't have ex-girlfriends you keep in touch with?"

"No."

Okay. Moving on. "How did you hear about this place?"

He looked around the dining room absently. "I wanted to take you and your brother somewhere nice so I did a little looking online. A client of mine also mentioned he'd taken his wife here and she enjoyed it."

"That was very thoughtful of you. If the food is as amazing as the view, we're in for a treat."

"The view is not nearly as amazing as the stunning woman in front of it."

Ugh. *Cheese anyone?* "Thank you."

Mercifully, our zealous teenage waiter brought our food. The aroma of my fish wafted underneath my nostrils and made my mouth water. I cut into my meal ravenously. The halibut melted in my mouth, its tender flesh falling apart and I closed my eyes and moaned softly in sweet appreciation. I loved a good meal. I finished my wine and Reid generously refilled my glass, its black cherry taste bold and rich in flavor.

I'm pretty sure I'd forgotten to breathe during the course of my meal. I scarfed it down in record time and then ordered another bottle of wine. By the time the second bottle was empty, I was feeling lightheaded and at ease.

"Do you want dessert?" Reid offered.

"I don't have any more room to put it."

"Then, let's get you home and let me show you just how much I missed you," he growled seductively, his blue eyes glinting with lust.

Everything below my waistline tensed at the thought. I tossed my cloth napkin on the table and hurriedly stood to my feet. Reid laughed out loud.

"Well, let me pay the bill first."

When we made it to the car and he'd pulled out of the garage, I could feel my eyelids getting heavy with sleep. I leaned my head back against the leather seat and shut my eyes. I felt Reid's hand on my knee.

"Tired babe?"

I nodded. My stomach was deliciously tight with food and the toll from the day's travels suddenly pressed down heavily on me.

"Just rest. You'll be home soon."

Feather light kisses against my cheek roused me from my catnap. I looked out the window and we were parked in front of my brownstone. A most welcome sight. Reid popped the trunk open, grabbed my luggage, and carried it inside.

I flicked the light switch and looked around. Dorothy had it right. There really was no place like home. I locked the door behind us and kicked my shoes off. A pair of arms reached over my shoulders and began unbuttoning my coat from behind me and then Reid spun me around roughly. I lost my balance with the sudden movement and the effect of two bottles of wine and he reached out to steady me. He continued his devastatingly slow removal of my coat and finally shoved it off my shoulders and it fell with a soft thud to the ground. I bit my lower lip in anticipation of his next move. His thumb grazed my jawline, down my neck, traced my collarbone. His hands made their way to the hem of my sweater and I felt a blast of cool air as he raised my sweater up and over my head.

"Do you want some coffee or tea?" I offered weakly.

He kissed the tip of my earlobe. "No, thank you. You know? I wouldn't have to leave if I lived here."

I repressed my natural inclination to grunt with annoyance. His hands moving down my backside distracted me from even my own irascibility. "But you don't have to leave now. Or tonight for that matter."

Lust blazed in his azure eyes and he slid his glasses off and placed them on the small table by the door. He grabbed me around the waist and lifted me up to meet his mouth. With one muscular arm he held me tightly against him while the other hand deftly undid the eyehooks of my bra. I felt the earth move as he carried me into the bedroom and laid me on the bed, his lips still joined with mine. He slid my bra straps down my arms and tossed it to the floor. He undressed himself while I tore off my jeans and panties. He settled his firm body on top of me and ushered me into sweet oblivion.

Reid stroked the hair at my temple as he spooned me from behind. We were both still naked and his sweltering body heat warmed me like a fiery, molten volcano. There was no better heater to chase the cold. Reid Blackmore: the natural electric blanket. Patent pending.

I pushed my bottom back against him and his grip tightened around me. I could feel myself drifting off to sleep. He planted kisses on my shoulder and I was safely tucked into the warm cocoon of his embrace.

Reid's breath caressed my ear and I traced the outline of my lips with my tongue, renewed desire surging through me. The nearness of him was constant, pure arousal. The wine had finally dulled my senses and I was blissfully relaxed with a heady combination of good wine and good sex.

"Sloane?" he whispered.

I murmured a disjointed reply.

"What did you say Tucker's last name was?"

"Stevenson," I mumbled and then floated into a peaceful sleep.

CHAPTER SEVEN

"Seriously? That key was for emergencies only," I grumbled Sunday afternoon as I heard my front door open and watched Dane saunter in.

"Relax, SloMax. Today I come bearing news and this." He grinned, holding up a six pack of beer. "I thought it was past time I replenished the stock I frequent from."

"Very generous."

"You want?"

"Do you have to ask?"

He pulled two bottles from the cardboard case and tossed me one. I fumbled the glass bottle and barely caught it.

"Nice job, Grace."

I took a huge swill of the beer and then my eyes popped wide. "What happened with Hilary? How dare you let twenty-four hours go by and not dish. What did you guys talk about?"

He plopped down on the sofa next to me and unzipped his navy North Face jacket. "That's the news I've come to share like the good, kind brother that I am."

"And you have no friends to tell this stuff to," I teased.

"On the contrary, I have plenty of guy friends but you're the only one who wants to hear all the details. Guys don't care about that stuff."

I pulled my sweatpants up to my knees and tucked my legs underneath me. "Start talking."

"After we left the airport we stopped for sushi and went home. She was her normal self during dinner. So much so that I thought maybe she'd changed her mind about talking to me. But when we got home she sat me down in the living room and laid into me."

"Where was Jane?"

"She was still out of town visiting her parents. We had the whole house to ourselves."

"And?"

"She told me she had feelings for me. Serious feelings. She told me how hard she'd been trying to keep them under control but that she couldn't do it anymore."

"I knew it! What did you say?"

Dane rolled to his feet and took a gulp of his beer. "I was floored. But I was also surprised—pleasantly surprised."

"What?"

"I know. She was so sincere and sweet and I've never heard anyone declare their feelings for me the way she did. It took a lot of guts for her to do that."

I squinted at him. "So what? You're proud of her?"

"I am, actually." I noted the sincerity in his voice. "I couldn't have done what she did. I couldn't have said all the things she did."

"But what does that mean? You want to hook up with her because she's courageous? Because she was open and honest with you? That's not a good enough reason to date someone. Not because you feel gratitude or something toward her."

"Who said anything about dating her?"

"You didn't have to. I can see it on your face that you're considering it. And if you want to that's fine. But only if you really care about her. Don't do it out of gratitude or guilt. Or because you're scared to let her down."

Dane stopped his idle pacing to look at me. "That's the thing. When I was sitting there listening to her, I realized how much I *did* care for her. More than I realized."

"And if it had been Jane telling you the same thing instead of Hilary, would you have suddenly realized you liked her, too?"

"Give me some credit, Slo."

I put my hands up. "Just asking."

"Hilary is smart and fun and I've always been attracted to her. I just don't know about taking the next step with her. But I think I want to."

"And if you do, where does that leave Jane? You think that'll screw with your *Three's Company* set up?"

He laughed. "That's the other part of this. I don't want the dynamic in the house to change—to be awkward for her."

I smacked my lips. "You can hang that up, bro. Things will definitely change. She's going to feel like the odd man out."

"Hil and I don't want that."

"You're already talking like a couple."

"Oh jeez," he moaned and downed the rest of his beer.

"So where did you two leave things?"

"I told her I wanted to think about it. But I knew what I wanted to do before she was even done talking. I like her."

I smiled up at him. "I'm happy for you. Really, I am. I think Hilary's a nice girl. But tread lightly with this Jane situation. You don't want to rock your happy little boat. And since you've already slept with both of them, I'm not really sure that's possible. Jack never slept with Chrissy, Janet, Cindy or Terri."

"But I bet he wished he had. Damn these good looks of mine!"

I shook my head in feigned disgust. "And the rest of the evening...?"

Dane smirked and his green eyes positively sparkled. "You said you didn't want details if it involved sex."

"Shameful," I kidded.

"How was dinner with Reid?"

I got up to toss our empty bottles in the kitchen trash can. "Really good."

"Do you think you'll let him move in?"

"No. That's already been decided."

"Was he okay with it?"

"Yep. Occasionally, he still mentions it, but I think he knows I'm not ready for that step."

"Do you think you'll ever be?"

"Maybe. With the right person. We'll see."

"Do you think he could be the right person?"

The house phone rang abruptly preventing Dane from questioning me any further and me from answering his question, but I ignored it.

"Aren't you going to answer that?"

"Nope. It's Sunday afternoon. My lazy day. And if someone's calling my house phone it's probably a telemarketer."

I reached for the remote to turn on the TV while my answering machine clicked on in the background. The beep sounded and a voice I didn't recognize began to leave a message.

"This message is for Sloane Maxwell. My name is Sam Brody and I'm calling to confirm your appointment with me tomorrow evening at 6pm. I can be reached at 212-555-9878 if you need to speak with me before our session. Thank you."

I watched as Dane slowly began to zip up his jacket and tried to make a beeline toward the door. I could feel my brain begin to pound with unbridled fury. My sisterly instincts had already alerted me to what he'd done.

"Please tell me that's not what I think it is," I spat out harshly.

"I should probably get home to the girls before it gets too late," he stalled, taking a cautious step backward.

"It's two o'clock. You're fine. Tell me who Sam Brody is and why he's calling me. What session?"

"How would I know? This isn't my house. He didn't call me; he called you."

"Dane Robert Maxwell! Explain!"

"I might have set up a counseling session for you. For us," he corrected.

I was almost at a loss for words. But not quite. "You can't be serious!"

"I've heard good things about this Sam Brody guy around campus and I thought we could see him together."

"Is he a teacher or a counselor?"

"Both. He teaches an English Lit course. But he also has his own practice counseling people."

I crossed my arms over my chest. "I'm not going."

"I know I went behind your back and set this up but I didn't think you'd seek out help on your own."

"What makes you think I need help?"

He made a very irritating sound in the back of his throat. "Do I really need to answer that?"

Both of us knew he didn't. "Well, you can tell me how it goes because I'm not going."

"Look. We'll be together. And if you don't want to say anything you don't have to. Nobody can force you to talk. But I don't want to go alone and open up to someone I barely know. I need you there. Please."

I gripped a handful of my hair in frustration. I felt like screaming at him. Instead, I pouted. He was nearly impossible to say no to and that alone frustrated me to no end. "I'm not saying a word to him. I mean it, Dane."

He grinned and rushed forward to hug me. "You don't have to. I'll text you the address and meet you after my class tomorrow night. You won't regret it."

"I doubt that."

"Wish me luck with Hilary today. I'm going to tell her I think we should give it a go."

"Luck."

Dane gave me an apologetic wink before he closed the door after himself. I really had to learn to stand my ground where that kid was concerned. And possibly see about a lock change.

Monday flew by in a hazy blur of ceaseless activity. The day was filled with business calls and spreadsheets, fashion catalogues, and fabric samples. I'd been inundated with emails, proposals, and sales meetings. Five o'clock came much too quickly and I wasn't ready for the surprise shrink session Dane had arranged. At least he'd be there with me and he was right about one thing—if I didn't want to talk (and I didn't) I didn't have to. Dane could conduct this little meeting all on his own. It would serve him right. I knew I was being stubborn and immature but I didn't care. To add to my annoyance, I had to take a subway thirty minutes into West Village. Blah.

I shut off my computer and stuffed the latest edition of Vogue, swiped from our reception area, into my briefcase and zipped it close. I looked around my office to see if I could find anything else to do to stall for time.

"You going home at five? That's unheard of for you," Tucker spoke up from the doorway, leaning casually against the frame.

"I have to meet my brother," I explained vaguely.

"I haven't see you all day. How was your holiday?"

"Uneventful. Yours?"

"Quiet. It was just me and Stewart."

"How cozy. What about your parents? And his?"

Tucker walked toward me and I took a self-preserving step back. He forever had a hold on me. I didn't want to slip back into old, unhealthy habits—not when we'd worked so hard on maintaining our platonic friendship.

"My parents went on a cruise to the Bahamas and Stew's parents went to visit an aunt of his in Jersey."

"Why didn't he go?"

"He wanted to spend the holiday with me alone. It was really pretty nice."

I put the strap of my briefcase over my shoulder and made an attempt toward the door but Tuck stepped in my path.

"What's your hurry?"

I looked up at him. "I told you I was meeting Dane. If I don't hurry I'll miss the six."

Tucker laughed heartily. "You're taking the subway? Also unheard of."

I shoved on his shoulder teasingly. "I hate it, but it's a necessary evil. I'm glad you had a good Thanksgiving with Stewart. And I'm glad you two are good."

"I thought about you the whole day," he admitted.

I smiled and stuck my index finger in the deep cleft in his chin. My finger fit perfectly there. "I'd be sad if you didn't. See you tomorrow."

He grabbed my arm as I passed him and turned me gently. "Listen to what I'm saying, Sloane. I missed you."

"I missed you, too. But why do we have to stop and have a conversation about it?"

Tucker tugged on his bottom lip with his teeth and released a heavy sigh. "I'm sitting at the dinner table with my boyfriend and thinking about you. Can't you see the problem there?"

"Only if Stewart knew what you were thinking."

"I know what we said about being friends but…"

"Don't," I interrupted quickly.

"Don't what?"

"Ruin a good thing. Ruin *us*."

"I think I already did that. I invited Stewart into our lives and it messed things up between me and you. I didn't take your feelings into consideration at all. But I care about you, Sloane. A lot."

I made another attempt toward the door. "I care about you, too. You wanted Stewart in your life and I get that. You should be with who you want."

"But I had to choose and I think I chose wrong. It's you I want."

Oh, good grief! Could anything be simple in my life? I didn't think I was strong enough to resist him if he moved any closer to me. My sexual attraction to him was palpable. I sidestepped out of his way, just out of the reach of his long arms.

"You don't know what you're saying. You and Stewart are great together. And if you feel like you're missing the female element in your relationship, find someone else. It's not my thing."

"That's what I'm trying to tell you. I'll give Stewart up for you. I want you and only you."

I felt queasy. "No you don't. And I have to go. I'll see you tomorrow," I decided firmly and flounced out and into the hallway. He called after me but I kept walking. I didn't know what was going on with him but he wasn't acting like himself. We'd always been flirtatious with one another but this was something completely different. Even when we were dating, he hadn't been as open about his feelings and it had been fine with me. People lie. People tell you what you want to hear and speak of love like a duty or responsibility. It's spoken with an emptiness, a glibness as if it didn't matter. I'd rather people not say anything at all rather than lie to me.

That's how my dad talked about my mom. Like loving her was a chore, a burden. Perhaps it was. I didn't want anyone to love me out of a sense of obligation or tell me what they thought I wanted to hear. Maybe that's why I'd never been in love. I didn't trust anyone to reciprocate my feelings at the same capacity as mine. Love should not be one-sided and if it was I considered that a terrible tragedy because someone was left in the dust. My dad had been left in the dust for many years and yet, he kept going back for more. I had no sympathy or patience for his cycle of foolishness.

Seemingly, my journey to self-discovery was going to begin before I'd even made it to the subway station. I forced my mind to contemplate other things. Like the woman who'd just passed me wearing the most unfortunate pair of wooden clogs. They clicked and clunked across the pavement in aggravating intervals. I stepped around her and hurried down the stairs to the platform.

Once settled on the hard, plastic benches of our fine mass transit system, I fished my pilfered magazine from my case and focused all my attention on next spring's color palette and floral prints.

The train whizzed with a rumble that shook under my feet and more and more people clamored on with each stop. A noisy hum buzzed around me that I was only marginally aware of. I glanced up periodically and read the same two posted advertisements about smoking and AIDS over and over again. "Quit to save a life. Yours" and "AIDS: Don't die of ignorance". What morbid topics.

Exactly thirty-one minutes later and several pages into which day bag to carry this season, the silver sub graced to a stop and I was one of many to rush to an exit door. I'd forgotten the chill in the air until the doors slid open and its frigid blast smacked my cheeks, frosting my face and ears. The cold air made my nose run and I sniffed unattractively.

I looked again at the texted address from Dane and walked three blocks from the station to a bright red, three-story brick building situated on the corner. It looked more like a slightly run-down apartment building and I entered the front door uncertainly. There was an old directory on the wall to my right and I found Sam Brody's name posted underneath his floor and office number. Walking two flights up, I turned down a narrow, dimly lit hallway. A fluorescent bulb in the ceiling blinked spastically and its flickering light danced on the grimy tile floors. I glanced at my watch. It was six o'clock exactly. I found office 202 and the door was wide open, so I stepped to the side to reach for my phone and check on Dane's whereabouts. But my phone rang in my hand. It was him.

"Hey, where are you?" I asked.

"My professor is holding me after class. He wants me to meet him in his office to discuss one of my paintings. I think he wants to enter it in some contest or something."

"So when will you be here?"

"That's the thing. I don't think I'll be able to make it. I don't know how long this will take. He seems really interested and it might be a good time to get him to discuss the internship with me for the spring. I'm sorry I can't be there."

I felt my ears turning red with aggravation. "This was your idea."

"I know. This was a last minute thing but it's important. Just reschedule the appointment and I'll be there next time."

"By yourself," I whispered curtly. "I'm not coming back. I was only doing this for you."

"This meeting with my professor could turn into something big, Slo. I know you understand. I'll make it up to you. Promise. I gotta go."

"Fine."

I pounded the end call button with my finger with the same intensity as if I were going to hurl it across the room. I leaned back against the wall. All I wanted was to be home on my couch with a bowl of tomato bisque soup and a roaring fire in the fireplace. My moderate sense of etiquette wouldn't allow me to just walk off, which is what I really wanted to do. So I stuck my head in the door to reschedule the session for Dane. Alone. I really wasn't coming back.

"Mr. Brody?" I said to the dark haired man sitting behind a worn oak desk.

He looked up from his desk and I was frozen where I stood as hazel brown eyes lifted to meet mine. It was the man I'd met on Madison Avenue. I felt my mouth drop open in disbelief and I fleetingly wondered if he was an illusion. He was far more handsome than I remembered. Not in the model-esque way Tucker was or the bodybuilding fitness way Reid was. He was handsome in a comforting way—like your favorite quilt and cup of chicken noodle soup way. He gave off warmth and genuineness. He rose to his feet.

"Well, this *is* a surprise. How's your knee?" he asked.

I managed to close my gaping mouth and licked my dry lips. "It's much better, thank you."

"What are the odds we'd see each other again in a city this big? Three times actually."

So I really did see him in Chelsea that day. I could only shake my head. Words escaped me again.

"You are my six o'clock, aren't you?"

I nodded.

He grinned and gestured toward a chair. "I'm Sam Brody. Would you like to have a seat?"

My common sense finally reemerged and my brain jumped into action. "My brother arranged this meeting and he's not able to come so I need to reschedule this session for him."

"But the meeting was for both of you. Right?"

"Yes, but it was really more for him."

Sam glanced at his appointment book and flipped through a couple of pages, pointing to a time slot. "I specifically remember Dane Maxwell made the appointment for both of you."

"He didn't tell me he made the appointment for me. I was really only coming for moral support."

"But you're here now so why not sit and talk with me?"

A peculiar feeling was pulling me to do just that. I'd be lying to myself if I didn't admit something was intriguing about this man. There was something compelling about him—but foreign and at the same time so conversant. No matter my inexplicable tug toward him, I didn't want to be analyzed and picked apart by him.

"Like I said, Mr. Brody, this was for my brother and not me. Since he's not coming, I don't see why I should stay."

He came from around his desk and stood in front of me. I had a clear look then at just how magnificent he truly was. His brown eye was the color of the earth, rich and deep and dark. And his hazel eye held flecks of green and brown. His lashes were long and thick under heavy eyebrows and lush brown hair. His philtrum was a deep groove right above a pair of full lips. I tore my gaze away from his mouth.

"Please, call me Sam. I know these sessions can be a little uncomfortable at first so if you don't feel like talking you don't have to," he said walking back to his desk. "Let me do the talking."

"What do you mean?"

"During this first session ask me anything you want. I'm an open book mostly. Then, maybe you'll feel more comfortable opening up about yourself."

I was interested. Not many people offered to expose themselves so freely with a stranger. His tactic was unique and I found his willingness to be vulnerable refreshing. Who was this man and what spell was he unwittingly beginning to cast over me? I couldn't deny I wanted to know more about him. I pulled up a chair and sat down.

CHAPTER EIGHT

I took off my coat and swung it over the back of my chair. I suddenly became hyperaware and preoccupied about my appearance. I pulled my sweater down and ran a hand through my hair nervously. I hoped I didn't look like I'd worked a nine hour day even though I had. I didn't want to *look* like I had.

"I'm the one being grilled, not you," Sam kidded, correctly reading my frequent body movements. "There's no reason to be nervous. Where would you like to begin?"

"Are you from New York?" I started. I felt like a reporter for the Times.

"No. Minnesota."

"What brought you here?"

"A job opportunity. I teach an English Literature class at Columbia. I believe that's how your brother found me."

I nodded. "Yes, it is."

"Why do you think he made today's appointment?"

I smiled and shook my head. "Nice try, doctor. I get to ask the questions. Not you."

Sam returned my smile with his own stunning white beam and I felt my heart flutter in my chest. *Oh boy.*

"My apologies. Please continue."

"Are you an actual doctor?"

"No."

"But you counsel people? Like a shrink?"

He leaned back in his chair and glared at me—his eyes gazing right into mine with a clarity he shouldn't have about me—a knowingness he couldn't possibly see and yet, it seemed he did. I felt naked before him and I shifted in my chair.

"I'm not a psychiatrist. But I am a licensed professional counselor. I studied sociology."

"Where did you go to school?"

"The University of Minnesota."

"Where did you spend your Thanksgiving holidays?"

"In St. Paul with my parents."

He didn't mention a wife, I thought to myself a little too giddily. And then I remembered I was the one asking the questions; I could ask whatever I wanted.

"Are you married?"

"No."

"Do you want to be?"

"Are you asking me to marry you, Miss Maxwell?"

I blushed. "Of course not."

He smiled softly as if he were amused by my obvious embarrassment. "I'd like very much to be married."

I shivered in my seat. His candidness took me slightly aback.

"Are you cold? This old building can be drafty."

"No, I'm fine. I'm sure there are teaching positions in Minnesota. Why did you choose New York?"

Sam leaned forward on the desk and his navy blue button down shirt stretched across his biceps revealing tight, muscular arms. "I think New York chose me."

"What do you mean?"

"I applied and interviewed for several positions in several places and received offers from almost all of them. But I felt led to teach at Columbia."

"Led?"

"You know? When it seems like everything is aligning to bring you to one place? When all the cards are stacked in your favor and the decision seems really clear? That's how I felt when I received the offer from Columbia. Like I was being led here."

"By some outside force?"

"Or in my case, an internal force."

I took a minute to mull that over. "Like your gut was leading you here?"

"Not my gut exactly. More like God."

"Oh."

Sam raised his eyebrows. "You don't believe in God?"

"Not really."

"Why is that?"

I smirked. "If this is going to work you have to let *me* ask the questions."

He upraised his hands in surrender. "Keep me honest, Miss Maxwell."

"Sloane, please."

"Sloane."

My name in his mouth did something to my insides. It sounded safe there—like it belonged. I was lucky I hadn't melted into a puddle of goo at his feet yet.

"Do you get along with your parents?"

"Now that's an interesting question."

"Just answer," I teased.

"Yes, I do. Quite well."

"Do you have brothers and sisters?"

"Two of each."

"Wow. Big family. I bet family gatherings at your house are insane."

He laughed and it echoed all around us, bouncing off the walls and submersing me in its warm sound.

"That's an understatement. It's noisy and chaotic and constantly buzzing. My mother had my youngest brother and sister late in life. They're only twelve and ten so they keep the energy level high in our house."

"I bet."

"Is Dane your only sibling?"

"Yes."

"And he's studying to be an artist right?"

"He's an amazing artist and I'm not just saying that because we're related. His talent is unbelievable."

A crooked smile graced his perfect lips. "I'd like to see some of his work sometime."

"Really? Some of his paintings are in the student museum on

campus. And I have a great piece at my house. I don't mean you should come to my house... I just meant that I have a great one to show you. But I could bring it here or meet you somewhere, if you want. Or not. I'll take a picture of it or something and email you. What I mean is..." *God stop me!*

"I know what you mean, Sloane. It's okay. I'd love to see any of his work. I'll make a point to stop by the campus museum."

I inwardly chided myself for being so daft and uneasy around him. He must think I'm a first class idiot.

"What do you do for a living? Surely, you'll answer one personal question for me since I've answered so many of yours."

"This was your idea, not mine. But to answer the question, I'm a fashion buyer in Manhattan. At Design 22."

"So you decide which clothes get put into the stores?"

I was impressed. Most men didn't know the role of a fashion buyer from their ass.

"That's right."

"That sounds very interesting. Do you like what you do?"

"I love it. I couldn't dream of doing anything more rewarding. Except maybe being a doctor and saving lives or something. And that's all I'm going to tell you about myself."

"You've told me more than you realize."

I cocked a curious eyebrow. "Have I?"

"Ask me something else."

"You really are an open book, aren't you? Why is that?"

He shrugged his broad shoulders. "Why wouldn't I be?"

"You're not afraid of the skeletons in the closet seeing the light of day? Or is it you just don't have any secrets?"

He leaned across the desk again and his eyes stilled me. "We all have secrets, Sloane. But nothing done in the dark stays in the dark. We may as well be open about who we are."

I glanced down. "Even if we don't like who we are?"

"Do you not like who you are?"

I pointed my index finger at him. "Generally speaking."

"Then generally speaking, I believe it's best to be honest even if you don't like who you are. Maybe by being honest we can start to heal some things and *begin* to like who we are. It's more important to face the truth than to live with the lies about ourselves."

I let out a nervous giggle. "Spoken like a true head doctor. You have all the answers, I guess."

"Not even close. I'm going through this life just like you are, figuring my way through it the best I can."

"You seem very sure of yourself."

"Was that a question?"

"No. An observation. Why did you choose to study sociology?"

"I wanted to understand people better and our effects on society and each other. It's a fascinating subject."

I twisted the hem of my sweater. "What have you learned about me?"

He linked his fingers together and stared at me over the bridge of his hands. "I'll only tell you this. You seem like a very bright young lady with a soft spot for family. You were willing to come here tonight for Dane's sake even though it was obvious you didn't want to be here. You don't let people in easily, which explains why you haven't opened up about yourself tonight. But when you do, your heart belongs to those you love. That's why betrayal and hurt wounds you far more than the average person."

His assessment made me squirm in my seat and I felt my cheeks blaze. I didn't know if it was the way he was staring at me or the fact that he could see through me, but he unnerved me on a level that was terrifying.

"It's impossible for you to know that. You sound like a fortune teller at a town fair," I remarked shakily.

"Then I'm right?"

"I didn't say that."

"You don't have to."

I ran my finger along the groove of his desk. "What are your hobbies?"

"You're touching one of them."

I looked around me confoundedly—at the chair, the floor, the desk. "What?"

"I built this desk we're sitting at. One of my hobbies is wood work."

I gawked at the worn desk with new eyes and more appreciation. Suddenly, it wasn't worn but well-aged. Its wood was no longer battered oak but perfectly rugged oak with character and distinctiveness. I admired the skill and time it took to craft something like this. I would never have the patience for it.

"That's really incredible. It's lovely."

"Do you have anything else to ask me?"

"I can think of tons of questions. But I've put you through enough," I said, standing.

"Not at all. I'm only asking because we're nearing our hour."

I glanced at the clock over his head in disbelief. I couldn't believe I'd been in his office for almost an hour.

"I really should be on my way then."

Sam stood and walked around to the back of my chair. He removed my coat and held it up for me while I stuck my arms in. His knuckles accidently grazed my neck as he straightened my collar and I felt lightheaded from just the gentle touch.

"I've enjoyed our conversation, Sloane," he said as I turned back around toward him. "When can we do it again?"

It sounded more like an invitation to dinner than a counseling session. Or was I imagining that? Or was I *hoping* that?

"This was really Dane's thing. I'll have him call you about rescheduling."

"So you don't think you could benefit at all from us talking?"

Briefly, I thought about mentioning Reid. I was growing increasingly concerned that I may not be wired to handle a committed relationship. Watching my father lay down like a doormat for my mother for years was not something I wanted for myself. Something about Reid made me uneasy and yet, I kept going back for more—just like my father did with my mother. I didn't know if it was truly that or something else. Whatever it was, I didn't want to get into it with the handsome shrink. I could think of several ways I could benefit from spending more time with Sam that didn't include Reid. Besides, he couldn't help me when I didn't understand it myself.

"I'll give it some real thought," I said honestly. I wanted to see him again.

"I'll wait to hear from you. And Dane," he added quickly.

He shook my hand with those powerful hands of his. Those hands that had caressed my knee when it was cut. Those same hands that had built that incredible desk. Those hands that pleaded with me to hold them, kiss them, touch them.

I held his hand for a moment too long, letting his warmth seep into me. I was sad to let it go—to let *him* go.

"Good night, Sam."

"Good night."

I buttoned up my coat and stepped into the hallway. I felt his eyes on my back and I wanted desperately to turn around one more time and see him again. But what excuse could I give for doing that? I'd already embarrassed myself enough with the half-assed invite to my house to see Dane's painting.

It was dark outside but the town was lit with glittering, twinkling lights. It was never truly dark in New York. Lights were continually blinking—crosswalks, billboards, marquees. I checked my phone and I'd missed two calls—one from Dad and another from Dane. I didn't return either. I didn't even bother to check my voicemail. I should really be thanking my brother; it was because of him I'd even met Sam. Maybe I'd been led to him. I didn't believe in all that divine providence but Sam made it sound feasible. I really should check my voicemail to see how Dane's meeting with his professor went. I was curious to know what he'd said. And I knew Dad wanted to know why we left Florida a day early. I knew Dane had given him some lame excuse and Dad would be calling to ask me about it. But I didn't call. I wanted to enjoy the quiet time of just walking through the city alone.

The subway ride seemed much longer getting home, but I was able to finish my copy of Vogue and vowed to return it to the lobby at work tomorrow. The streets were fairly empty by the time I was leaving the station and heading toward home. I didn't feel rushed like I normally did by the hordes of people pressing and pushing against me on my early morning commute. There was a peace, a rare calm that I didn't get to experience often on the streets of the Big Apple. A few people milled about but it was a relaxed stroll, not the typical heave of impatience. I enjoyed the city when it was like this. And as I neared the steps of my brownstone, it happened. A single, cool flake of snow fell on the bridge of my nose and melted. I couldn't help the smile on my face as I glanced up into the night sky. Soft, white flurries began to rain on me and I inhaled that crisp, cold air I loved so much. Snow drifted down in gentle swirls, cascading and floating, dusting the earth with silent flakes. It was what I'd been waiting for.

I sat down on the top step of my porch and crossed my arms, rubbing my hands up and down my arms to keep warm. I watched the first snow fall in beautiful, tranquil morsels of white, whispers of things to come carried in the gentle wind. Lights were snuffed out in the windows across the street and I sat there infinitely letting the snow transport me into its pure, magical world.

An obnoxiously large vase of red roses was delivered to my office right before lunch the next day. There were so many flowers, the smell actually overwhelmed me and caused a dull throb in my head. I stuck my hand inside the monstrous arrangement and dug out the card.

Thinking of you and hoping you have a great day. Love, Reid.

I didn't know whether to be touched or disgusted. The fact that he thought to send me flowers touched me. The size of the gesture annoyed me. Or was I being my usual, ungrateful self?

"Did I miss your birthday?" Tucker laughed as he strolled through my door.

I rolled my eyes. "No. They're from Reid."

He frowned. "I figured as much. I followed the stench in here. Did you two have a fight or something?"

I moved the arrangement to the side of my desk so I could see him. "I think he was just being sweet."

"Or territorial."

"What?"

"There are only two reasons a man would send an arrangement that enormous. Either you got into a fight or he's marking his territory. He wants everyone to know you belong to him."

"I'm my own person. I don't belong to anyone."

"I know that, but does he?"

"It was a nice gesture. A little over the top but sweet nonetheless."

Tucker flicked his finger at one of the petals. "Does he know you at all? Because if he did he'd know you're not impressed with these grand gestures."

I leaned back in my chair and smirked. "And you know me so well?"

He came around my desk and leaned against it. "I know you

better than he does."

"What makes you think so?"

"I *know* so, baby. You need a man who can challenge you intellectually as well as take care of you physically. You need someone who understands what makes you tick—what makes you, you. And I do. I get you."

His arrogance never ceased to amaze me. "Reid is brilliant and he takes care of me physically. I assure you I want for nothing."

Tuck grimaced and a hand flew to his chest in mock outrage. "Spare me the details. You can't honestly tell me you haven't thought about me when you've been with him, can you?"

I knew I had. But I wasn't going to give Tucker the satisfaction. "No. I'm happy with him."

"You're lying to yourself or to me or both. What's the harm in admitting your feelings for me?"

"Because I don't have any. At least not the way you want me to. Do I find you attractive? Of course, I do. But so are thousands of men in this city and it doesn't mean I want to jump in bed with all of them. So stop with the assumptions and let me enjoy my boyfriend and you enjoy yours."

His green eyes glinted as he leaned forward. "I told you I'd give up Stewart for you and I will."

"Let me make this clear. I don't want you to give up anything for me. You and I are better as friends. Let's leave it at that."

"What if I said I couldn't?"

His proximity was having that effect on me again. I felt myself being sucked in. "Then, I'd say we could no longer be friends. And I don't want to do that. I value what we have. So much, Tuck. Please don't make this awkward between us."

He leaned back giving me a moment to regain my senses. His sexual vibe was too much for me.

"Okay, if that's what you want. I'll try and stop wanting you. To stop myself from pulling that sweater dress right over your head and laying you across this desk. I'll try if that's what you want."

I felt my insides overheat with want. In that moment it was only the glass walls that kept me from letting him do just that. I was so freaking, unattractively pathetic around him and I was annoyed with myself.

"I do," I said unconvincingly.

He leaned forward again and I instinctively pressed myself against the back of my chair to create as much distance between the two of us as possible.

"I want to taste your mouth right now," he whispered hungrily and my stomach tightened with desire. "And I think you want me too. But I've always been one to listen to what women say despite their obvious body language. My mom raised me right. And I respect you enough to do what you've asked, even though I know you're lying."

"Thank you and thank your mom for me," I mumbled.

A glimmer of a smile flashed across his lips as he straightened. "I'll leave you to do your work. We okay?"

I nodded. I didn't trust my voice. And my panties were damp with a yearning for him I obviously couldn't control.

"Am I interrupting?" a voice said from the doorway.

I glanced up as Reid strolled into the office. My cheeks were already flushed with heat and I felt them turn scarlet when Reid eyed me questionably. I jumped to my feet too quickly.

"Not at all. What are you doing here?"

"I came to surprise you and take you to lunch. From the looks of it, mission accomplished."

I didn't miss the note of irritation in his voice. "That's very sweet of you."

"Are you going to introduce me to your friend?"

Tucker stepped up and outstretched his hand before I could. "Tucker Stevenson."

"Reid Blackmore."

I watched Tucker's eyes narrow. "I've heard good things about you. Good to know you."

"Likewise."

"I was just on my way out. Enjoy your lunch."

Tucker sauntered out of the office and I was left standing face to face with Reid. I felt like I'd just been caught with my pants down, or my dress raised, in this particular instance.

"I see you got my flowers," he started.

I fondled a rose absently—anything to avert my gaze from his very serious, suspicious blue one. "Yes, thank you so much. It was very thoughtful."

"So that was Tucker?"

"Yep."

"It looked like you two were deep in conversation."

"Not really. Just work stuff," I lied.

"Can you get away for lunch?"

"I can't. I'm swamped."

"Then I'll bring lunch to you. I'll run to Pastrami Queen. What do you have a taste for?"

"I'm not really at a good stopping place."

"I'd really like to have lunch with you."

Then you should have called, I thought wryly.

"You have to stop for lunch some time, right?"

Pastrami Queen did sound delicious. Reid was trying so hard. Maybe too hard? Or maybe I wasn't trying hard enough.

"Okay. Pastrami on rye with mustard."

"You got it. Be back in a minute."

He dashed out of the office and I took the opportunity to move my colossal bouquet from my office to the lobby. I placed them carefully on the coffee table.

"You and Reid have a fight?" Rebekah, the receptionist, asked nosily. "Are those apology flowers?"

Did no one get flowers unless there was an argument? What a cynical world we lived in. "No. He was just being thoughtful," I said, defending him. Maybe I was being too hard on him, too.

"They're big."

Oh, Rebekah. Always one to state the obvious.

"I'm going to leave them here so the whole office can enjoy them," I fibbed.

"I'm not watering that jungle. It's not in my job description."

Actually, I think it is. "I would never ask you to. I'm sure the cleaning crew will take care of it."

"Cool."

I dismissed her without another thought and returned to my office. Reid came back fifteen minutes later with two brown bags bulging with food. The smell of sandwiches permeated my office and made my mouth water. He closed the door behind him and pulled a chair up to my desk. He handed me my sandwich and a bottled water.

"Thanks."

"I know I'm going to regret eating this, but I'll work it off later."

Reid chuckled as he bit into his roast beef sandwich and sighed. "This is good."

The tender folds of my pastrami sandwich combined with the crusty bread and tangy mustard was perfection for my palate and I moaned in contentment. My taste buds were so glad I didn't bypass this spur-of-the-moment lunch date.

"You have plans this weekend?" he mumbled over bites of food.

"I'll probably catch up on some work since I didn't get anything done over Thanksgiving."

"Do you think you can squeeze in some time for me? We can see a movie or you can come hang at my place."

I dipped into my creamy coleslaw. "I'll let you know. I told you I'd be pretty busy with the new store."

"I know. I guess I can't get enough of you. Anything wrong with that?"

I winked at him. "No." His attentiveness was charming at times.

"Where are your flowers?"

His attention to detail, however, was not. "I took them to the lobby so everyone could admire them."

"Oh." He paused and then took a deep breath. "I don't want to rock the boat, but since you've decided we shouldn't live together, would you consider coming to my house for Christmas and meeting my parents? That is, if you and your brother don't go visit your dad again."

I felt a piece of pastrami get lodged in my throat as I inhaled sharply. I began to cough harshly and Reid handed me my bottle of water. I took several swishes, washing down my lunch.

"Is that a no?" He tried to kid. "You don't have to answer now. I just want you to think about it. I don't want to waste time with you, Sloane Maxwell. We've been together six months and you're the girl for me and I hope I'm the guy for you. I want you to meet my parents. I want them to know how important you are to me."

I was starting to feel pressured, caged. First, moving in together and now meeting his parents—I was scared to think what he may suggest next. I liked him, I did. Just how much, I still wasn't sure at this point. I vowed to try with Reid but I felt like I was being dragged into a whirlpool that was circling out of control and carrying me away with it.

I shoved myself back in my chair. I suddenly couldn't eat any more of my oversized sandwich. His impromptu suggestion had my mind racing. It was time to come clean.

"I'm not the girl who rushes into things, Reid. Six months is nothing to me. It could be six years and I could still feel exactly like I do right now about you. I have to do things in my own time. Living together and meeting parents has never really been my thing. It's *not* my thing."

I watched as his handsome face soured. I knew I was disappointing him and I hated it.

"So you're telling me we could be together six years and your feelings not have changed at *all* toward me?"

"I was just giving an example, but yes. I can't promise I'll ever feel as strongly for you as you do for me. But I also don't know that I won't. I just need more time. What we have now, this pace, is good for me. Can we not rush into meeting parents and merging our lives just yet?"

Reid rewrapped the uneaten portion of his sandwich and stuffed it into his bag. He looked at me thoughtfully. "I get what you're saying. And I'm a patient man. We'll go as slow as you need to. No more mention of moving in together or meeting parents."

The fact that he understood made me breathe a little easier.

"I didn't mean for this to be such a heavy lunch date. I just wanted to surprise you."

I stood as he did and smiled softly. "I appreciate the lunch, the flowers, and you."

Reid took me in his arms and crushed his lips against mine. I always welcomed his kisses but it immediately felt different this time—his kiss was hard and punishing. His mouth pressed so tightly against mine I couldn't move my lips. He pinned my arms against his wide chest and with one hand held the back of my head so I couldn't turn away. His other hand was at the small of my back pressing me to him. He managed to capture my lower lip in between his teeth and bit down hard. I winced in pain and tried to break free but his hold was unforgiving. He finally let me go only moments later and I took a wary step back.

"What the hell was that?" I whispered angrily, holding the back of my hand against my injured lip.

He smiled but it never reached his eyes. "I'm sorry. I guess I get a little carried away when it comes to you. That's what you do to me.

You make me crazy, Sloane. See you later?"

He turned and waltzed out of the office with his leftovers in his hand before I could think of a response. What the hell had just happened?

I glanced out into the hallway and my coworkers were jokingly giving me a quiet round of applause. From the outside looking in it must have appeared that Reid and I were entangled in a lovers embrace. But that kiss had been anything but loving. That kiss had been cruel.

CHAPTER NINE

"I thought you were ignoring me." Dane sulked as he waltzed into my house Friday evening carrying a bag of Chinese takeout. "Your phone broken?"

"What am I? Your girlfriend?"

He shoved me lightly. "Whatevs. Why haven't you been returning my calls? Where've you been?"

"Nowhere. I've just been laying low."

"How come?"

"No reason," I lied. I was becoming too good at lying.

"You okay?"

"Enough with the twenty questions. Let's eat."

Dane shrugged and grabbed some paper plates from the pantry and two pairs of chopsticks from the island drawer. When we were settled at the breakfast bar, our take-out boxes brimming with sticky rice, spicy crispy beef, pineapple duck, fried rice, steamed vegetables, and a bottle of Pinot, I began my own interrogation.

"How's it going with Hilary?"

He rolled food to the side of his mouth. "She's pretty great. She started sleeping in my bed and I can't say that I mind."

"How is Jane handling this shift in the house?"

"She seems to be okay. I definitely don't want to alienate her because I like her and we can't afford to live there without her."

I took a sip of my wine. "You mean *you* can't afford to live there without her. Hilary has a job. Was Jane happy for you guys?"

"I think so. Initially she sounded really excited for us. But she's been pretty quiet the past couple of days. I don't know. You're a girl. How would you feel?"

I chuckled. "If I was Jane and I had feelings for you, I'd either be pissed or hurt. Maybe both. But if she truly views you as a friend, and I doubt she does because you've slept with her, she'll be happy for you. My advice would've been not to shit where you eat. But that ship has sailed."

He tore open a packet of soy sauce with his teeth. "I hope I haven't screwed things up for all of us."

"As long as you and Hilary don't flaunt your relationship in Jane's face and give her some time to process, she may be okay with it all. What happened with your professor the other night? And it better be good since you ditched me," I added frankly.

He rolled his eyes at me but his smile beamed and I knew it was good news.

"He really liked a painting I did for my abstract project and he wants to enter it in the Chelsea International Fine Art Competition."

"Dane, that's incredible! I'm so proud of you."

"Thanks. Professor D thinks I've got a good shot at winning. Top prize goes to three artists. If I win my painting will be displayed in the gallery, I'll get art promotion, press, ads, listings in New York publications and all sorts of other stuff. My painting may even be sold."

"Professor D?"

"Professor Danner. Nobody calls him Danner, though."

"That's really amazing. When do you enter?"

"Not until spring but it could really be another great opportunity."

"Definitely. What did he say about the internship?"

Dane's eyes brightened and his enthusiasm was contagious. He loved what he did and I loved that he loved it.

"He agreed to write me a letter of recommendation."

I lunged forward and hugged him, knocking his broccoli off his chopsticks. "He must think so highly of your talent. I told you, you were amazing. This is just the beginning for you. I know it. Just by being entered in the competition you're going to get so much great exposure."

"You've always been my biggest fan."

"And I always will be."

He scissored his broccoli floret again and shoved it into his mouth. "I'm sorry I had to leave you hanging on Monday. What happened with the shrink? Did you reschedule my appointment for me?"

My heart lurched at the thought of Sam and his mesmerizing eyes. There was no reason in hell my body should have a physical reaction to just the thought of him. *Oh, but it did.*

"He's not a shrink. He's a licensed counselor."

He raised an amused brow. "Excuse me. Did you guys talk?"

I took a huge gulp of wine, letting the cool, floral flavored liquid relax my senses. The mention of Sam set me on edge.

"I didn't talk. He did."

"About what?"

"Everything. He let me ask him whatever I wanted."

Dane snorted. "Thank God those sessions are free. What a waste of time."

"It wasn't," I argued quickly and with far more assertion than I intended. "It was very informative and interesting. *He's* very interesting."

"And unhelpful it would seem. I can't believe you stuck around."

"He wanted me to be comfortable and I was. I told him you'd call him and set up another session."

Dane stuck his chopsticks inside his rice and leaned back in his seat. "What aren't you telling me?"

I blushed. "Nothing."

"Liar."

"I think he's attractive, that's all," I admitted quietly.

He bit his trembling lower lip to keep from laughing. "I see. So then you're not opposed to going back with me on Monday for my session when I reschedule?"

I wanted to. I knew I did. "For moral support? Absolutely."

"Moral support—sure, that's what we'll call it."

I tossed a chunk of duck at him and grinned. "That's what a loving sister would do."

"Yeah. A loving sister who has a crush on her hot counselor."

"Shut up. It's no big deal. And he's not my counselor. He's yours."

"I don't really care how you feel about him. I'm just glad you're coming with me."

I raised my wine glass. "Cheers to that."

"Have you talked to Dad?"

"No. You?"

He polished off his wine and refilled his glass. "No. I don't know what to tell him."

I buried my head in my food. I knew where this conversation was headed.

"I rattled off some piss poor excuse about why we were leaving but I know he didn't buy it. What happened to you at the house? We still haven't talked about it."

"That's because there's nothing to talk about."

"Stop, Slo. Please. You know as well as I do something's off and you sweeping it under the rug is not going to help. I'm not going to let you keep brushing it off."

"Brushing what off?"

"Whatever's going on. That's why I made that appointment with Brody. We have to talk about our fucked up childhood. I can't keep going in circles like this."

"Then *you* do that and leave me out of it. I said I would go with you to at least one session and I will. But I don't want help because I don't need it." I could feel my pulse spiking.

He stood from his bar stool and stepped within inches of me. He loomed over me and his voice dropped to a somber low. He was playing the part of overprotective brother but that was my job. I shield *him*, I watch out for *him*—not the other way around. It had always been like that.

"What made you break down in Florida?" he asked softly.

I chewed on the inside of my cheek.

"Was it being back in the house? Did Dad say something to upset you?"

He had me stuck between his body and the kitchen island. I felt myself growing anxious. I looked everywhere but at him. I guzzled down the rest of my wine and attempted to swing my stool around to the other side. But Dane stepped back instead, allowing me to stand and walk briskly to the living room. He was eyeing me like some wild thing—like some animal that might pounce and tear his flesh with my teeth. Had I put that fear in his eyes? Or was I imagining it all?

"Dad didn't say anything," I murmured. "And I think you're making more of all this than is necessary. That house is too small. I felt claustrophobic—like I couldn't breathe."

"Then it didn't have anything to do with Mom either?"

I walked back to the kitchen and started shoveling leftovers into plastic containers. "You want some of this to take home to Hilary and Jane? I'll never eat all this."

"It didn't have anything to do with Mom?"

"No, Dane, it didn't," I barked. His troubled expression was too much for me.

"I just want to help you."

"Then stop hounding me. When I talk to Dad, I'll smooth things over for us both. Don't worry."

"You think *that's* what I'm worried about? That Dad is angry we left early? Screw that. I'm worried about the sister I love who's acting more and more like our mother every day."

His admission wounded me and at the same time jerked me into a reality I wasn't ready to confront. I wanted to sink into the floor, amalgamate into the walls, anything to go unnoticed, unseen. I felt that familiar sliding sensation again, the one that allowed me to go to my dark place and reside there. I was starting to seek it, to crave it. It was taking on color and shape and texture. It was becoming my new reality. But Dane wouldn't let me stay there.

"I'm sorry. I-I shouldn't have said that," he stammered hurriedly. "Forget it. Sloane, did you hear me? Forget I mentioned Mom or Florida or anything. You're fine. We're both fine. We'll be okay."

The next thing I knew I was consumed in his embrace and I felt myself relax in his soporific hold.

"You told me *I'm* your home, remember? And you're mine, too. You're my home, too," he whispered against my hair.

My eyes burned with unshed tears. I closed my eyes and concentrated hard on the muffled thud of Dane's heartbeat. It was steady and constant and strong—like him.

After several moments I felt like myself again. I backed out of his grasp and finished putting the food away. I packed some of the containers into a plastic grocery bag and poured myself another glass of wine.

"If Brody can fit me in on Monday night, you still okay to come with me?" he questioned warily.

I nodded. I was tired of talking—of feeling.

"Cool. Thanks for the leftovers."

He tossed on his coat and shoved a black knit cap over his head. He tugged on a pair of discounted designer leather gloves I'd bought him from Frenzy and grabbed the to-go bag from the kitchen counter.

"Hey, I meant to ask you what happened to your lip. It's kind of bruised."

I sucked on my bottom lip gingerly. It was still tender. "I bit it," I lied. I was covering for Reid when he didn't deserve it. To admit his mistake would only shine a light on mine. Even *I* couldn't quite explain why I was still dating him.

"Jeez. Take it easy."

"Get home safely."

"I will. See you later."

I closed and locked the door behind him. I sipped my last glass of wine, savoring it, while I waited for a small load of laundry to finish up in the dryer. I wiped down the counter with some bleach and a sponge, cleaned the sink, and then washed my hands. The dryer buzzer sounded and I took the laundry basket from the top shelf of the laundry room and dumped in my hot, clean clothes. I took the basket to my bedroom and began to fold and put away my clothes and undergarments. There was something soothing about mindless work. It was mechanical, thoughtless, automatic. It didn't require me to think or feel or talk or listen but it kept me moving and occupied. *Always stay moving, always keep going.* Movement kept the memories at bay. Movement kept me sane. When I stopped, I had too much time to think; too much can happen when I'm not moving. Fear and pain and disappointment happen when I stop for too long.

I got to the bottom of the basket and was left with one brown sock and one black sock. I sighed. I jogged back to the dryer and opened the door, searching for the missing articles. But it appeared the dryer had eaten my missing socks. I strolled back to my bedroom and took out the black and brown sock and held them up. And then I grinned to myself—much too widely I realized. The mismatched socks reminded me of Sam and his mismatched eyes. I could picture his face, his smile, his hands. A mismatched man for this mixed-up girl. Sounded like a match made in mismatched heaven.

I was jolted from my sleep by a boisterous pounding on my front door. It took a second for me to gather my thoughts as I shot up in bed and when my eyes finally focused on the clock, I saw it was two-thirty in the morning. I untangled myself from the sheets, tugged on the cotton robe tossed over my desk chair, and padded into the living room with my heart in my throat. I tiptoed to the front door and squinted through the peephole. It was Reid. His hammering was echoing through the house and I was scared the neighbors would call the police. What was he doing here? And should *I* be scared, too?

"Sloane! Open the door! I know you're in there!" he shouted.

His words were slurred and I knew immediately he'd been drinking. My hand rested on the doorknob but I was hesitant to twist it open.

"Sloane Maxwell! Open up!" he garbled. "I want to see you."

We hadn't spoken since having lunch in my office. I'd ignored his calls. I didn't particularly want to talk to him now, either. But I couldn't leave him out in the cold and I didn't know how long he'd stand there shouting in the streets. Even worse, I didn't want him driving home in his condition. I unlocked the deadbolt and took a step aside as he tumbled in.

"Slo… n," he mumbled, "it's freezing out there."

"Yes, I know. What are you doing here?"

He leaned forward to kiss me. He smelled of cigarettes and rum.

"Some friends and I went for drinks after work. I thought I'd stop by and see my girl."

"It's two-thirty, Reid. Have you been drinking since you got off? That was like eight hours ago."

He collapsed on my coach, his legs thrown wide apart, and tried unsuccessfully to unbutton his coat.

"It's hot in here," he complained.

I turned on each lamp on either side of the sofa and leaned down to unbutton his coat. A wolfish grin slid across his face as he eyed me lustfully, his gaze gliding from my face down to my toes. His hand reached out between the split of my robe and caressed my inner thigh. I took a step back.

"Take your coat off. I'll make you some coffee."

He didn't fight my obvious rebuff of his advance. He was too smashed. I piddled around in the kitchen until the coffee was ready and steamed out into a ceramic mug. I thought about adding cream and sugar but decided it was best for him to take it black.

"Here," I said, thrusting the cup at him.

He didn't move. His head was thrown back against the back of the sofa and I rolled my eyes in disgust. I'd never seen him like this. I understood getting sloshed—I'd been there before in my college days. But in six months, I'd never seen Reid drunk—and I didn't like it.

I bent my leg and sank onto the couch holding the cup of coffee under his nose. The strong scent had the effect of smelling salts because Reid opened his eyes and raised his head. I held the cup to his lips and he sipped carefully. He swallowed and his head lolled back against the sofa again. I sighed.

"You're so good to me, Sloane Maxwell," he muttered. "Really, you are. I guess that's why I love you because you're so good. You take good care of me."

His declaration of love made my stomach drop. Most women would've been ecstatic to hear their boyfriends profess their love for them. It made me queasy; it terrified me. But then, I wasn't most women.

"You don't mean that," I debated as if I could change his mind. "You're drunk out of your skull."

He inhaled deeply and yawned. "Mean what?"

I was relieved. People say alcohol is a truth serum but in Reid's case it seemed to have caused amnesia instead. It was a mere slip of the tongue, an accidental avowal he'd never remember.

I made him sit up and drink the rest of the coffee until his bloodshot eyes begin to clear some. I removed his glasses and placed them gently on the coffee table and then fought with his heavy, uncooperative body until I'd pulled his coat off. I tossed his shoes on the floor and Reid's long frame swayed slowly downward until he eventually made contact with the couch. I lifted his hefty, cumbersome legs and covered him with a pale blue cashmere throw blanket. He covered his eyes with his forearm.

"The lights. Please, Sloane," he moaned. "So bright."

I turned out the lamp near his head and reached for the cord on the other lamp when his next words stilled my hand.

"I meant what I said before. I love you."

I glanced at him from the corner of my eye. His eyes were closed. I didn't speak; my mouth was shut with shock. *Holy shit.* He hadn't been rambling after all; it hadn't been his drunken stupor. *Reid* was doing the talking—not Captain Morgan.

"Say something," he breathed faintly. He was drifting to sleep.

"You've had too much to drink. We'll talk tomorrow."

He turned over on his side. "Give me a kiss."

"No thanks. We've tried that before. It still hurts."

A stupid grin floated across his lips. "I'm sorry about that. I got carried away. I'd never hurt you."

The room blurred as tears welled in my eyes. "You did," I replied, my voice barely audible.

"I'll never let you go, Sloane. Never. I hope you know that," he slurred. "You belong to me."

I reared back. "I don't belong to anyone and especially not you." I nearly choked on the words as fear trickled in, wearing me down like a water drop on a rock, slowly but steadily.

He reached for me blindly, his hand opening and closing around air, searching for something now beyond his grasp. And then he nodded off in sleep, his soft snores rhythmic and even. I stood over him for a minute as he slept and watched him. He appeared so peaceful, so young and strong. He was incredibly handsome in sleep; everything about him softened. His lips parted slightly and his hands were lax, his brow unfrowned. There was such vulnerability in sleep—he was totally exposed and open. He was no longer cruel or funny or intimidating or charismatic. He was like everyone else. People were equals in sleep.

I turned off the other lamp and went back to my bedroom, and instinctively locked the door behind me. I wasn't sure what made me do it.

My feet were cold and I grabbed my black and brown sock and smiled as I pulled them on. It made me feel better to think about Sam.

Something else was making me restless, though. Something about Reid's admission, triggered a reaction deep in my gut. I couldn't shake it, couldn't quite place the feeling, yet I knew I was afraid. Something about Reid frightened me terribly.

CHAPTER TEN

Dane actually beat me to Sam's office Monday night. He was leaning casually against the wall with one strap of his backpack slung over his shoulder. He was dressed in perfectly torn jeans, a long sleeve white tee and a black puffer vest. His brown curls shaded his face as they fell over his forehead. I could have taken his picture right then. He belonged in a Gap ad. He looked up as I approached and grinned.

"Hey," he said.

"Hey."

"You ready for this?"

I was ready to see Sam. I'd thought of little else all day. I didn't know what my fascination with him was but I couldn't wait to get there. That feeling was aided greatly by the fact that I knew I wasn't under the microscope tonight. But it also unnerved me to think about what Dane may divulge to Sam. How open about his childhood would he be? And would I be able to sit there passively and relive it all? Suddenly, I was beginning to second guess the whole thing.

"You owe me so massively big for this. You should clean my house for like six months," I exaggerated jokingly.

"I just got really nervous," he said abruptly. "Let's just get this over with."

My smile faded into a frown as I walked in the office after Dane. Sam stood when he saw us and grinned broadly. Dane leaned close to my ear.

"I see what you mean," he whispered and I flushed furiously.

"You must be Dane. Glad to meet you. I'm Sam."

"Nice to meet you," Dane greeted softly.

I looked at him sideways. His face had paled. He was really nervous. He'd opened this can of worms but now I felt bad for him.

"Good to see you again, Sloane. Both of you sit, please."

Dane eased into his chair like he was sinking into a tub of hot bath water—anticipating the burn. Jeez. He was more scared than I thought. I moved my chair a little closer to his.

"Let me tell you how I'd like this to go." Sam closed his office door and perched on the edge of his desk in front of us. "I want you both to feel comfortable here—to feel free to say whatever you like. But Sloane, since you're here for moral support only, I'd like you to remain quiet and let Dane have the floor. This is his session. Dane," he continued, "you can speak as little or as much as you want. I'm here to facilitate and I'll follow your lead. We'll only discuss what you're comfortable discussing and I'll help you process anything I can. I'm not a miracle worker—deeply rooted issues are not mended overnight. But I promise I'll be here to listen whenever you want. That goes for you too, Sloane, when you feel ready."

We both nodded and stared blankly at him like two kids in the principal's office.

As if he'd heard my thoughts, Sam chuckled and said, "Relax guys. I can only help as much as you let me in and trust me. Dane, I'd be remiss if I didn't make the same offer to you as I made to your sister. If you'd like to forego your session and question me instead to make it easier to open up, I'm game."

Dane cracked a smile and raised his hand in refusal. "No, let's do this. Besides, I don't think I could get her to come back here a third time."

I turned quickly to look at him. "You know I'd do it for you," I whispered.

Sam moved around the desk and sat in his chair, his eyes darting from mine to Dane's. "You two seem close."

"She's my best friend."

"That's wonderful to hear."

"I think our friendship was born out of necessity."

Sam nodded. "What does that mean?"

I felt a heavy breath fill my lungs as I inhaled sharply and Dane patted my knee reassuringly.

"We didn't have the easiest childhood," he began.

"What made it so difficult?"

"Our mother for starters. She was an adulteress—a repeat offender. Different men would come in and out of our house when our Dad was at work. I don't know where or how she met them, but there seemed to be a revolving door to her bedroom."

I cringed as unwelcome memories invaded my thoughts. I tried to concentrate on anything else: the clock, the humming of Sam's laptop, the snow globe paper weight on his desk. Anything but what Dane was saying.

"How old were you when this was going on?"

Dane cracked his knuckles. "Five. Sloane was eight."

"Go on if you want."

Please don't go on, I pleaded silently. I felt him tense beside me.

"There was one night in particular I remember very clearly. One of my mom's scumbag boyfriends came into my room late that evening. It was so dark I could barely see. He'd just finished fucking our mother. I guess she was passed out or something, I don't know."

Sam's face didn't flinch; he didn't even blink. "What happened?"

"He pulled the sheets off of me and it startled me awake. He'd scared me, so I started screaming. He told me to shut up and yanked my pajama pants down."

Dane's knee was bouncing up and down furiously like a paddleball. I began reading the titles on the bookshelf behind Sam's head. Tolstoy, Keats, Shelley, Whitman…

"He was leaning over me, getting ready to—" He broke off as if the memory was too much for him. "But Sloane heard me yell and came into my room."

"What then?"

Plato, Aristotle, Plutarch, Virgil, Tacitus… Sam seemed quite well read.

"He shoved her to the floor and told her it was her turn next. But for now she could watch."

I dug my fingernails into my palms until they left half-moon shaped indentions in my hands. Dante, Chaucer, Montaigne, Freud…

"He reached for me again and Sloane started screaming at the top of her lungs. She screamed bloody murder for what seemed like hours. I've never heard anything like it—like she was in excruciating, unbearable pain. She just stood there and screamed. The guy thought she was crazy and said I wasn't worth the trouble and left. We didn't know if he'd come back, so we hid in the hall closet all night until Dad found us in the morning."

I rubbed my palms up and down my thighs, the friction causing my legs to burn.

"What did you tell your dad?"

"We tried to explain what happened but we were scared shitless. He didn't believe us. He didn't *want* to believe us. He thought we were playing a game. My mom never said a word. Sometimes it was like she didn't even remember—like she blacked out. And Dad worked a full time job and two part time jobs. He was hardly ever home and she continued to get away with it."

"How long did this go on?" Sam pressed.

Please, God, make this stop!

"For a while, a long while. I don't remember how long."

"Did he try anything else with you? Did any of the other men who visited your mother?"

My brother's head dropped as he nodded sadly and some fragile thing in me shattered. I rolled to my feet and turned, tripping over Dane's backpack in my haste.

"I'm sorry. Everything I say affects her, too," I heard him explain as I scrambled to my feet and opened the door.

I tore off down the hallway but my legs felt like lead. I wanted to run but I felt heavy, stuck—like I was standing in quicksand. I didn't get far before I felt hands on my upper arms halting me.

"Sloane." It was Sam.

I didn't want to turn and face him. My eyes were watering, my hands were shaking, and I felt ridiculous for running out of his office. The inside of my mouth ached from how hard I'd been gnawing on the soft tissue there.

"Sloane," he repeated softly. "Look at me."

His voice was compelling, inviting, and I turned despite myself. It was like something inside of me was answering something inside of him—something primordial and instinctive. Familiar.

"Are you okay?"

"I just needed some air," I mumbled feebly.

I felt his hands, *those* hands, on my face. He cupped my cheeks and forced my eyes up to his. His breath was warm against my face and I breathed him in.

"I'm sorry about what happened back there. If I'd known what Dane was going to say and how it would affect you, I would've told you not to come here tonight. I can see you're not ready to face the things of your past yet and that's okay. When you are, I'll be here."

Before I could reply, Sam took his hands down and took an embarrassed step back.

"I'm sorry. That was completely unprofessional of me."

"It's okay. I…"

"No, it's not okay. I'm your counselor. You're supposed to be able to trust me. I wouldn't blame you if you wanted to find someone else."

I stilled his flailing, animated hands by grabbing one and holding it in my own. "Technically, you're Dane's counselor—not mine. I wanted to come with him I just wasn't prepared for all this," I confessed. "I want to be there for him but it's a lot for me to deal with."

"I understand. It's normal to be nervous or afraid to open up about things that are painful. Anything I can do to help, I will. Any way I can make you more comfortable, I'll try my best."

"If I was going to talk to anyone about my past, it'd be you. I'm more comfortable around you than I probably should be. I don't understand it, but it's true."

Sam smiled and my heart raced with hope.

"I'd like to stay here and talk more but I have to get back to Dane. I need to finish my session with him. You're more than welcome to come back and join us if you want."

"I've had enough for one evening."

"Are you okay to get home by yourself? I mean, are you okay?"

I knew what he meant. Was I emotionally stable enough to see myself safely home? I was emotionally drained and all I wanted was to climb into my bed and have an early night.

"I'm fine. Please tell my brother I'll call him tomorrow."

He pursed his lips together, nodded, and then walked down to his office and shut the door. I was so tired all of a sudden, overwhelmed. I couldn't sit through another session like that—not even for Dane. It was too much for me. I wasn't as strong as him. I'd had to be strong when I was too young to even know what it meant and I'd depleted my resources. My tank was empty. My childhood had robbed me of all my strength, of everything.

I woke up in a dark mood the next morning. After I showered, I dressed in a black turtleneck, black slacks, black boots, my black coat, and shoved a pair of dark sunglasses on top of my head. It felt like a cloud was hanging over my head, so I dressed for the occasion.

As soon as I arrived at work I was swept into a meeting, which lasted over an hour, thankfully keeping my mind occupied and my thoughts engrossed in other things. Afterward, I had a brief meeting with merchandising, a conference call with Dallas, and an arduous negotiating war with one of our suppliers. Through the miasma of busy work I noticed I hadn't seen Tucker all day. I ordered lunch in and had something quickly delivered so I didn't have to confront the avalanche of snow outside or the biting wind. I'd just put my work phone on privacy and picked up my fork to spear a shrimp from my shrimp and avocado salad when Tuck waltzed in. I put my fork down.

"Where've you been? You missed Sandra's big announcement. We got the Winston account." I paused as the look of distress on his face registered. "What's wrong?"

He sat down across from me. "I'm late because I had to take my car to the garage."

I picked up my fork again and began eating. "Is that all? Did you need an oil change or tune-up or something?"

"No. I needed four new tires because all of mine were slashed."

I put my fork down again. "What? Did you and Stewart have some sort of blow up and he took it out on your car?"

"No."

"Did you leave it in some sketchy neighborhood?"

"No. It wasn't even broken into. But the tires were shredded. Like brutally shredded. I think it was personal."

I was never going to finish my lunch this way. "Personal? Like who? A jealous ex? I wasn't aware you had any enemies."

"Nor was I. But the police seem to think it was intentional—like someone trying to send me a message."

I leaned back. "I don't get it. Who would do something like that? Do you have any idea?"

"Nope. But I'm pretty pissed off about it. I just shelled out eight hundred bucks."

"I'm sorry that happened, Tuck. I never understood why you had a car anyway. You can get anywhere on foot or by subway. Maybe it's time to get rid of it."

"I think you're missing the point, Sloane," he replied dryly. "Who the hell did I piss off?"

"Sorry. Let me know if there's anything I can do to help."

"So we got Winston's?"

"Yep. We found out this morning."

Tucker rested his ankle across his knee. "That means we'll all be buried alive until way after the new year. Winston's wants a completely original collection."

"But it's great for the company. It means the big wigs at Winston's see the value in what we do here and they trust our work. Design 22 will never be the same after this. We'll get tons of business. Besides, more work is good for me."

"Why?"

"I like to be busy. You know that."

"We have that in common. But we like to be busy for different reasons."

I ignored him and attempted another try at my salad.

He leaned across the desk. "I like to be busy because I love what I do. You like to be busy so you don't have to think about your feelings for me."

I nearly spit out my food at his superciliousness. "You have some nerve. I love what I do, too."

"Hey, you okay? We never did talk about your little break down in here before Thanksgiving."

Why did it seem everyone wanted to discuss my personal life? "I'm great. Never been better."

"You're perhaps one of the worst liars I know. I really think you should consider seeing someone."

"I'm an excellent liar and I am sort of seeing someone," I admitted.

"Really? How's it going?"

"It's hard. It's really hard. And we've barely scratched the surface."

He reached for my hand and squeezed it. "It'll get easier, I promise."

I shoved my salad aside. I was slowly losing my appetite.

"Are you going to finish that?"

I snapped the lid on and slid the plastic bowl across the desk. "Help yourself."

"I didn't have time to get lunch, obviously, since I was tending to the act of vandalism on my car. I better get going. I assume Sandra's going to want a ton of new sketches and designs in the not too distant future."

"Swing by her office and let her fill you in."

"I will. And keep up with the counseling. It'll pay off in the end; I know it."

I forced a tight smile. For the first time I could ever remember, my heart was not in my work today. It was teetering on one o'clock and I was already mentally checked out. Being at work had done nothing to lighten my foul mood. When I woke up the morning after Reid's drunken intrusion, groggy from a lack of sleep, Reid was heavy on my mind. He was gone when I awoke. He'd scratched a note saying he'd call me later but I'd woken up innately knowing what I needed to do. I needed to cut Reid loose. I'd be lying to myself if I said Sam wasn't a factor in my decision. My mind had been engrossed with thoughts of him for the past week. But more than that, I didn't want to keep living with the sinking feeling in the pit of my stomach every time I thought of Reid. It was time to face facts. I didn't want to be in a relationship with him anymore. Not only did my instincts tell me so but my heart did, too. There was something I didn't trust, something I didn't quite understand about him. I'd given myself a full week to mull it over and I knew what I had to do.

I met Reid in a coffee shop around the corner from my work at six. He blew in with the snow, his coat freckled with tiny melting flakes. He brushed his shoulders off as he spotted me and came to the table. He leaned down and brushed my mouth with his lips. I flinched unintentionally.

"I was surprised you called—but glad. Why didn't you let me

take you to dinner instead of meeting for coffee?"

"I just needed to talk briefly."

He sat down and wiped off his snow speckled glasses with the tail of his shirt. "I didn't get a chance to thank you for taking care of me the other night. I got carried away with the guys. Thanks for letting me crash. I missed not being in the bed with you when I woke up."

I knotted my fingers. "Reid, I wanted to meet you because I needed to tell you I don't think it's a good idea we see each other anymore."

The space between his brows crinkled but he didn't comment. I pushed on. "I've enjoyed our time together, really, I just have some personal things going on that I need to figure out. I hope you can understand." *God, I was awful at this.*

"Is this about asking you to meet my parents over Christmas? I told you I was okay with us slowing things down."

"No, it's not about that," I fibbed. It was that and a dozen other things. "It's me and all the things going on with me. I need time to process without the added distraction of a relationship. It's too much for me right now."

"It has nothing to do with the other night? I'm sorry I drank too much. You know that's not like me."

"It doesn't have anything to do with that either. It really is all me. Please understand."

His gaze raked over my face. "I understand," he growled softly, his eyes beginning to flash with ire. "I understand I've wasted six months with you and I've got nothing to show for it. You've completely wasted my time."

I clenched my fist under the table. "I'm sorry you feel that way. I certainly don't."

"How gracious of you," he drawled, his voice dripping with acerbity.

"Look, I wanted to be honest with you. I didn't want to keep doing this thing with us and making it harder in the end. I just need to take some time for myself."

"*This thing* with us? Is that how you view what we have?"

Poor choice of words. "Maybe later down the line we can try this again." I realized I was trying to pacify him. Why? "I just need my space now."

He smiled at me then and it chilled me to the bone. Through

gritted teeth he replied, "I told you the other night I would never let you go and I meant it."

I threw my shoulders back in a futile attempt to appear more self-assured than I felt. "That's not your call to make. Let's not make this harder than it is."

His face was a mask of contempt and then quickly, almost imperceptibly, he relaxed and his shrewd grin returned. He stood and I looked up at him in shock.

"This isn't hard at all, but it will be. Especially for you. I'll see you around."

His exit was so unexpected, so hurried, I didn't have time to remark. He'd gone from angry to mild tempered in seconds and his veiled threat unsettled me. Where was his switch? And had I unknowingly just flipped it?

CHAPTER ELEVEN

Is it normal to obsess about a man you barely know? Less than twenty-four hours ago, I'd broken up with a relatively decent guy and instead of having a good cry, I couldn't stop thinking about Sam. There was no explanation for my bizarre behavior other than I liked him. I was entranced, enthralled by him. Something about his presence drew me in; I didn't even know what. It was absurd and a little fanatical to be this spellbound by someone I'd just met. I'd had exactly two real conversations with the man, and they were under less than ideal circumstances. And if he knew anything about me or my family he'd never be interested in damaged, disturbed me.

But if I shut by eyes I could still feel his hands upon my face—warm and reassuring and strong. If I concentrated long enough my mind could conjure up green and gold flecks in a hazel eye. If I listened closely I could just make out the sound of his voice. I wanted Sam Brody with an impractical yearning, a foolish craving, an unexplainable desire. Perhaps it was the unknown—the excitement of getting to know someone new. Or maybe I was intrigued by his all-American upbringing—so unlike my own. Maybe it was some sort of twisted doctor-patient crush because I'd convinced myself he could heal me, fix me. It could be good ole fashioned desire and lust for a sexy man or a combination of all those things. I wasn't sure. But I was sure I wanted to see him again. That much was crystal clear.

However, I didn't want to go to counseling in order to spend time with him. I knew my brother wanted me there, but I didn't possess the mental fortitude it took to keep unburying memories that should've long been forgotten. And what would Sam think of me if he knew all my secrets? I wrestled with my mind and my heart and they each desperately wanted different things. The internal tug-of-war would drive me mad if I didn't come up with a solution.

My cell phone rang, jarring my thoughts back to the present. I glanced at the face of my phone. It was my dad. I hadn't talked to him since Thanksgiving and I'd been ignoring his calls. Sooner or later I'd have to face him; it may as well be now. I quickly jogged over to shut my office door and answered the phone.

"Hi, Dad."

"Hello yourself."

He didn't sound too pleased with me. "What's going on?"

"That's what I'd like to know."

I played dumb. "What do you mean?"

"I think you know very well what I mean. You and your brother flew out of here so fast it made my head spin. What happened?"

Why had I answered the phone again? I didn't know what Dane had said to him because I was waiting in the cab to go to the airport while he was making our excuses. I heard Sam in my head advising me. *Maybe through honesty we can start to heal some things.* The last thing I wanted to do was open that door but I thought I'd give his novel tactic a try.

"It's difficult being back in that house, Dad. I couldn't take it. I felt too closed in."

I heard him sigh heavily and I instantly regretted being honest. My truth always seemed to hurt other people.

"Why didn't you tell me that, angel? I would've understood. Sometimes it's hard for me to be here, too."

I'd never considered that before. He always seemed so sure of himself and his choices. He'd chosen to stay in that house and I thought it was because he wanted to be close to *her*. He'd chosen her over us so many times, I assumed he was comfortable in his decision. It never occurred to me he had his own demons to face in that house. But then again, why wouldn't he? He'd lived through his own hell. We'd all been tormented one way or another. Even my mother. She was still living in her own nightmare. We all were.

I didn't say anything and he sighed again. "There aren't enough ways I can say I'm sorry for everything that happened to you."

"Dad, please. I don't want to talk about it." I was on the brink of beginning to, slowly gathering my strength and courage, but not with him and not now.

"Then just listen. I was a fool. I didn't protect you the way a father should. I was so blinded by what I *wanted* to believe, I ignored what was. I'll never forgive myself for it. And you've paid the price your entire life. My mistakes affected you in ways I can't even imagine. So yes, I understand why being in this house is hard for you. I'll understand if you never want to come back here."

"If you knew all this, why didn't you leave her?" I snapped. It'd been the question I swore I'd never ask. I wasn't always sure I wanted the answer.

He didn't miss a beat. "Because I thought I could save her. That's why I didn't get her help sooner. I believed she'd come back to me. I was wrong."

His reply gave me pause. In a twisted sort of way, it made sense. Didn't we all want to believe we could bring the people we loved through anything? That they'd always come back if we just waited or asked just the right way? Maybe he did understand me better than I thought. "I'm not saying I'll never come back. I just need some time."

"Take the time you need, angel."

"And you came through as a father when I needed you most," I added quietly.

I could almost hear him shudder over the line. We never talked about that night. What was there to say?

My father's tone changed to light and breezy in an instant. "How's work?"

I was thankful for the change in topic. "Really busy. We just landed a major department store account so business is picking up."

"And how's Reid?"

I flinched at the mention of his name. I reached for a stack of papers on my desk and absently folded the edges of the papers into triangles. "Reid and I are no more."

"What happened?"

My jaw clenched. Just the thought of him made me tense. "It just wasn't working for me. I needed a time out."

"Is there still hope you two might reconcile?"

"I doubt it. I've moved on." As soon as the words left my mouth I wished I could suck them in again.

"Moved on? So fast? Am I overstepping my fatherly boundaries to ask who with?"

I scratched my head. "His name's Sam, but it's complicated."

His raspy laugh made me smile. "Love is not complicated, sweetheart. People are. If you like him and he likes you, there's nothing simpler than that."

"I like him but I don't know if the feeling is mutual."

"Then he's an imbecile."

"Thanks, Dad."

"I want you to know I'm not going to force you down here for Christmas. I'd love to see you but if you don't come, I'll understand. Maybe I'll come up north after the new year."

"That'd be nice. I'll talk to Dane about Christmas and see what he wants to do."

"Okay, sweetheart. I'll let you get back to work. I love you."

"Love you, too."

I turned to a cost analysis report I'd been ignoring for three days and decided to crunch the numbers when my phone lit up again. It was a text from Dane.

Forgot 2 tell u all the art majors r putting on a showcase this Fri. nite at 7pm. Can u make it?

I texted back.

Wouldn't miss it.

Should b pretty swanky. Invite any1 u want.

OK. Just talked 2 dad.

His reply was quick.

How'd that go?

Good.

Things r ok between u 2?

Yep.

Can u do me a favor and snag something from ur design dept. 4 me 2 wear on Fri.?

I'm pretty sure that's against all regulations but I'll c what I can do.

Thx sis.

C u Fri.

I picked up my desk phone and dialed the extension to Tuck's office. He answered swiftly and I could hear the smile in his voice.
"Hey gorgeous."
"What are you and Stewart doing Friday night?"
"Anything you want us to," he growled.
I rolled my eyes. "Not that. My brother is having an art showcase this Friday. It should be cool. You in?"
"Sure. I'll check with Stew and see what he's got going on."
"Dress code is nice."
"Do I know any other way?"
I giggled. It was true. Tucker was more stylish than me on my best day. "Touché."
"And maybe afterward the three of us can get drinks."
I pulled a calculator out of my desk drawer. "Sounds good."
"And then maybe after that…"
"We can all go home," I interrupted and laughed.
Tuck let out a low moan and my body responded in its usual shameless way. "Will I finally get to meet Reid?"
"No. We broke up."
"Was it because of me?"
I laughed so loudly the girl across the hall turned to look at me.
"It's good to hear you laugh, Sloane. Even if it's at my expense. For a split second after my tires got slashed I thought it might be him."
I frowned. "Why would you think that? What reason would

Reid have to slash your tires?"

"I don't know. It was just a thought. He seems like the possessive type. I thought he might've been jealous of our friendship. Sending that ridiculous flower arrangement and all. I told you that's how men mark their territory."

Just then I remembered Reid's icy gaze at dinner when I received Tucker's text message and the recollection was chilling. "I hadn't thought of that. But I highly doubt he'd go to those lengths."

"I'm sure you're right. Like I said, I didn't give it a second thought. I don't know why I thought of it at all. Why don't Stew and I pick you up Friday night so you don't have to take a cab?"

"That would be great. I'll give you the details when I know more. I've got to get back to work."

"Later."

I hung up the phone and started calculations for the cost analysis so it would be ready for Dallas that afternoon.

I was just putting the final touches to my makeup when the doorbell rang Friday night. I gave myself a final once over in the bathroom mirror and nodded appreciatively. I'd slicked my short, dark brown hair back with styling gel to give it a sophisticated, evening look. My designer ash gray, silk pantsuit was artfully belted at the waist and accompanied by a fabulous four strand, soft pink and gray necklace. I stuck a tube of lipstick, a compact, my cell, and debit card in my silver clutch and went to open the front door.

"Wow. You look like a million bucks," Tucker complimented.

I curtsied jokingly and then raised my eyes to admire his white button down shirt, opened at the collar, and black slacks. And in typical Tucker fashion he'd added an orange, blue, and black bow tie untied and tossed casually around his neck. He managed to look thrown together and graceful all at once. He was simply decadent.

"You don't look so bad yourself. Where's Stewart?"

"He couldn't make it. You'll have to suffer through my company tonight."

I narrowed my eyes at him. "Did you even invite him or did you arrange to have us be alone?"

Tucker's face dropped in feigned shock. "You think highly of yourself don't you?"

"Pot, kettle—kettle, pot."

Tuck smiled that charming grin of his and I almost dropped my panties right then and there.

"Let's go."

The art showcase was near Columbia's campus at an old converted warehouse on Broadway. Its white brick exterior was besieged with colorful, graphic graffiti and vibrant artwork. As Tucker neared the curb, I noticed they'd laid down a thick red carpet which led from the street to the canopied doorway. An attendant took the car to park and Tucker guided me inside placing his hand on the small of my back. A pulse of electricity jolted through me, even through the thickness of my coat. I was seriously considering having sex with him tonight.

The gallery was huge and each wall was cluttered with various paintings of still lives and abstracts, modernists and postimpressionists. Toward the back of the building were sculptures made of iron and clay, and others, recycled materials and wood. Everywhere you turned there was talent and creativity. I imagined these students felt much like Tuck and I did about our industry. A chance to reveal yourself through your art, your ideas, your inspirations. Their work jumped to life and took on an energy of its own, much like what I felt when a simple thread was woven into a finished product.

Tuck slipped off my pink wool coat and handed it to the young coat check attendant, along with his coat and scarf. A waitress came by carrying a silver tray of wine and Tucker took two glasses from her and handed me one.

"This is pretty impressive for a university," he commented as he sipped on his white wine.

I grabbed two cocktail napkins of tomato and goat cheese on crostino crudités. It was lightly drizzled with basil olive oil and I inhaled it in one bite. I heard Tuck chuckle beside me but I ignored him. I hadn't eaten dinner yet.

I felt a light tap on my arm and turned to see Hilary standing next to me. She was dressed in a killer purple, sleeveless dress that nearly swept the floor. It clung to every single curve of her young body and she wore a dainty, multi-layered gold chain. Her hair was swept back from her face in a messy up do, showcasing her wide brown eyes and full, nude painted lips. She represented my brother well and together they made a sickeningly handsome couple.

"Hi, Sloane. You look terrific," she gushed as she leaned in to give me an air kiss.

"You too. This is my friend, Tucker. This is Hilary, Dane's girlfriend," I introduced. It felt strange introducing her as his girlfriend. My brother had never had a serious relationship in his life.

She beamed. "Nice to meet you. I'm so glad you could come tonight."

"Where's Dane?" I wondered.

Hilary looked over her shoulder vaguely. "He's being bombarded by professors. I've barely gotten a chance to speak to him."

"Where's his work?"

"His main piece is hanging in the center but he's got some other paintings scattered around. Come with me."

We followed Hilary to a free standing wall in the middle of the gallery. A small crowd was gathered around and in the midst of it all, there Dane stood. He was explaining to the group the materials he'd used, why he'd chosen the subject matter, and answered various other questions about the piece. I couldn't have been more proud of him. He looked so calm, so self-assured and confident; I thought I'd burst with delight. He was also trendily dressed. I'd brought him a garment bag full of clothes yesterday and dropped it at his house for him to choose. He'd chosen to wear a pair of black skinny jeans, a vintage white tee with a faded picture of Marilyn Monroe on it, and a black blazer. He'd thrown on a pair of leather, high top black Converse and he splendidly looked the part of the stylish artist. His brown curls framed that gorgeous face and his green eyes danced in the light.

I squeezed my way to the front of the throng and Dane acknowledged my presence with an amicable wink but I'd barely noticed. The wall behind him held one massive painting, taking up nearly all the space and I was immediately absorbed into the realm he'd created. Depicted on a wide canvas in oil paints was a woman sleeping in a bed underneath a veil of inky night skies and muted silver stars. The four poster bed was at the forefront of the painting at the lower bottom corner. My eyes were instantly drawn there but the bed was small in comparison to the moon and stars. The woman was covered with a rumpled blanket and her pallid face glowed in a creamy beam of chalky moonlight. She was shrouded in a mollifying pall of silence. There was a tranquility Dane managed to capture, a beautiful stillness that made you envy her peaceful, uninterrupted sleep.

I took a step closer—drawn into the mysticism and wonder of the black and silver and gray colors; those bold brushstrokes that came together to form this masterwork. The woman's face was intimate and as clarity began to slowly dawn, I realized the woman in the painting was my mother. A younger, purer version of her former self. I noticed how much my own face was like hers. Even in sleep the shape of her mouth and chin were so well-known.

I wanted to avert my eyes; I didn't want to remember who she was because it hurt to recall that. She was no longer that tranquil creature—she hadn't been in years. How odd my brother had chosen to remember her that way. It was almost a farce to present her in that light. However, at one time that's exactly who she'd been.

The pounding in my chest began to also ring in my ears as I stood there staring at her. And very quickly the conversations around me became muffled and distorted. I felt myself slipping unwillingly as my mother's face stared back at me. She activated something dark inside of me—or maybe it wasn't her at all. Maybe it was just who I was. Dane was still talking but his eyes locked onto mine and he nodded almost unperceptively at me, as if he were giving me permission to leave or maybe a nod of acknowledgement that he understood my disdain for our mother. I took a clumsy step backward and felt Tucker's firm grip on my elbow as he steadied me. As I turned I was met with searching hazel brown eyes and instantly my reeling senses stabilized. I was again focused, transfixed on something else—someone else.

"Are you okay?" Sam asked leading me gently out of the crowd and to a semi-empty corner of the room.

"What are you doing here?" I muttered distractedly.

"I told Dane I'd try and stop by. He wanted me to come see his work and I haven't had the chance to stop by the campus museum. What happened to you while you were looking at that painting?"

I fiddled with the pearls at my neck, intertwining the strands, tangling them with one another. "It's my mother."

Sam peered over the heads of the group gathered around. "She's very beautiful. You look like her."

Did he just tell me I was beautiful? It was too much to ask, too much to hope for. I'd only be disappointed.

"What specifically about seeing her upset you?"

I licked my dry lips and grabbed another glass of wine as a tray passed by. Perfect timing.

"Sorry, professor. This is not a counseling session. I'm fine now. Thank you."

Sam leaned down to me and he was close enough that I could smell his shampoo and aftershave. It had to be what perfection smelled like.

"You're not okay and the sooner you admit it, the better. Are you sure you won't reconsider coming back to my office to see me? I think I can help. At least I want to try."

I shuffled back and forth nervously. His persistence was beginning to wear on me. I just didn't know if I was capable of going through with it.

"Listen," he went on, "I have a spot open on Tuesday evening at six. I won't book anything else that night and I'll be in my office waiting for you. If you come, great. If not, then I'll know the reason why."

I didn't know if it was the second glass of wine on an empty stomach or the irrational fluttering of butterflies churning in my belly, but I giggled. "That offer sounded a lot like a scene from *An Affair to Remember*."

Sam's face brightened with a lazy grin. "But let's pray you don't get hit by a cab on your way to see me."

From the corner of my eye I saw Dane making his way toward us. His green eyes were filled with concern and I put up my hands to thwart his next words. I didn't want anything spoiling his moment and certainly not my peculiar behavior. Besides, Sam had managed to calm me down quite effectively.

I rushed into Dane's arms and hugged him tightly. "*That* is amazing. I'm so proud of you."

His arms circled me fiercely and his body relaxed in relief. "I should've told you about the painting. I wasn't thinking," he said, looking contrite.

I reared back and grabbed his handsome face in my hands. "Are you kidding? You don't owe me any explanations. You're a genius, Dane, and your painting is beautiful. She would be just as proud of you as I am."

He swallowed hard and took my hands in his. "That means a

lot. Hi, Sam," he said turning. "I'm glad you could make it."

Sam shook his hand firmly. "You're a very talented young man."

"Thank you."

Hilary and Jane joined our group and after introductions were made, Dane was again dragged away by a professor and his groupie roommates followed. I was left alone again with Sam.

"Your brother shows incredible promise."

"I couldn't agree more." The proximity to him was becoming unsettling. Every nerve ending was alert with his nearness; every part of me came alive when I was close to him.

A large mass of people moved past us and I bumped into Sam's chest in an awkward attempt to create more space for them to squeeze by. His breath mingled with mine as I gazed up into his eyes. I heard his breath catch and my own labored under his penetrating stare. Something shifted in the air between us—a charge was ignited and then inflamed as we stood there face to face, the contact between us profound and electric. I felt my pulse quicken and then my body tremored as his fingertips brushed a wayward strand of hair away from my forehead. I saw a glimmer of a smile touch his lips as he opened his mouth to speak.

"Hey, I was looking for you beautiful," Tucker interrupted suddenly and my heart sank.

Sam took a wide step back from me as if he were intruding on some unspoken connection between Tuck and I.

"I lost you in the crowd. Who's your friend?"

I flexed my hands behind my back. "This is Sam Brody. Sam, this is Tucker Stevenson, my colleague."

Tucker grinned devilishly and draped an arm over my shoulder. "Is that what we're calling it now?"

I flushed three shades of pink and watched Sam's face twitch slightly with unease.

"It's nice to meet you," he greeted tightly. "I think I see a colleague of my own. I'll see you both later, I'm sure."

Sam departed and the loss of him was felt deep inside me, a gaping chasm.

"Who's the guy with the weird eyes?" Tucker quipped.

"He's a professor at Columbia. And his eyes are incredible."

Tuck glanced at me and then shrugged indifferently. "Let's look around."

Several flutes of wine later and after walking every inch of the gallery, the crowd began to thin out and disperse as the night came to an end. The artistry and talent in the room far exceeded my expectations. I'd been to several of these gatherings since my brother started attending school, but the level of work this year surpassed anything I'd seen outside of an actual museum.

Columbia professors, students, and a writer and photographer from the school newspaper, had been clamoring for Dane's attention all night. I felt bad for his classmates and the other artists who hadn't garnered nearly the same amount of attention. I watched my little brother float around the room naturally, making witty comments and giving intellectual remarks, posing for pictures, praising other artists, giving the occasional kiss on the cheek to Hilary, and putting everyone at ease. He belonged in this world. He owned it.

"We're all going to The Brewery for drinks. You wanna come?" Dane offered when he eventually made his way to me. He was beaming but I couldn't help notice the displeased look on Jane's face. Seeing Hilary and Dane together couldn't be easy for her.

"I'm not in the mood to drive into Queens. But you guys go and have a good time."

Dane kissed my temple swiftly. "Thanks again for being here."

"Be safe."

I said goodbye to him, Jane, and Hilary while Tucker went to grab our coats. I meandered toward the entrance, still oohing and ahhing at the amazing collection of artwork and noticed Sam standing near the exit. I walked up to him with an offbeat sense of urgency. I felt I needed to explain to him that Tucker and I were not romantically linked in any way. True enough, I'd considered going to bed with him a mere three hours ago, but I was past that now. I wanted Sam to know I was unattached.

"Did you enjoy yourself?" I started bravely.

"Definitely. I had no idea the level of talent Columbia was producing. You should be really proud of him."

"I am." I paused a beat. *Why was it so hard to talk to him?* "I thought you were going to say something earlier. Did you have something to tell me?"

He opened his mouth again to speak but must have thought better of it. I watched as his posture changed—stiffened.

"It was nothing."

Disappointment was imprinted across my forehead and I stuck my chin out like a petulant child. Something had just transpired between us—altered, but I didn't know what it was. And I still hadn't explained about my friendship with Tucker.

Sam looked over my shoulder and gave me a ghost of a smile. "Maybe I'll see you Tuesday."

He walked off just as Tuck approached and I felt like stamping my feet in frustration. I tugged my coat on angrily, annoyed with my lack of initiative and inability to form words when necessary.

"You okay?" Tuck asked.

I nodded and let him take my hand and lead me outside.

"You want to come in for a nightcap?" I offered as Tuck entered the brownstone behind me.

"You know it."

I flicked the light switch on the wall and froze. Tucker bumped into my back, pushing me forward. When I'd gathered myself, I stood motionlessly surveying my living room.

"What's wrong?"

I glanced around, taking in my surroundings, and something was off. I sensed it in every fiber of my being and the hair prickled on my forearms confirming my suspicions. Something was out of place but I didn't know what. Everything seemed to be where I left it but I felt an uneasiness that was either completely irrational or completely founded.

"Sloane, what is it?" he asked again.

"Someone's been in here."

Tucker stepped in front of me protectively, his eyes scanning the room. "How do you know?"

"I just do."

"Stay here."

Before I could protest, Tucker did a thorough sweep of the house. I heard him opening closets and recognized the rustling of my shower curtain. I heard the banging of doors and I stood in the open doorway trying to figure out what was different. He bounded around the corner and checked the kitchen and laundry room while I stood rooted to the ground.

"There's no one here and from what I can tell nothing's been taken. All the windows are locked tight. Look around and see if anything's missing."

I did as he suggested, conducting an exhaustive, systematic search of every nook and cranny. I didn't notice anything out of place in my bedroom or bathroom but I couldn't shake the feeling someone had been there.

"Anything?" Tuck asked upon my return to the living room.

"No. But something's off, Tuck. I feel it."

He closed and bolted the front door and helped me take my coat off.

"You're shaking," he said. "Do you want me to stay the night?"

I eyed him suspiciously.

"On the couch, I mean. I will if you want me to."

I thought it was a good idea. "Yes. Thank you."

As I tried to collect my thoughts, I started toward the kitchen to grab two wine glasses and suddenly I began to tremble uncontrollably. I pointed to the kitchen island as my voice quivered with alarm.

"Tuck."

He was by my side in an instant, staring down at the butcher knife lying on the countertop.

"Did you leave that there?" he asked quietly.

"No," I breathed.

"Is it yours?"

I glanced at the butcher block of knives I kept on the other side of the kitchen and one of the knives was missing from its place.

"Yes, it's mine."

"That's strange," he mumbled.

It was more than strange, I thought to myself. I was positive I hadn't left it there. And if I didn't, who'd been in my house?

CHAPTER TWELVE

It was remarkable how far Dallas' new store in Chelsea had come in only a few weeks. All of the electrical work had been completed, counters and shelves were installed, the roof had been repaired, and the walls had been painted a bright, stark white. The white tiled floor, speckled with gold flecks, glistened underneath bright halogen lights. Shiny metal clothing racks had been delivered over the weekend and waited in cardboard boxes to be unpacked and assembled. Containers of merchandise I'd personally handpicked were ready to be opened, unfolded or hung, and put on display. It was one of my favorite parts of the job; setting up the store just the way I wanted and laying out all the stock for prospective customers gave me a thrill. But first I had to weed through the massive inventory list and triple check everything I'd ordered was shipped correctly and none of the accessories were damaged. It was a long process but one I enjoyed. I liked the methodical task of ticking off boxes and crossing things off a list. It kept my hands and my mind busy.

Dallas had bribed his two, college-age sons to come and do the heavy lifting. They were unpacking boxes when I arrived, assembling racks, and installing glass doors in the display counters. A massive, gold gilded mirror stood in a crate waiting to be mounted on one of the walls. Dallas greeted me in his usual, gruff manner as I entered the store.

"Morning, Sloane. What've you got for me?"

I pulled out a detailed diagram of the store layout and briefly discussed my ideas with him. I had very definite plans about how I wanted the store to look and much to my delight, Dallas agreed with them all. With that out of the way, I grabbed my clipboard and inventory checklist and began counting and sorting through merchandise. Dallas locked the front door, plugged in his iPod at the docking station, and the store became a funky little dance club. I eyed Dallas warily. This was not at all like him.

He shrugged his shoulders and said, "What? We have to make all this hard work as fun as possible, don't we?"

His sons groaned in agreement, clearly unhappy about having to be there, and I laughed. I began slicing open boxes and bobbing my head to the electric house music pulsating through the room.

We broke for lunch well after two o'clock. I sat on the cool floor and leaned up against a counter, sweaty and exhausted. Dallas treated us all to pizza and we sat around in silence, heaping food into our mouths hungrily.

"This is really starting to come together," Dallas remarked with an orangey shimmer of pizza grease shining from the corner of his mouth.

I wiped my mouth and looked around the room. He was right. The store looked amazing. A minimal selection of winter items were in the back of the store and the display stands at the entrance held the majority of the collection of bright, floral prints for spring. Everything I'd ordered had arrived in pristine condition and nearly all of the accessories, too. I found some damaged necklaces and rings that had lost their stones and they would have to be returned to our supplier. But everything else was just as it should have been. Almost all the clothes were unpacked but the large mirror still needed to be hung as well as the mirrors for the fitting rooms. There were still mannequins to assemble and clothe for the front windows, registers to connect, and the sound system still needed to be installed. There was still plenty to do before the store could open, but it was a good day's work and I was satisfied.

"It looks great," I finally commented after several more bites of pizza and a thorough inspection around the room.

"Word on the street is Design 22 landed Winston's. Any truth to that?" Dallas asked bluntly.

I didn't know if the news was public knowledge yet or if Sandra wanted to make an official announcement. And where was he getting his information?

"Where'd you here that?" I dodged.

"So it's true."

"I didn't say that."

"I just want to know if my best girl is still going to have time for me. Frenzy's success depends on your brilliance and eye for fashion."

I was almost moved by his uncharacteristic remark. Rarely did he issue a compliment; unconstructive criticism was more his style.

"I care about Frenzy's success as much as you do. You gave me my first real chance to show what I can do and I won't forget that. You won't lose me."

"Glad to hear it."

We settled back into a comfortable silence, broken only by the occasional grunt or belch from the men in the room. After I'd taken a few minutes to digest my lunch, I brushed off my blue jeans and got back to work.

My legs were sore on my walk to work Tuesday morning. I'd overtired my muscles breaking down boxes and moving heaving cartons all around Dallas' store yesterday. Manual labor had never been my thing and now my body was paying the price. But it had been worth it. When I finally left at seven that evening, everything was in its rightful place, right down to the sunglasses on the mannequin. There were still minor details to attend to but nothing Dallas couldn't handle on his own. I would be in attendance at the store's soft opening on Sunday and the grand opening on Monday.

I narrowly avoided slamming into the same fire hydrant I'd hit several days ago, but I sidestepped quickly and avoided another run in and ruined pair of pantyhose. I was left with a sense of wistfulness as I passed the very spot where I'd met Sam. The place where he'd fascinated me with those mismatched eyes, the place where I first saw those strong, builder hands, and the place where time gave the impression of completely standing still. I still remembered how I felt in the moment and how I'd felt every day since. He had a hold on me. An inexplicable, incomprehensible, confounding grip on all that I was. I didn't know what intangible thing he possessed that I was so drawn to, so hungry for. My feelings for him defied rational thought and logic, yet they were the realest emotions I'd ever felt.

The thought of him waiting on me tonight played over and over in my mind. It pained me to think of him sitting alone in an empty office and me knowing I'd never show. How could I go? How could I subject myself to the shadows I'd tried so hard to cast off—willingly allow myself to let the darkness creep in? I didn't know how I'd ever recover if I let it in. It would consume me—take me prisoner and break me. But my desire to see him was beginning to prevail even over my fear of exposing my past. I was so mixed up. My thoughts ran in twenty different directions but in the end, they always came back to Sam. It was his face I imagined when I needed to quiet my mind. It was his voice I heard and his smile I saw when I needed to escape from myself. He somehow provided an outlet I didn't know I needed; he was the answer to questions I didn't know I'd been asking. If I was going to face the foul fiends of my past I wanted to do it with him. I just wasn't sure I wanted to.

Tucker bombarded me the minute I walked in the door at work and wrapped his arm around my shoulders snugly.

"What are you going to do about the knife thing?" he whispered as we passed the receptionist desk.

I'd tried to forget about that little incident. "What is there *to* do?"

"I think we should have called the police."

I stopped at the entrance to his office. "And tell them what? A knife was left out on my countertop? They're going to look at me like I'm crazy."

"It might've had fingerprints or something on it."

"I doubt it."

He eyed me seriously. "You're sure you didn't leave it out by accident? You're positive?"

I exhaled heavily. "I don't know. I don't think so. But I can't say for sure."

"The other night you were so sure and now you're not?"

"Which is exactly why we're not going to waste the police's time. They'd kick me out of the station before I could get a word in edgewise."

Tuck nodded. "It still makes me uneasy."

It made me uneasy, too. "Don't worry about it," I reassured him with a conviction I didn't feel. "I'm sure I'm just being forgetful." Deep down I knew that was a lie. But I didn't want him to worry. I was freaked out enough for the both of us.

"If you say so."

"Dane is the only other person with a key, so if it wasn't me, I'm sure it was him."

"Did you ask him?"

I looked sheepishly down the hallway. "I asked him in a roundabout way so he wouldn't get suspicious but he said he never touched it."

"Sloane…" he started thoughtfully.

"Let's not panic yet until we really have something to worry about."

He paused as if he'd just thought of something. "You remember in October when your purse was stolen? What if someone made a copy of your house key? It's possible."

I hadn't thought of that. And now that I had, my fear was escalating to hysteria.

"I don't want to scare you to death but I do want you to be realistic and careful. If you need me to come stay with you, let me know. Or better yet, you can come stay at my place. Don't try and be a fucking hero."

"Thanks, Tuck. I won't. I promise."

Plopping down in my office chair, I thought about what Tucker said. What if someone else did have a key to my house? I booted up my laptop and Googled locksmiths immediately. After I'd found a reputable company and read the reviews, I put in a call and scheduled an appointment for the same day. I shot Dane a text to let him know I'd be issuing a new key to him, grabbed my purse, and headed back home to meet the locksmith in an hour.

I ended up staying home for the rest of the day once the locksmith left. I called Sandra and told her I was feeling under the weather but I'd continue to check my emails in case anything pressing popped up unexpectedly. Home was really the last place I wanted to be. Even though the locks were changed, I only felt a small sense of relief. The idea that someone had been in my house, possibly going through my things, made me queasy. I would've felt better if it had been a robbery. At least that way I could explain the intrusion. But leaving a knife on the countertop was a threat, a fierce threat, and I didn't know what to do with that. Who in the world would want to harm me? Or at the very least want to intimidate and frighten me? I hadn't made any enemies that I was aware of. I didn't know who I could've offended so greatly. The other part, the part I desperately wanted to believe, was that I'd left the knife out by accident. I *had* been chopping vegetables the other night. Perhaps I'd overlooked putting the knife up. *That's what I choose to believe,* I decided resolutely. I needed to believe that. The only other thought I could entertain, I didn't even want to utter. What if it had been someone I knew? What if it had been Reid?

It was nearing six o'clock and I was still sitting on my couch with the lights off and a quickly setting sun in the background. I'd long finished working and Alanis Morissette was singing angrily from my wireless speakers. Her angst filled voice was one I could relate to presently. I lost myself in the lyrics, in the edgy guitar rhythm and drum cadence. She gave voice to an internal melee, my personal life soundtrack. I'd opened all the blinds facing the street and hazy yellow streetlights streamed through, but I stared unseeingly, just me and Alanis. I'd had nearly an entire bottle of wine and I was starting to feel relaxed but sleepy. Through cloudy eyes I watched the clock in the living room tick from six to six ten, six fifteen, six-thirty. I chewed on my lower lip distractedly and drummed my fingers on my propped up knees. Suddenly, I surged to my feet. I didn't care what we did or didn't talk about. Sam was waiting for me and I wanted to go to him.

I practically ran all the way from the subway station to Sam's building. I was too impatient for the elevator and opted for the staircase, taking two steps at a time. I was out of breath by the time I reached Sam's door and it was closed. I knocked louder than was necessary but there was no answer. I could see it was dark inside from the crack underneath the door and I glanced at my watch. Seven thirty. I could've kicked myself. What was I expecting? Him to wait for an hour and a half?

I stood outside his door for a few minutes; it helped to imagine him on the other side, sitting behind his handmade desk, looking at me with a curious glint in his eyes. Standing next to his space, his things, made me feel oddly closer to him. I leaned against the wall and closed my eyes for a minute, trying to rationalize my deep disappointment and catch my breath.

"Sloane?"

I was afraid to open my eyes for fear what I'd heard wasn't true—wasn't happening. I wanted so badly to see Sam that now I was imagining his voice. I'd rather have stood there and imagined him than open my eyes and he not really be there. But I sensed his presence and then I felt his body heat next to me, his breath on my face, and my eyes shot open.

"Are you okay?" he asked.

I wasn't. My heart was pounding furiously but my senses were dulled by the bottle of Chardonnay I'd had. It was a strange sensation and I wanted to giggle with the ludicrousness of my situation.

"You're here. I thought you'd left," I managed to squeak out.

"I did leave. I left my phone inside and I came back to get it."

He reached around me to unlock the door and I pressed myself against the wall. He stepped inside his office and retreated quickly, locking the door behind him. He paused to look down at me and I felt that familiar shock of electricity crackle in the air between us. I was sure he felt it, too, because he inadvertently leaned in to me and I heard his rapid breathing.

"I waited for you," he admitted softly.

It wasn't accusatory; it sounded more like a declaration. He wanted me to know he was expecting me, waiting on me to arrive. He'd been exactly where he'd said he be and he'd waited—on *me*. He wanted to see me as badly as I'd wanted to see him. Or, I could be reading all the signs wrong. Was I seeing and hearing only what I wanted to?

"I know. I'm sorry. I went back and forth all day if I should come or not."

"What made you finally decide?"

This, I thought. Standing here next to you breathing you in. *This* is what made me come.

"I don't know," I fibbed. "I was doing okay until I got here."

My stomach took this inopportune time to grumble loudly and I glanced down at my feet.

"Why don't we get some food in you? We can talk over dinner," he suggested and I leapt at the chance to spend time with him outside his office walls.

We walked four blocks up to The Spotted Pig. The Tuesday night crowd was relatively light and we were seated after a short wait at a table with low bar stools. The atmosphere was lively and eclectic; pictures of fish and pigs were scattered haphazardly on brick columns and a colorfully tattooed wait staff meandered around the room, friendly and unrushed. Sam pulled out my bar stool for me, its patterned seat colored in a faded, turquoise chevron. We sat and a waitress with a silver nose ring handed us two menus.

"What do you have a taste for?" he asked me.

You. "A good salad I think."

"What happened when you got to my office?"

I looked up quizzically from my menu. "What do you mean?"

"You said you were doing okay until you got to my office. What happened when you got there?"

I was still buzzed from my wine and I took a hesitant, but brave breath. "I was disappointed you weren't there."

He put his menu down and gave me his full, undivided attention. "Then you wanted to talk?"

"I don't know if I did or didn't. But I couldn't stand the thought of you sitting there waiting on me not knowing if I was going to show up or not."

Sam smiled. "So you felt bad for me?"

"Yes. Well, no. I'm not s-sure," I stammered.

"Do I make you nervous, Sloane?"

He said my name like it was a delicacy. It dripped off his tongue and he caressed it, stroked it skillfully.

"A little."

He leaned back and frowned. "That's not good. If this is going to work you have to feel like you can trust me. And I haven't done a very good job of making you comfortable, I'm afraid. What can I do?"

I shook my head wildly. "It's not you, trust me. I'm a mess."

"You're not. And through our sessions I'll prove it to you—if you want to continue seeing me."

"It was good to see you the other night at the showcase. I know my brother appreciated it," I said, artfully changing the subject.

"I'm really impressed by his talent and the talent of his classmates. It was exceptional to see." He paused. "Your friend Tucker seems nice."

Did I hear a hint, the slightest hint, of jealousy? I couldn't be sure but it was the opening I needed to clear the air.

"He is. We've worked together for a few years but we're not dating or anything," I explained awkwardly.

"You're not? Because he seemed quite fond of you."

"I'm sure it was the three glasses of wine he'd already had. We're definitely not dating."

I thought I saw relief flicker in his eyes but I wasn't sure. Everything Sam did was with the utmost subtlety. I couldn't read him easily and it frustrated me.

I wanted to shift the focus. "Tell me more about your family."

"What do you want to know?"

"Tell me about your siblings."

"My oldest brother is Daniel. He designs software and he's pretty much a nerd. But he's got a great sense of humor, kind of a dry wit and he cracks me up all the time. Then there's my sister, Laurel. She owns her own greeting card business in a little store in Minnesota and she's the exact opposite of Daniel. She's very serious. She's also a very talented writer. I'm in the middle and after me is my twelve-year-old brother, Liam. He's a great kid—kind of a typical boy. He plays football and likes girls. He takes after me with woodworking and he's becoming really good at it. When I'm home, I try and spend as much time with him as I can because he seems to be taking a real interest in it. My ten-year-old sister Hannah is obsessed with all things One Direction related, Nick Jonas, and every preteen show on the Disney Channel. She's also really involved in ballet. She's pretty good."

"Is it hard being away from all of them?"

"Sometimes, especially Liam and Hannah because they're so young. Me, Daniel, and Laurel all got to grow up together but Liam and Hannah only have each other in the house. I wish I could spend more time with them and be a more active part of their lives. But my life, at least for now, is in New York and I'm really starting to love it. I have great colleagues, great students, and I meet a lot of interesting people."

Was I included in the head count of interesting people?

"Why don't we try this? For every personal question you ask me, I get to ask you one in return. And I promise I won't dig too deep tonight."

I guess it was only fair. I knew far more about him than he knew about me.

"I'll give it a try."

"If you feel too uneasy at any point, we stop. The goal is to make you more comfortable with me and to learn to open up at your own pace. Do you think you can do that?"

Our waitress popped up to take our orders and placed two glasses of water with lemon on the table. I was going to need something stronger than water.

"Who goes first?" I asked.

"Well, I already answered the first question so it's your turn."

I already knew I was going to regret this. But at least it afforded me more time to spend with Sam and learn everything I could about the handsome counselor. Knowing I could stop at any time was also a relief. I took a gigantic breath and a sip of water.

"Shoot, professor."

CHAPTER THIRTEEN

"Where did you grow up?"

"Middletown, New York. What do you do in your spare time?"

He chuckled. "I grade a lot of papers. I just moved to New York so I spend most of my time unpacking and trying to get my apartment in order."

"Still?" I questioned.

"I went to work two days after I moved here. I haven't really had the time to unpack. I'm living out of boxes."

"Do you need any help?" I offered before I'd even thought about the implication. He was going to think I was nuts. "I like that kind of stuff, is all." I tried to explain. "I like interior design and organizing things."

"I may take you up on that."

I breathed a sigh of relief as my glass of Nouveau was delivered to the table.

"Tell me about your relationship with Dane."

"Why?"

"I'm trying to establish why you feel the need to protect him."

"Do you think that I do?"

"I think *you* think that you do. It's evident in the way you interact with him and I'm curious to know where that stems from."

"I'm sure you know all about us. Didn't he tell you everything there is to know?"

"You know I can't discuss our sessions with you. But for the record, Dane talks about himself, not you. I can only discover *you* from what *you* tell me."

I took a large gulp of the red wine. This was the least romantic date I'd ever been on. "He's my little brother. I think it's natural for an older sibling to want to look out for their younger one. Don't you feel like that about your brother and sister?"

"In a way, yes. Especially Hannah."

"Then you understand."

"Are you going to answer any of my questions directly or are you going to skirt around them all?"

Sam was smiling at me but I heard the serious undertone in his voice. He was right. I had to quit dodging him.

"As you probably know, our childhood wasn't an easy one. I tried to shield him as much as I could from my parents arguing and the constant fighting. I guess the need to protect him has carried over into adulthood. That's unhealthy, right?"

Sam leaned across the table and I could smell him. I inhaled deeply.

"Not necessarily. And the reasons you protected him are not unhealthy at all. You wanted to protect him from the verbal abuse in your house. Do you feel as if you accomplished that? Like you kept him safe?"

"I believe it's my turn to ask a question."

He nodded his head in agreement.

"Do you have a girlfriend?" I asked bluntly.

"No. Now answer."

"Yes. I kept him safe," I confessed quietly. I didn't like the memories that were on the brink, the edges of my mind, pugnaciously wanting to come forth. I wanted to give this counseling thing a chance, truly, but I was already starting to feel uneasy and unsafe. Sam didn't make me feel unsafe but the topic of conversation did. It wasn't my comfort zone, wasn't my happy place. I drank some more of my wine, determined to keep trying. It was my turn to ask a question. Since I couldn't read his expressions, I thought I'd ask point blank how he felt about me. I'd had just enough wine to give me the courage to ask and just enough curiosity to want to know.

"Do you find me attractive?"

He didn't blink. "Yes. Very. Tell me how the painting of your mother made you feel the other night."

Damn. I couldn't even process his compliment or how my heartrate increased instantaneously because I was already focused on my next reply. He was good. He was really good at this.

"I felt like the painting was a lie."

"Why?"

"Because that's not who she is. That beautiful, sleeping, peaceful thing he painted is not how I see her."

"Then how do *you* view her?"

"She's manipulative and cunning. She lies and deceives and she hurt all of us. For years, she did nothing but cause irreparable damage. Dane's painting was beautiful but it was all a lie."

"Did you always feel that way about her or was there ever a time when you had fond memories of her?"

"My turn, professor. What do you find the most attractive about me?"

This time I saw Sam flinch. I was beginning to get under his skin.

"I don't think I should answer that."

"Why not? You want me to tell you my life story but you don't want to be open with me? Answer, please."

"Your eyes."

"What about them?"

"My turn. Tell me about a positive experience with your mom. How did you feel about her when you were a little girl?"

It seemed like such a long time ago it was honestly difficult to recall a time when my mom seemed normal. Nearly my whole life I'd demonized her, looked down on her with such hateful disgust and complete disregard that I wasn't sure I *ever* liked her.

"My earliest memory of her was when I was about four or five. She was walking me to school and I remember her holding my hand so tightly, like she was afraid to let me go. She was near tears but I couldn't understand why. I don't remember being particularly scared or nervous to go to school so it wasn't like she was comforting me. She just seemed to want me close to her. It was almost as if she were scared or frightened of something, but I don't know why."

"And that's your earliest positive memory of her? Nothing after that?"

I shrugged. "No. So to answer your question I don't remember ever feeling anything for her except contempt."

The waitress came back and set down an apple and walnut salad for me and a burger with Roquefort cheese and shoestring fries in front of Sam. The smell of his food made my mouth water and slightly regretful I'd ordered a healthy meal. We both took a minute to dive into our food and I needed the reprieve. There was so much more to uncover, so much more I would have to let myself feel if this line of questioning continued. But he hadn't answered my last question yet and I desperately wanted to know.

"I believe you were saying something," I teased, "about my eyes?"

Sam licked mayonnaise off the corner of his mouth and my entire body tensed. I wondered if he knew how incredibly attractive he was. He took his time swallowing and then reached for his water glass. He was stalling, I realized, and I couldn't help but smirk. It was about time he had his feathers ruffled; he'd certainly made me nervous on more than one occasion.

"This conversation is completely unprofessional," he argued decidedly.

"It's a good thing you're the professional then and I'm not. You keep your questions for me professional and I'll ask you whatever I like."

"That hardly seems fair."

"I didn't make the rules, professor."

He shifted in his seat. "They're golden."

I squinted at him. "What?"

"Your eyes. They're light brown with these incredible gold flecks in them. It was the first thing I noticed about you when I saw you. Well, the second thing I noticed. The first thing I noticed was how clumsy you are."

I threw a crouton at him and laughed. "I'm not really. I was *that* particular day but not usually."

"Should we continue our session?"

I sighed and stuffed my mouth full of lettuce and walnuts.

"Had enough?"

I nodded. I just wanted to sit and stare at him. I didn't want to talk; I wanted to soak him in.

"Can you at least admit now that you need me? Can I put you on the books indefinitely on Tuesday nights at six?"

I could admit that I needed him but not in the way he meant. But something about having a set day once a week excited me. It was the only way I could guarantee I'd see him. How pathetic was

I? Scheduling painful counseling sessions just to gawk at a man I didn't know? I was ashamed of myself. But I did it anyway.

"Okay. If you really think you can help. I'm willing to give it a try."

The pleased look on his face was enough confirmation I'd done the right thing. At the very least I got to see him on a regular basis. At the very most he could save me from myself once and for all.

"Do you think maybe we could see each other outside of your office?" I ventured boldly, my liquid courage again allowing me to speak my mind confidently. What did I have to lose? I'd fallen in front of the man twice and told him at least some of the details of my troubled youth. If he was willing to accept me with the knowledge he'd already ascertained, there was hope for us yet.

Sam cast me that lazy half grin I was growing to love and leaned across the table toward me. As soon as he opened his mouth to speak I heard my name but it hadn't come from him.

"Sloane? What are you doing here?"

I looked up to see Reid standing over our table, his cobalt eyes piercing into mine. I blinked frantically like I was seeing a ghost. I hadn't seen or heard from him since our awkward breakup and now here he was. After several seconds, I finally found my voice.

"Just grabbing some dinner. You?"

"The same." He turned toward Sam and stretched his hand out. "I'm Reid."

"Sam," he said politely. "You're a friend of Sloane's?"

"We were more than friends just a week ago. Now I'm not sure what we are. Sloane?"

They both looked at me and Reid's uncomfortable declaration caught me completely off guard. I felt my cheeks turn an embarrassed shade of crimson.

"Friends," I muttered quickly, "definitely friends."

"Well, there you have it. We're friends," Reid repeated mockingly. "I saw you over here and just wanted to stop and say hi. My food's ready. I'm sure I'll see you around."

I gaped after him, inwardly fuming at his derisive behavior and at the same time mortified to look Sam in the eye.

"Bad breakup?" Sam began gingerly.

"Sort of."

"And recent, too?"

"Yep." I tried to steer the conversation back to happier topics. "About us spending time together outside of your office hours…"

"It's not a good idea. We should keep our relationship strictly professional."

I didn't know if he could hear my heart breaking but the sound of it resembled something like the crushing of a Coke can. Dammit, Reid! His timing was incredible!

Sam and I fumbled our way through the rest of dinner with surface conversation and awkward pauses of silence. His body language had changed again—the same way it had at the art showcase when Tucker interrupted us. He probably thought I had men crawling out from every fissure of my life. I decided to try my fool proof, faithful approach. I moistened my lips and gazed up at him from under my lashes. I gave him my best wounded-puppy look and smiled softly.

"I disagree with what you said earlier. I think it's a great idea we see each other and I'd like to get to know you without the invasive psychoanalysis and therapy sessions. I want to know who you are."

Sam cleared his throat and leaned forward again. His eyes softened as he looked at me and I knew I had him.

"I want to know you, too," he said in a low voice and my toes curled inside my boots. "But only professionally speaking. I want to help you sort through the things that terrify you and are keeping you from living your life. Your past is holding you back and I want to help you move forward."

His rebuff stung and it made me angry. I was used to getting my way with men and the fact that he was obviously immune to my charms frustrated and confused me. "I'm not some head case you can just fix over a few sessions in your office. And I'm happy the way I am," I snapped.

"Are you?"

His condescending tone was too much for me and I grit my teeth. "Yes, I am. At least I was before you started prying into my life unasked."

"You're not a head case, Sloane. And I only want to help."

"You keep saying that but you can't."

"Only because you won't let me."

Logically, I knew my anger stemmed from Sam not wanting to spend time with me outside of Tuesday nights in his office. My disappointment overwhelmed me and it didn't allow me to think clearly. All I wanted was to deflect the pain so I didn't have to think about his rejection of me.

"I've hurt you," he said quietly.

His intuitiveness was spot on. "No," I lied.

"I didn't mean to and I'm sorry. I just think its best we keep things platonic."

"Why? Why are you so desperate to keep things professional between us?"

"Because I know I could fall in love with you."

Somehow I managed to keep breathing even though the air had been sucked from my lungs. The earth seemed to stand still and everything around us gave pause—held in an ephemeral suspension. My heart ached and raced at the same time. I was so incredibly moved by his pronouncement and saddened because somewhere inside I knew he'd never act on it. He wanted me but he didn't *want* to want me.

The waitress dropped off our bill and Sam laid down his credit card. The silence was thunderous between us.

"Is that a bad thing?" I questioned but I was afraid of his answer.

"For me, yes, I believe it is."

"Because you think I'm insane and you don't want to get involved with me?"

It was his turn to look wounded and my heart melted. "Of course not. I think you're perfect—flaws, imperfections, family secrets and all. But being with me can be complicated in more ways than one and I won't drag anyone down with me."

His honesty took me aback and aroused my curiosity. "And you think my life's not complicated? I'm the poster child for complicated."

The waitress returned his credit card. He signed and stood up hastily making it very clear our conversation was over.

Sam walked me to the subway station keeping a safe, two feet of distance between us. I jammed my hands into my coat pockets, angrily clenching and unclenching my fists for a good five blocks. I was having a hard time processing my rampant emotions. He walked me down to the platform and turned to me, his beautiful eyes staring into mine, burning into me.

"This is where I leave you."

Why did it sound like he was saying goodbye forever? Even standing in the freezing cold there was a heat radiating between us. It was undeniable, palpable. It burned with a wild frenzy—widespread, all consuming. I couldn't deny it if I tried and I didn't think he could either. I saw him bristle when I moved closer to him; his body tensed in reaction to my movement. He was as in sync with me as I was with him.

I moved toward him instinctually, as if we were magnets being pulled together by an involuntary force. I was linked to him in some ridiculous, unexplainable way. I didn't even know when it'd happened but he felt like the missing piece to my twisted puzzle. I heard his breathing stop and his lips twitched with the same voracious yearning I felt. I saw the delicate skin on his throat move as he swallowed, repressing his words, fighting the same desires that were raging inside of me. He looked over the top of my head, avoiding eye contact.

"I'll see you next Tuesday night?"

I was torn between crying and yelling, but all I could do was nod. Sam bit his bottom lip and turned on his heel. I stood on the platform and watched him disappear into the crowd of people. I knew he wasn't gone forever but it felt so final as I stood there alone watching him. I moved my leaden feet and stepped into the next sub as it glided to a stop. I walked on blindly and sat down, replaying the last half hour we'd spent together. He had feelings for me—that much was obvious. But he was determined not to act on them. And what did he mean being with him was complimented? His secrets could in no way compare to mine. I could see he was scared, it was the same fear I recognized in myself, but I wanted him. I wanted him with a fierceness and an urgency I'd never experienced before. I knew I had to get a hold of myself but I didn't want to. I *wanted* to think about Sam, wanted to let my heart feel what it wanted for him, wanted to love him. I could love him. I knew I could. I was in danger of falling so hard it frightened me to the core. I'd never been in love before but suddenly my heart only wanted Sam.

He wasn't going to make it easy on me. He wanted to relegate our relationship to weekly therapy sessions and nothing more. I would never be satisfied with that. I wouldn't be satisfied with anything less than having him in my life the way I wanted. Committed, all in, all mine.

I almost missed my stop thinking about my next move with Sam.

I squeezed through the subway's automatic doors before they closed on me and started my walk home. A light dusting of snow was falling and it lifted my spirits. It had been snowing for over a week now and the ground was covered in four inches of white powder. The snowfall in the street had been decimated by cars and trucks and turned into dirty, gray slush and the sidewalks had been conveniently shoveled. But the rooftops and tiny front lawns were blanketed in untouched, snowy wonder. It was hard to stay frustrated when the world was covered in snow—the sounds of the city and the voices in my head all but silenced underneath its white covering.

My tranquil daydreaming was interrupted by the blaring of my cell phone and I reached into my purse to retrieve it.

"Hey, what are you doing?" Dane asked and I could hear the smile in his voice which was completely infectious.

"Headed home. What's up?"

"I thought you'd like to know you're talking to a paid artist."

"What are you talking about?"

"One of my paintings from the art showcase sold!" he practically shouted, his voice oozing with enthusiasm.

"You're kidding! I thought it was just a project for your final grade. I didn't know you could actually purchase pieces."

"None of the pieces were up for sell. In fact, Professor D told us that wasn't even an option. Some legal mumbo jumbo about copyrighting or trademarking or whatever. Basically, any art we create belongs to the school until we graduate."

"So what happened? Who bought it?" I asked excitedly.

"I don't know. Professor D said it was anonymous. But whoever it was wouldn't take no for an answer until they came to an agreement with the dean and the chairman of the art department. Once all the legal stuff was settled, they called and asked me if I'd be willing to sell and of course I said hell yeah."

"That's unbelievable! I'm so proud of you."

"I can't believe someone fought to buy something I did. It's unreal."

"Not even. You're so uber talented it's ridiculous. How much did you get for it?"

"That's the best part. I got a check for fifteen hundred dollars."

"Holy shit, Dane!"

"Right? I can't believe it. I want to take you to dinner with my new riches for always being my biggest supporter."

My cheeks hurt from grinning. "You don't have to. Take Hilary out and do something nice for her. Or better yet, offer to pay some rent." I joked.

"Not gonna happen. And of course I'll take Hil out. But for all the years I took beer from you and ate all the food in your fridge, I can finally repay you back, at least in a small way. I want to, Slo."

"You're still drinking all my beer and eating all my food but I'll let you take me to dinner. Which painting sold?"

"I don't know. I didn't even stop to ask."

"That's so great. Let me know what night works for you for dinner."

"Cool. Talk later."

He hung up the phone and I couldn't stop smiling. I'd been waiting on the day Dane would be a huge success as an artist, when someone would recognize his unparalleled talent, and it looked like that day was coming sooner rather than later. I was so beyond proud of him it nearly burst my heart. It was exactly the news I needed to cheer me up and end the day on a high note.

Somewhere behind me, I heard a metal trash can lid hit the cement and rattle to a stop. I looked back over my shoulder but the streets were empty as I neared my brownstone. *Maybe it was a cat digging through the garbage*, I thought to myself. I kept walking, my mind engrossed with thoughts of Dane's bright future, when I heard another sound—this one more like the rustling of material. I paused only briefly to see if I could identify the noise but when I stopped, the noise stopped, too. I felt the hairs at the back of my neck stand on end and I quickened my step toward my house. I fiddled with my keys, trying to still my shaky hand long enough to get the key in the door. I finally did and swiftly stepped inside, locking the door behind me. I didn't turn on any lights immediately. Instead, I peered out the window between the slats of the blinds and waited, watching the street. I only waited a few minutes before I felt my lungs constrict and my body tremble as I watched Reid walk past my window.

CHAPTER FOURTEEN

"He's stalking you?" Tucker exclaimed the next morning.

I rolled my eyes at him. "I didn't say that, Mr. Overdramatic."

"Then how do you explain him showing up at The Spotted Pig *and* walking past your place on the same night?"

"Coincidence?" I asked sheepishly.

"Don't be daft, Sloane. We should call the police."

"And tell them my ex-boyfriend was at a public restaurant and walked on a public sidewalk? I have nothing to go on. I would sound ridiculous."

Tucker shut my office door. "I'm serious. What if he's the one who left the knife in your kitchen?"

I'd had the same fleeting thought but I'd dismissed it immediately in order to maintain my sanity. "Why would he do that? We only dated six months and we got along great. He'd have no reason to want to come after me."

"Reason has nothing to do with it. People who are unstable are not reasonable, Sloane. Maybe he's more upset about your breakup then he's let on. I think you should take precautions."

"Like what?"

"I don't know. Maybe you should consider staying with Dane for a while. Or me, if you want."

"I just had the locks changed so I don't think that's necessary. And please stop trying to get me in your bed." I kidded.

He perched on the edge of my desk and swung his leg beside my chair. "I'm serious. Maybe you should think about buying a gun."

I cringed at the thought. "Not for me. Guns terrify me."

"Well, you can't just sit back and do nothing."

"Actually, that's exactly what I plan on doing. I don't know if Reid is after me or anyone else for that matter. I saw him twice on the same night, so what? I'm not going to overreact and neither should you. I appreciate your concern but I have no proof and until I do I'm not going to worry about it."

Tucker looked at me warily and sighed. "Okay. But promise me you'll be safe. If anything even looks a little bit off to you, promise me you'll call the cops. I can't stand the thought of anything happening to you. And if you need me…"

"I know. You're there. Thanks."

He shook his dark head at me and waltzed out of my office. I watched him go, absently thinking how much I valued our friendship. He really was good to me. He'd never wanted anything but the best for me and I appreciated it. It was good to have someone looking out for me—even if he was being paranoid. At least I *hoped* he was being paranoid. There'd been some questionable moments in mine and Reid's relationship, some instances where I felt apprehensive, but I didn't think he was capable of hurting me. I hoped I wasn't being too naïve.

I turned my attention elsewhere. Frenzy's grand opening was in a few days and there was still some work to be done. On top of that, Sandra had asked me to head up the collection for the women's department at Winston's which was a great honor and a greater responsibility. There was enough work to be done to last me weeks on end and our contract was set to start in the first quarter of the new year. There were fabrics and prints to be chosen, suppliers to contact, and cost projections to be made. Sandra was going to want most of that information ready for her by our Friday meeting so I forced Reid out of my mind and went to work.

It was seven o'clock before I looked up again. I hadn't even noticed the dimmed lights in the hallway until I heard the vacuum running in the front lobby, alerting me to the fact that the cleaning crew was there and it was well past closing time. I swiveled back and forth in my office chair idly, wanting to go home but feeling too lazy to move. It was quiet in the office; all of my coworkers long gone for the evening. Even Tucker hadn't stopped by to say good night like usual and it was peaceful being there alone. But too much quiet time allowed my mind to wander to thoughts of Sam. I wondered what he was doing and where he was. Was he working in his office in West Village or was he sitting in his barren apartment? Was he eating dinner alone or buried under a mound of college essays? I craved him—wanted to share the same space and air as him. I unraveled when I was near him; I simply came undone. And I couldn't wait until next Tuesday to see him. I didn't want to. Part of me, the prideful side, was telling me to go home. The other part, the part of me that operated under emotion, was telling me to call him and talk. I needed to know we were okay. We'd left things so open ended and unsettled. I felt like there were things left unsaid. On the other hand, I was on the edge of appearing desperate and I didn't do desperate. Although my heart was shouting at me to find him, I decided not to.

I shut down my computer and listlessly packed my belongings, all the while talking myself into walking straight home and not heading toward his office. *He probably wasn't even there*, I told myself. It would be a wasted trip.

With that settled in my mind, I gathered my things and headed out. I saw my massive vase of flowers still sitting on the table in the lobby and I motioned to Brenda, the cleaning lady, to remove her headphones and switch off the vacuum.

"Hi, Miss Sloane. You're here late. I haven't seen you in a long time."

"I know. I'm just heading home now. Would you do me a favor? Please get rid of those flowers. If you want to take them home you're more than welcome to."

Brenda grinned and adjusted the red bandana tied around her blond head. "They're lovely, I will. Are you sure you don't want them?"

I buttoned my coat and tugged on a wool hat over my short, bobbed hair. "Quite sure. Enjoy them."

"Thank you."

As I stepped onto the sidewalk, I glanced down to fasten the last button on my coat and slammed right into the chest of Sam Brody. I dropped my purse and briefcase in the collision and it lay on the snow soaked sidewalk as I stared up into his face, baffled. Had I dreamt so hard I'd made him a reality? He stooped down to retrieve my things and I stood there in astonishment, a cloud of cold air forming in front of my gaping mouth. He handed me my purse and I took it from him stiffly, my limbs frozen with shock. He looked at me searchingly, his colorful eyes dancing around my face and he reached out to tug my hat down over my ears.

"What are you doing here?" I murmured. My heart was singing but I was fighting to appear composed. I was anything but. "How did you know where I worked?"

"You told me in our first session together and I looked up the address. I honestly didn't expect to catch you here this late but I took a chance. I didn't like the way we left things yesterday," he explained.

"You mean the part where you told me we couldn't see each other outside of our sessions?"

He nodded. He was feeling the same way I was. It wasn't just my imagination. We *were* connected to each other.

"I wasn't fair to you. I feel like I might have misled you in some way."

I crinkled my eyebrows in confusion. "In what way?"

"It was never a good idea for me to counsel you. I knew it from the moment you walked into my office. I think it would be good for you to talk to someone—just not me. I can recommend some people to you."

I wondered if my face looked as stunned as I felt. I wasn't expecting this conversation to go in the direction it was headed.

"So what changed?" I whispered. I felt my breathing grow shallow as if an elephant were sitting on my chest.

"My feelings for you," he admitted, running an exasperated hand through his dark locks. "I can't keep seeing you—professionally or otherwise. You were right when you said I couldn't help you."

"But I don't understand. Why not? If you care about me and I care about you, why can't we be together?"

He scowled as if he were angry with himself for caring for me. "Do you know the physical restraint I have to incur in order not to kiss you right now? Every time I see you?"

I took a step closer to him and he instinctively moved back. My face fell.

"You don't have to fight me, Sam. Kiss me. Please."

His face twisted uncomfortably, his lips slightly parted with wanting. He was battling me so hard. But he didn't have to, not me. Didn't he know I wanted him just as badly? He lifted his arm as if he were going to reach out and stroke my cheek but he didn't. I needed to feel his hands on me, needed to feel physically connected to him. Shamelessly, I grabbed his hand and placed it on my cheek. I heard him inhale harshly and he cupped my face in his hand. I closed my eyes and leaned into his palm. He offered only a small part of himself and I took it all in, as much as I could. I didn't know how long it would last. His face was inches from mine, our lips close, pleading with each other to be touched, tasted.

"Don't you think I want to?" he asked softly.

I leaned up on my toes and closed my eyes and I felt his hand drop away. I opened my eyes slowly, reluctantly. He was staring down at me with such desire in his eyes I could barely contain my lust for him. He was driving me mad with an insatiable longing I could no longer control.

"Sloane, it's because of my faith I don't think we should see each other anymore."

That snapped me back into reality. I blinked rapidly as if I didn't comprehend. I was at a loss for words. Again.

"Did you hear me?"

"Yes. Your faith is why we can't be together?"

"One of many reasons."

"Did you think I'd have a problem with you being religious or something?"

"Don't you?"

I didn't have a problem with any part of him. "No. Have you taken some vow of celibacy that I need to know about?"

He chuckled at that and I was grateful for the lighter mood. "I think only Catholics and monks take vows of celibacy. But I am practicing abstinence."

My eyes grew large and I was horribly unsuccessful at hiding my stunned reaction. Who practiced abstinence in the twenty-first century? No one I'd ever dated, that's for sure. And certainly not me.

Before I could stop I heard myself inquire, "You're not a virgin are you?"

"No."

I breathed an unintentional sigh of relief. "Then if you're not a virgin why are you practicing abstinence? You've already done the deed."

"But it doesn't mean I have to continue doing it. It's a tenet of my faith to wait until marriage. And even though I've already done the deed, as you so eloquently put it, I plan on waiting until marriage to sleep with anyone else. Not everyone understands this or the reasons why I'm doing it."

"Your reasons are your reasons and I respect that." No one had ever asked me *not* to have sex in a relationship. But if that's what he wanted I was okay with it. Actually, I was interested in the challenge, although it wouldn't be easy. I could tell he was relieved by my response because his shoulders and face relaxed. Was that the obstacle he thought we couldn't overcome? Was that the complicated part of his life he spoke of? That was nothing. Easy breezy.

"I'm glad to hear you say it. But it doesn't change anything. I only came here tonight to say goodbye and wish you well."

If he was going for the shock factor he'd certainly achieved it tonight.

"Wish me well? That's all you have to say to me? You tell me one day you could love me and the next day you don't want anything to do with me? I don't get it and I don't buy it. You could have told me this over the phone. Why did you come here?"

I could feel tears stinging the back of my eyes but I didn't cry. I refused to let myself break down in front of him. Sam shifted his weight to his other foot.

"You're right and it wasn't fair to you. I could've called you but I wanted to see you again. You're my weakness, Sloane. I realize now coming here was a mistake, too. It just made everything harder."

"But you still haven't told me why," I argued. "Why are you doing this?"

"I'm sorry if I hurt you. That was never my intention. And I'm sorry I didn't stop this before it got out of hand. I thought I could handle it and I was wrong. Please, forgive me."

I didn't know what I was forgiving him for. I didn't understand any of it. What I did know was he was walking out of my life and breaking my heart. I didn't know how to convince him to stay or even if I should try. This man owed me nothing—not explanations, not apologies, nothing. And yet here I was, expecting everything. My vanity wouldn't allow me to keep standing there—vulnerable, quivering with tears and on the periphery of losing my mind. I had to make my feet move. I had to get away.

"You did stop whatever this is before it got out of hand so don't worry about it. And there's nothing to forgive you for," I bit out. The best defense is a good offense. "Take care of yourself."

I turned to storm off triumphantly, head high. But he called after me and I turned back around. I was so weak around him and I hated myself for it, particularly when I was trying to stomp off with any shred of dignity.

"Please don't leave angry with me. I couldn't stand it," he pleaded and the sorrowful look on his face broke my heart.

"I'm only doing what you wanted. You don't get to dictate to me *how* I do it."

I walked off and barely made it to the next block before hot tears streamed down my cheeks. I wiped at them angrily but they continued to roll in searing torrents. I couldn't get home fast enough and when I did, I stripped down and climbed into bed. It was barely eight o'clock and I hadn't eaten dinner, but I didn't care. I wanted to be in the dark and underneath the covers. But there was no escaping Sam. I was like a puppet on a string and he pulled and moved me every which way; he controlled my every move, orchestrated my next thought and breath. Something about me had scared him off. Was it my messy past? Was it because I'd never truly opened up to him in our sessions? Or was it Tucker and Reid showing up at inopportune times and staking their claims on me in front of him? Maybe he thought my breakup with Reid was too raw, too new, and he didn't want to get involved with me. Maybe he thought I was on the rebound. I could play "what if" all night but I didn't want to. The bottom line was Sam made the decision for both of us that he didn't want me in his life and I had to live with it. I just didn't know, presently, how I was going to do that.

My week sped by in a muddled haze. I remembered showering and dressing and eating. I could even recall conversations with people and shows I'd watched on TV. But everything I did was mechanical, robotic. I moved through the week on autopilot—never really feeling or seeing or thinking. It was a strange feeling to be mentally detached from the world you lived in—to be alive and not feel, to see and be sightless, to exist and survive only by rote memory. My body still knew what to do; my heart still beat and pumped blood, the neurons in my brain allowed me to move my feet and arms and legs. But I felt like an empty shell. Sam had done this to me. In all actuality, my childhood had done this to me. Sam had just delivered the final blow, the TKO. If this was what love felt like it was no wonder I'd never ventured into that arena before.

My cab pulled to a jerky stop half a block away from the new Frenzy boutique in Chelsea. I swiped my debit card and exited, bidding the driver a good evening. Tonight was a big night for Dallas and for me and I wouldn't let my foul mood sour the evening. At least I was going to try. Most of my coworkers would be in attendance and they were always a fun bunch to be around. And Tucker would be there. He did wonders for me. I'd be glad to see him.

I was in awe as I stepped inside the store. Everything gleamed, shined with newness and originality. Multi-colored strobe lighting zoomed around the room, casting fluorescent beams of light on everything and Bruno Mars blasted from the stereo system. It was bright and energetic and fresh—everything I'd hoped it would be. The room was filled with people and formal clad waitresses passed around glasses of champagne. I spotted Tucker coming toward me with two glasses in his hand. My hero.

"This looks amazing," Tucker exclaimed, handing me my glass. "The collection is great. It fits right in with the feel of the neighborhood. Already people are buzzing about the clothes."

I guzzled the bubbly liquid. "Thank you."

"I wonder if Dallas knows what a gem he has in you. Success is written all over this place."

"I do, indeed, Mr. Stevenson," Dallas interjected coming up behind us. "You did a great job, Sloane. But then I knew you would."

What a chameleon that man was. If he wasn't critiquing me he was complimenting me. I couldn't keep up with his mood swings.

"The place looks great," I agreed.

"I see some people who are waiting on me for a quote and a picture. You okay with a few pictures, too?"

"Absolutely." I was wearing a silk blouse and pants from Frenzy's clothing line just in case there would be photographers. A little extra publicity never hurt.

"I'll come find you when they're ready."

Dallas dashed off to greet the media and I gave the store a quick once over to make sure everything was in its proper place. It really did look fantastic.

"Damn. You finished with your drink already?" Tuck exclaimed jokingly. "I'll go get you another glass."

I handed him my empty champagne flute and bent down to refold a rumpled shirt on one of the display tables. A pair of hands handed me another glass and I accepted it eagerly as I stood.

"This is really nice," Reid remarked, clinking his glass against mine. "Congratulations."

He'd caught me off guard again. Nervously, my eyes darted around the room. "What are you doing here?"

"It's a soft opening, Sloane. Every small business in a fifteen mile radius was invited tonight. What did you think? That I was stalking you?"

His comment made my pulse race and I felt my hands begin to perspire. I looked up at him defiantly and answered. "Yes."

He took another swig of his drink and sneered crudely. "If I am, who'd believe you?"

Reid gave me a polite nod and left me there quaking uncontrollably. I glanced around the room to see if anyone had noticed the exchange between us. But everyone was absorbed in their own conversations, laughing and talking and the music was so loud, I was sure no one had overheard us. He was the one. I knew it now with a certainty like never before. He'd been in my house and left the butcher knife on my counter for me to find. He'd left it there for me to see, to frighten me. But why? What did he want?

"You couldn't wait long enough for me to bring you back a drink?" Tuck kidded me as he squeezed through the crowd toward me. I took the glass he offered unthinkingly in my trembling hand and it slipped through my fingers, the glass shattering across the new floors like twinkling crystals. Tucker looked down at me quizzically.

"Hey butter fingers, watch it."

I stood there motionless as mind numbing clarity set in. Reid was after me.

CHAPTER FIFTEEN

The inside of the New York Police Department was like something out of a movie or eighties cop show. Uniformed policemen sipped on lukewarm cups of coffee, their feet hiked up on paper strewn desks. The building smelled old and musty and corkboards were lined with faded posters of the FBI's most wanted. No one paid any attention to me as I followed behind Officer Paul Danby past rows of desks and water coolers. Telephones rang incessantly with frantic callers reporting crimes and other various misconducts. Officer Danby led me to an empty table in the corner of the station. He was too big and his navy blue polyester pants stretched wide across his buttocks. He moseyed with no great sense of urgency, his rubber soled shoes squeaking under his weight as they crossed the dingy linoleum floor. My eyes were riveted to the back of his shiny, balding head. There was a perfect circular patch in the center where hair had once grown. I wondered absently what made his head shine so.

The table was sticky with old food particles and dried coffee rings stained the worn wood. He sat down wordlessly and I sat across from him, clutching my purse tightly in my fist. He slid a clipboard and pen across the table to me. Danby smacked his gum and the scent of minty wintergreen hit my nose.

"Write down everything that's happened up to this point. The more detailed the better," he instructed dryly.

"I don't have a lot to go on," I admitted. "Just my instincts, really."

"Just write."

I could already see this was a waste of my time. Reid could get away with stalking me the rest of my life. I had nothing on him and I probably never would.

I took the grimy ball point pen in my hand and took a minute to think. My hesitation must have broken some unspoken rule because Danby was quick to comment.

"Don't you know what happened?"

I raised an insolent brow. "Of course I do. I'm just trying to figure out how much to write down. Do you want me to tell you how Reid and I met?"

"Just the reasons why you think he's after you, Miss Maxwell. That'll do."

I felt like I was keeping him from something more important and I was becoming increasingly annoyed with his impertinence. "If you have something else to do, don't let me keep you."

"Nope. Nothing."

I frowned. This was already difficult enough without the crappy attitude of an apathetic cop. I wondered if there was anyone else I could talk to.

I filled out all my personal information first: name, address, telephone number. There was a huge white space where I was supposed to describe the incidents that had occurred. I knew I wouldn't fill up a third of the box. This was a mistake. But now I felt like I owed it to Danby to at least write something down. Otherwise, I knew he'd make me feel like I'd wasted his time. I wrote down all my suspicions, even the lip biting thing, and slid the paper back across the table. I waited patiently as Officer Danby skimmed the paper. I watched his brow furrow and then he glanced up at me over the sheet. He took a pencil from behind his ear.

"When was the last time you saw Mr. Blackmore?"

"Last night at the grand opening of the store."

"And this is a direct quote from him? 'If I am, who'd believe you?'"

I got chills even now hearing the phrase. "Yes. Should I be worried?"

Danby leaned back in his chair but his belly still touched the table. He jotted some notes down.

"I think it's an odd thing to say. But it's not enough for me to do

---

anything about it. He hasn't actually threatened you, has he? Verbally or physically?"

I bit my lip. "No."

"He hasn't broken any laws. And there's nothing to prove he left the knife out in your kitchen. The most I can do is send someone to your home to dust for fingerprints and even that's a stretch. I doubt I could get the chief to agree to it."

"That won't do any good. Reid's been to my house a million times before. His fingerprints are everywhere and I touched the knife when I put it away."

He blew a tiny bubble with his gum and popped it. "If you're feeling unsafe the only advice I can offer you is to be more cautious. Be aware of your surroundings at all times, let someone you trust know where you're going, try not to stay out too late at night, that kind of thing."

I fought the urge to crack the clipboard over his shiny bald head. I stood hastily and glared at him. I didn't know why I was so angry. I already knew the police wouldn't be able to help me. Not unless Reid had actually attacked me and by then it could've been too late.

"I just wanted to file the report so it would be on record in case anything should happen," I explained defensively. "I thought the chances were slim anything could be done. I just thought I'd try."

"That was smart of you. And if he does anything else that causes you concern, let me know."

He pulled a business card from his chest pocket and handed it to me. I took the card, damp from his sweat, and thanked him for his time.

"Miss Maxwell?" he called after me when I'd retreated a few paces. I turned to face him.

"Be careful out there."

Seriously? Thanks, Kojak. If that wasn't a scripted line from a cop show I didn't know what was. I would've laughed if I hadn't been so scared for my safety. I crumpled his business card and shoved it in my pocket.

It was twenty degrees and gray outside. Department stores that had gotten a late start were decorating their display windows with cheery Christmas motifs, dispelling the hovering gray gloom of the city. City workers were coiling green garlands around lamp posts and stringing white lights across the street from one building to the next. There was a flurry of holiday activity. People walked the streets with heavy laden shopping bags and to-do lists. Wreaths with red bows hung from every available door and oversized glittery ornaments dangled precariously overhead from various buildings. New York was already a vibrant place to live but at Christmastime it was transformed into something else; it became enchanted and wondrous. It rekindled a childlike amazement and optimism that was regrettably absent the other 364 days of the year. The world felt different at Christmastime—hopeful, safe. How ironic that during the season known for kindness and forgiveness and love, I was trapped in my own world of malice, fear, and loneliness. I felt anything but safe. Reid wanted to hurt me and I didn't know why or to what extent. He could be watching me now. I turned distractedly to peer over my shoulder. And I was without Sam. His dismissal of me hurt in a way I didn't expect. There was a constant void I felt in my chest—a sort of abyss that was too deep and wide to bridge with work or friends or frivolities. Only Sam could stitch me back together again and he was gone. He'd become such a salient part of my life in such a short time that without him I felt a sense of loss I couldn't explain away. I was missing a piece of myself. The absence of him was felt as strongly and as deeply as my feelings for him; it was cogent and constant. I had to find other ways and people to distract myself. I couldn't let myself sink any deeper into despair. I had enough to focus on with Reid lurking somewhere out there.

I felt a huge sense of relief when I'd made it into work safely. I didn't know where Reid was or what his intentions were toward me so I was glad to finally be in a public place surrounded by people. Reid's unpredictability was distressing. I didn't know what would set him off. I didn't even know what I'd done to trigger his current behavior. Is this what my life was going to become? I was going to be looking over my shoulder indefinitely—waiting on Reid to hurt me?

I was accosted by Tuck in the hallway and he pulled me into his office and shut the door. I felt the curious glances of my colleagues from behind the glass walls. Tucker's green eyes roved over my face hurriedly like a madman and I chuckled inwardly. Thank goodness for Tuck.

"Did you go to the cops?" he started wildly.

"Yes. And as I expected they can't do anything at this point."

"What'd they say?"

I unbuttoned my coat. "A very unsympathetic Paul Danby told me to be careful out there."

He wrinkled his dark brows. "You can't be serious. That's it?"

"What did you expect, Tuck? They've got nothing. *I've* got nothing."

"Even after what he said to you last night? I swear to God I almost punched him in the jaw."

His machismo was endearing. "Who heard him say it but me? It was too loud for anyone to overhear. Reid is smart. He's going to play this to the hilt if that's what he decides to do. I'm hoping he'll get bored with the whole thing and move on."

"*That's* your plan? You hope he'll move on?"

"What would you have me do? I went to the police. There's nothing else for me to do."

"The hell there isn't. Come stay with me. At least for a while. I have a two bedroom and at least that way we both know you're safe."

I reached out to touch his shoulder affectionately. "Thanks, but I'm okay for now."

Tucker laughed and I looked at him peculiarly.

"I'm sorry. I realize that must have sounded like a request. Let me rephrase that. You're coming to stay with me. Just for a while. Maybe your inane theory is right and Reid will lose interest in you. We'll know soon enough. Until then I'm not taking no for an answer. If I have to toss you over my shoulder and drag you home I will and you know it. In fact, it would give me great pleasure to do so."

I opened my mouth to protest but he continued on.

"I'll take you home after work, where you will pack some clothes for the next couple of weeks. You will then get dressed and I will escort you to Frenzy's grand opening tonight. Afterward, I will deliver you to my house and deposit you safely into your bed for the night."

How could I argue with him? His concern for me touched my heart.

"You're the boss," I said brokenly, blinking back hot tears.

"And don't you forget it. Now go do some work."

He turned me around gently and gave me a slight shove, shooing me out of his office.

Frenzy's grand opening was a major success. Dallas grossed nearly six thousand dollars in sales, which was a feather in my hat and money in his pocket. People were clamoring in off the streets to browse around. The raucous music enticed some of them and the rest were lured in by the fashionable clothing prominently displayed from every available space. It was so busy with customers I ended up working the register and helping Dallas' new sales associates maintain order. Frenzy had had two successful nights in a row and I was over the moon. At this rate, Dallas could open stores all over the country and we would both be two very rich people. Sadly, I'd spent most of my time watching the front door in fear that Reid would come back a second time and it prevented me from fully enjoying myself.

As promised, when the last bottle of champagne was uncorked, the sales receipts had been tallied, and the last patron had gone, Tucker was by my side waiting to take me to his place. I couldn't disagree that I felt considerably better and profoundly safer knowing I wouldn't be alone for the next few nights. I would have preferred being in a house with Sam but I was eternally grateful to Tuck.

"Will Stewart be at your house?" I wondered vaguely as I stared out his car window on the drive to his apartment.

"If you want him to be. You feeling adventurous?"

I smirked at him. "Not particularly."

"You'll let me know, though? If you change your mind?"

I laughed. "You'll be the first."

Twenty minutes later, we pulled to a stop in front of Tucker's building on the Upper West Side and parked on the street. He grabbed my small case and I followed closely behind him into the glass enclosed lobby and to the bank of elevators. We whizzed up thirteen floors and exited onto a thickly carpeted hallway. Tucker unlocked the front door and I was hit with the strange sensation of peace and security. I'd forgotten how well secured his building was and how being with this brawny man immediately calmed me. I was glad he hadn't listened to my stubborn refusal not to stay with him. I already felt better.

I'd also forgotten how fabulous Tucker's apartment was but then

I wouldn't expect anything less from him. His white and gray-veined marble floor shone under recessed lighting and his small entryway opened up to a large, sparsely furnished living room. Tucker was a minimalist. He owned little furniture: only a long, creamy white leather sectional couch, a massive, shaggy, slate gray rug, and two cylinder shaped coffee tables decorated the room. Two built in lamps were fastened on either side of the sectional giving the room a dull, soothing glow. Three rectangular abstract pieces of art hung on the wall and his balcony opened up to sweeping views of the Hudson. He'd told me once there was no reason to fill the space with needless clutter and bulky furniture; it would distract from the view. And he was right. I walked to the glass doors and peered out over the bridge and into the black, churning waters. The city seemed small from here and at this height, I towered over it like a giant. I wished I felt like a giant with the supernatural ability to stomp out my enemies, crush them under my feet.

"How about something to eat?" I heard him ask behind me.

"No, thanks."

"You didn't eat dinner and you didn't eat anything at the opening. You must be starved."

I was. But I didn't want food.

"Make yourself comfortable and I'll fix us something. It won't take me a minute. You remember where the bedrooms are."

I could have found the bedrooms blindfolded as many times as I'd been there. I picked up my bag and walked down the hallway to what would be my room for the next two weeks, maybe more.

Cream and sea foam green striped wallpaper served as an accent wall behind the oyster-colored, tufted headboard. Another soft, shaggy rug lay underneath the bed and a single table and lamp rested beside it. A cream bench sat at the foot of the bed and a foam green chaise stood by the balcony doors. There was also a private bathroom and I tossed my bag on the bench in contentment. I could've done much worse than this.

I pulled off my boots and socks and curled and uncurled my toes in the fibers of the carpet. I hung my clothes up in the closet, stuck my personal garments in the empty dresser drawers, and opted for a hot shower before dinner.

When I was dressed in my favorite oversized, yellow and black Pratt sweatshirt, a pair of black leggings and socks, I padded into the kitchen where Tucker was blasting U2 from a Bluetooth speaker. I sat down on the bar stool with quiet relief. I didn't realize how wound up I'd been over this whole Reid thing until now.

"How was your shower?"

I rolled my shoulders, stretching the muscles there, and then poured myself a glass of wine. A steaming shower was exactly what I'd needed. "Perfect."

"Good. I'll be done in here in a sec."

I twirled a piece of hair around my index finger. "I could get used to this. Are you going to cook for me every night?"

"Would you stay here indefinitely if I did?"

"That's a real possibility."

"Then the answer's yes."

I giggled at him. "I'm a pretty good cook. I'll take over tomorrow night."

"Deal."

He placed a plate of food in front of me. I still wasn't hungry but I forced myself to take a couple of bites of my fish taco so as to not hurt the feelings of my hospitable host.

"Eat up. I don't want you wasting away. Not on my watch."

I took three more bites and then drank the rest of my dinner. I poured myself another glass of wine and then another after that. Before long I'd reached my goal; I'd reached the zenith of complete calm and blissful unawareness. I wanted to shut my thoughts off or at the very least dull them until they were misty thoughts and hazy memories. I caught Tucker staring at me over the rim of his wine glass.

"What?" I asked as his gaze moved over every inch of my face.

"You feeling okay?"

"Better than I have the past few days."

"Did I have anything to do with that?"

I licked my lips. They tasted of sticky, warm pears. My head was cloudy and I could feel my eyes getting heavy with sleep.

"You had everything to do with that. I feel safe with you, Tuck. You're my best friend."

He stood to clear our plates. "I think that distinction belongs to your brother."

I nodded and my head felt too heavy. "You both are."

"You're mine, too. I'd do anything for you, Sloane." He paused briefly. "Do you know what amazing eyes you have? Even when they're a little bloodshot."

My heart ached as I thought about Sam's mention of my brown irises. "I might've heard that before." I sighed wistfully. "I think I should try talking to Reid. Maybe I can reason with him," I suggested randomly. Must be the wine talking.

"I don't recommend that approach. We have no idea what he's capable of."

"I dated him for six months and he never once hurt me. I think if I just talk to him and make him understand..." The alcohol in my system would no longer let me complete a thought. I was awfully drowsy.

"He may have never hurt you before but I'm certainly not going to give him the chance now. We'll wait and see what comes of it all. I forbid you to talk to him."

"Forbid?" I giggled again. "You can't forbid me to do or not do anything. I'm a big girl."

"You're a drunk girl and you need your sleep. I can't have you at work tomorrow fighting a hangover."

"But I'm not tired," I argued weakly. "Let's stay up and talk."

"Another time, sleeping beauty. Come on."

I felt the earth tilt and I was in Tucker's arms in one swift movement. He carried me into the guest bedroom and laid me on the bed. I curled up instantly into a ball on the cloudlike mattress and he covered me with the thick, down-filled duvet. The high thread count sheets rubbed softly against my skin. I was wonderfully warm and safe tucked in by Tuck.

"I think I could get through to him," I moaned softly. "He'll listen to me."

"Have you already forgotten that I forbade you to seek out Reid?"

"I'll use my powers of persuasion—appeal to his feelings for me."

"I have no doubt that works on most men. You certainly cast your spell over me. But we're not dealing with most men. He may try and hurt you and I won't let you do it."

"And how, pray tell, are you going to stop me?"

I felt the bed move as his weight settled beside me. "If I have to tie you to this bed I will, Sloane. I mean it."

"Kinky."

"I'm serious. It's not a good idea. Promise me you won't try and talk with him. I don't want you aggravating the situation. Promise."

I sighed heavily as my final glass of wine started to hinder the last of my thoughts. I could no longer fight the shroud of sleep hovering over me.

"I didn't hear you promise, Sloane. Say it," he urged me.

"Okay, bossy. I promise."

"Thank you," he whispered gratefully.

"Make sure you lock the door," I mumbled.

"Don't worry. You're safe here."

I felt him kiss my forehead and then the room went dark. I heard the door close and as tired as I was, and after four glasses of champagne and three glasses of wine, I couldn't escape my thoughts of Sam. Imageries of him sliced through the alcoholic fog like a knife cutting mist. His face shown even through the haze of alcohol and the blur of fear. I yearned to feel his hands on my face and watch his mouth turn up in that languid half grin. I was consumed with thoughts of him, plagued by my own unquenchable thirst. I could almost sense him next to me now, his kaleidoscopic eyes burning into mine, setting all of me ablaze. I didn't want to go on like this—not without him. I had to find a way to keep him in my life, even if it was just in a small way.

Maybe I wasn't a commitment phobe at all. Maybe I just didn't want to be with Reid the way I wanted to be with Sam. Sam felt different—more different than any man before him.

This had to be what love felt like, real love, I thought with a peaceful surrender. I had fallen in love with Sam.

CHAPTER SIXTEEN

I slipped away unnoticed while Tucker was in a design departmental meeting. He'd watched me like a hawk for over a week and I was starting to feel smothered. I was grateful to him for caring so much and for looking after me, but I needed the chance to breathe on my own, to find some space to think. He was like a fierce mama lion watching over her cubs, ready to devour anything that dared come near her baby.

I hailed a cab and headed to Lower Manhattan toward the financial district. Against Tuck's warning and my own prudent reservations, I decided to find Reid. I thought if I could just talk to him, I could get to the root of all of this. Maybe there was some misunderstanding I could clear up or hurt feelings I could rectify. I would do what it took to reestablish normalcy in my life and make amends with him. He'd cared for me once and I, him. Surely, we could work out any differences or confusion. We were (mostly) level-headed adults.

Twenty minutes later, I was on the sidewalk outside Reid's building. Very quickly, I'd become jumpy and overly nervous. I stood staring at the signage on the windows, not moving, not breathing. I inhaled a large, crisp, cold breath of wintry air to steady myself. I moved through the revolving doors and across the wide lobby. His office was on the first floor of a high rise and in seconds I was standing outside the glass doors. If I wanted answers, I had to start here. I pushed on the front door and walked up to the bright eyed receptionist. She was alone in the tiny waiting room and I greeted her with an obligatory smile.

In a rush, I asked, "Is Reid Blackmore in?"

"No, he isn't. Can I take a message for you?" she asked politely. Her voice was too high pitched and it grated on my already frazzled nerves.

"When do you expect him back?"

The baby faced receptionist shrugged her boxy shoulders. "I don't expect him back at all."

"Why is that?"

"I'm only a temp but I've been here for a week and I've never seen him come in to work. I don't think he works here anymore."

"This is *his* company. Why wouldn't he come back?"

Baby Spice stood up and leaned across the desk. She glanced around her as if she were afraid we'd be overheard. "Like I said, I'm only a temp. But I've heard office rumors that Mr. Blackmore was asked to leave temporarily for personal reasons," she whispered as if she were divulging state secrets.

"Who asked him to leave and why?"

She leaned in even closer and her obnoxious rose-scented perfume made me want to vomit. The smell was permeating from everywhere.

"I don't know who said he had to take the time off. But the reason—," She glanced around again and I sighed. "—is because the receptionist, the one I'm replacing, filed sexual harassment charges."

My jaw dropped. This couldn't be happening.

"Are you sure? Are you positive that's what you heard?"

She sat down again and started chewing on her thumbnail like she'd regretted sharing with me. She was definitely not the person one ought to entrust confidential information. She'd sung like a canary.

"From what I can tell, that's what's going on. I shouldn't have said anything. I really like this job. Are you a friend of Mr. Blackmore's?"

"Yes, very old friends. And don't worry, I won't repeat what you've told me." Except to the police. "What's your name?"

"Jessica. You promise you're not going to say anything? I haven't even met Mr. Blackmore and I'd like to keep this job. I certainly don't want to get him into any trouble."

"It sounds like he's done that all on his own. What was the receptionist's name? Do you know where I can find her?"

Jessica opened a drawer and handed me a business card. "This is her card. I don't know where she is or if she's coming back. I've said enough. What did you say your name was?"

"Thanks for the information, Jessica."

I turned and left before Jessica developed a conscience and became overwrought with guilt, as I suspected she would. Once she'd realized she'd jeopardized her job by sharing personal company business and didn't even get my name, she'd feel bad and probably squeeze some tears out of those huge blue eyes of hers. I didn't want to wait around for that. She'd given me what I needed.

It sounded like Reid had a history of bothering women. Shocker. But that didn't help me. I still didn't know where he was. I grabbed another cab and headed to his apartment. I was determined to speak with him. Somewhere in the back of my mind, I realized I pitied him. I thought maybe I could help him or convince him to seek help before he destroyed his life. Our relationship hadn't been all bad; he just wasn't for me. And I understood more than most what it felt like to be pushed to the breaking point and snap. If he felt like that because of me, I wanted to right it. No one should go through that alone—not even Reid.

I'd found a new resolve by the time I made it to his apartment building and walked up to the front desk. I was still scared of Reid but my fear was lessoned by my unexpected empathy for him.

"Good afternoon, Ronald," I started boldly, glancing at the name tag of the man behind the desk. "Can you ring for my boyfriend and tell him I'm downstairs?"

He reached for the phone. "What's his name?"

"Reid Blackmore."

Ronald, who was old enough to be my dad, frowned at me. "I can't do that, miss."

I was taken aback but not deterred. "Why not? I really need to see him. What's the harm in calling upstairs for me? That's not against the rules is it?"

Ronald shook his graying head. "No. But Mr. Blackmore doesn't live here anymore."

I felt the wind get knocked out of me.

"What do you mean? I just saw him the other night."

"Well, you didn't see him here. He broke his lease two days ago. The place is empty."

"Did he leave a forwarding address?"

"No. And if you want my opinion, you're better off without him. He was an odd duck."

I raised curious brows at Ronald. People were certainly forthcoming today. "Why do you say that?"

But Ronald wasn't as naïve as Jessica. "Just a feeling. Good luck to you."

And I was dismissed. Ronald wasn't going to give me anything else. I took what little information I had and went back to work.

"Are you fucking serious right now, Sloane? Where the hell have you been?" Tucker ranted as he stormed into my office and slammed the door.

I jumped to my feet. "Calm down. What's wrong?"

The look of astonishment on his face confounded me.

"I come out of my meeting to find you gone. I called your cell phone no less than six times and you didn't answer. You had me going out of my mind with worry. I almost called the cops."

I picked up my cell phone and scrolled through my missed calls, finding Tucker's name several times in my call log. "I'm sorry, Tuck. I must have put my phone on silent by accident. But as you can see, I'm fine. I'm sorry I worried you."

"Worried me? You nearly gave me a heart attack. You were gone for over an hour."

"I'm sorry," I apologized again.

He shoved his hand through his hair. Jeez. I'd really scared him.

"Where did you go?"

I bit my lip hard. "I'll tell you but you have to promise not to get angrier with me."

"We're past that point. Talk."

I knew not to mess with irate, stubborn Tuck.

"I went to see Reid and before you blow a gasket, I didn't find him."

I saw the muscles in his jaw clench tight. "Keep talking."

"I went to his work and they said he'd been asked to leave because his receptionist filed sexual harassment charges against him."

Tucker relaxed some and I breathed a sigh of relief. I didn't like it when he was mad at me. I continued on.

"Then I went to his apartment only to find out he doesn't live there anymore. Like, as of two days ago. I don't know what to think. It's like he's disappeared."

"Or he's given everyone the slip."

"What do you mean?"

"Think about it, Sloane. If he's really stalking you, he's not going to make it easy to find him. And if he has a shady past, or certain things he doesn't want anyone else to know, and all of a sudden it started coming to light, wouldn't you skip town, too?"

I took a moment to mull that over. "Maybe. I don't know."

"The threat to your safety just increased tenfold. At least before we knew where we could find the bastard, now he's MIA."

"I didn't think of it that way," I admitted dejectedly.

"That's why you have me because I think things through. And that's why it's important I know where you are at all times. You can't just go out on your own like that, at least for now. I know it's a pain in the ass but it's the only thing I can think to do to help keep you safe. Maybe Reid's going to drop this whole thing and maybe he's not. But until we know for sure, you're stuck to me like glue. Understand?"

He certainly had a point. Reid could be out of my life or he could be laying low waiting to make a move against me. Until we knew for sure, I had to be smarter.

"I'm sorry I worried you."

Tuck grabbed me roughly into his arms and I buried my face against his hard chest. "I know. No more playing detective, though."

"I won't. I swear."

He pulled back from me and kissed my hair. "It's noon. Wanna grab lunch?"

I nodded eagerly and we left the building together, hand in hand.

When the weekend arrived, I was granted a reprieve from Tucker's watchful eye but only because I'd told him I was tree decorating with Dane and that he was going to stay the night with me. I was surprised by how much fun I was actually having staying with Tuck but I missed my things, my bed. I also wanted to allow him some uninterrupted time with Stewart. It was particularly difficult to have a romantic date when you had a third person in the house. And truthfully, I'd never been good living with other people. Not even in college. My college roommate was stellar but by sophomore year I was done with the whole roomy situation and I rented an apartment by myself. I'd lived on my own ever since. I needed my space and although Tucker's place was more than large enough for the two of us, he was beginning to hover like a mother hen. So it was good to be back in my house where I felt more like myself.

I debated telling Dane about Reid and finally decided I wouldn't. I wasn't going to tell him for various reasons. The most important one being I didn't want him to worry needlessly and I knew he would. There was no serious cause for alarm yet, despite what Tuck seemed to think. I didn't want to worry Dane unless I had to and right now, I didn't have to. Decorating our Christmas tree together was a tradition he and I started when we moved back to New York and it was one that was very special to me. I didn't want the day marred by my stalker ex, if that's even what he was.

Dane was in charge of choosing the tree every year and he'd just arrived, dragging in a sage green fir. He left a trail of needles from the front door to the living room, as usual, and I was ready with my broom, as usual, to sweep up behind him. He sat down on the floor with a pocket knife and sawed through the tightly wound rope. I was in charge of baking cookies, making spiked apple cider, keeping the Christmas music blaring, and making sure we stayed in the holiday spirit.

When the tree was finally upright, Dane hoisted it into its stand and stood back to eye his work. He straightened the pine scented fir and maneuvered branches until the tree achieved optimal fullness. He was a perfectionist when it came to decorating the tree and it tickled me every year. When he finally got it the way he wanted, he would stand back, stick his hands in the back pockets of his jeans, and nod to himself. When I took note of his familiar stance, it was my cue to break out the boxes and boxes of ornaments I kept in the basement and we'd get to work.

"It looks good, huh?" he asked, admiring his handiwork.

I grinned. "Perfect as always."

"Then let's decorate."

I saluted him. "Yes, sir."

I opened the dusty boxes of white lights and began to untwist the tangled cords.

"You okay not going to see Dad for Christmas?" I wondered aloud.

"Yep. I think it's better this way. At least this year. Maybe next year will be different. Anyway, you and I have a good thing going on."

I didn't know what would be any different between this year and the next. I still hated that house. Dane took a strand of lights from me.

"I guess. If you want to invite Hilary over for Christmas, I'm cool with that," I offered.

"She's going to visit some cousins in Maryland. But thanks."

"How are things going with you two?"

His nimble fingers worked out a complicated knot. "She's an awesome girl. We have a lot in common."

"Like what?"

"Like me, for instance. We both like me."

I tossed silver tinsel at him playfully. "Seriously. What do you have in common with her?"

"We like the same foods and music and stuff. We share the same sense of humor. And she comes from a screwed up family like me. I can talk to her about stuff."

"You can talk to me, too. Whenever you want," I added. I sounded like a jealous girlfriend even to my own ears.

Dane unhinged the ladder and climbed the rungs to start stringing lights from the top. "I know. But it's harder with you because you lived through it with me. She's not so close to the whole thing."

"Does she know everything?"

I saw him hesitate just a smidge. "No. Nobody knows everything except—" He stopped.

"Yeah. I know. Only the people who had the misfortune of having to live through it."

"This topic is not keeping me in the Christmas spirit, which, I believe, is the task assigned to you."

"My apologies, sir. Some apple cider should do it."

"Right you are. Hop to it."

I went to the kitchen and filled two red plastic cups with rum-laced cider. I handed one to Dane and he took a deep swig. I followed suit. It was delicious.

He grinned. "Feeling more Christmassy already."

"When are you finished with classes?" I asked as I took out the next strand of lights to hand to him.

"My last final is on Friday and then we're out until mid-January."

"You have plans for New Year's?"

"Hilary wants to hang out in Times Square so that's probably what we'll do. What about you?"

"No plans. I'll probably hang out with Tucker." *Since we're practically shacking up anyway*, I thought wryly.

The smell of cookies wafted through the air and I set the lights down, grabbed my cup, and jogged to the kitchen. I hit the oven light and peered inside. The sugar cookies were done. I reached for an oven mitt and grabbed the cookie sheet.

"You want green and red sprinkles?" I hollered from the kitchen over the melodious, crooning sounds of Bing Crosby.

"You know it. Don't tamper with tradition."

"You're like a big kid."

I reached for the sprinkles from the top pantry shelf. I liked that some things hadn't changed with Dane. In a lot of ways he was still like the sweet little boy I used to know. I'm glad a piece of that still existed in him—an optimism and carefreeness that still shone in his eyes. It hadn't yet been destroyed by the things of his past and I'd be damned if I ever let it.

"Have you talked to Sam lately?"

I closed the oven door with my foot and took down a red and white striped plate shaped like a candy cane. I transferred the cookies from the sheet to the dish.

"No. Why?"

"I met with him earlier this week and I've seen him around campus but he seems a little off. I just wanted to know if you'd noticed."

"Off in what way?"

He paused to think for a minute. "Distracted. He even cut my session short with him on Monday night. His mind was definitely somewhere else."

I felt an ache in my chest at just the mention of his name and I couldn't help the defeated sigh that escaped from my mouth. With my peripheral vision, I saw my brother stop to look at me.

"What?" he questioned.

"What?"

"What was the sigh for?"

I took another sip of cider for courage. "I'm in love with him."

I thought Dane was going to tumble off the ladder. He jumped five rungs down and rushed to the kitchen.

"Pass me a cookie."

I did and he took a bite, crumbs falling from his lips. I passed him a napkin.

"Where the hell have I been that I missed you falling in love with the shrink? When did this happen? And how?"

"I don't know when it happened exactly, it just did. And I don't know if I can explain *how* either. I just know that I do."

"How do you know? You've never been in love in your life."

The image of Sam's face flashed before me and I couldn't help but smile. He was so spectacularly handsome. I missed him in a way that was completely absurd, illogical, and kind of scary. He infiltrated my thoughts. Even when I was focused on other things, he was in the recesses of my mind, just on the outskirts of every thought and emotion.

"He's all I think about," I answered honestly. "I know it sounds crazy but I'm drawn to him in a way I've never been drawn to anyone before. From the first minute I met him it was like I was being pulled to him. I know I love him because it consumes me. *He* consumes me."

"Wow, sis. That's heavy."

"I know." I sighed again.

"Did you tell him?"

"Of course not."

"Why not?"

"He doesn't want to have anything to do with me."

Dane rolled his eyes. "I doubt that."

"He told me so point blank. I know it for a fact."

"You're kidding."

I drank the rest of my cider and poured another cup. I felt like getting loaded.

"I wish I was. He told me it would be a mistake getting involved with me professionally or otherwise."

"Why would he say that?"

I shrugged.

"I'll tell you why. Because he probably has feelings for you. If he didn't, why would he push you away? That's a classic guy move. We all do it when we get scared."

"That's a jerk move," I retorted.

"Agreed. But it's like jackass is in our DNA. We run before we get too deep."

"But you jumped right in with Hilary. You like her and you weren't scared to take it to the next level."

He smirked. "I'm more evolved than most men."

It was my turn to roll my eyes.

"I was scared getting involved with Hilary, you know that. I didn't want to ruin our friendship. But I liked her enough to give it a shot and I'm glad I did. The reward outweighed the risk."

"So Sam thinks I'm not worth the risk?"

"I think he does and that's why he bailed. He probably doesn't trust himself around you."

I vividly remembered Sam saying how badly he wanted to kiss me and how hard it was for him to stop himself. Maybe Dane had a point. Maybe Sam was scared. But so was I and I was willing to give it a try. Fear didn't excuse his behavior or make it sting any less.

"Well, whatever the reason, he made his point clear and there's nothing I can do about it."

Dane snatched another cookie. "That really sucks."

"Yep."

He came around the kitchen counter and draped an affectionate arm around my shoulders. "Do you want me to beat him up for you?"

I laughed and shoved him away good-humoredly. "I don't think that will be necessary."

"I'll stop seeing him if you want. I'll find another head doctor."

"Absolutely not. If he's helping you I want you to keep seeing him as long as you need to. I'm sure my feelings for him will subside over time."

He gave my arm a squeeze and returned to the tree to finish hanging lights. I knew I'd just told another lie. My feelings for Sam weren't going to wane. They were as strong and as deep as anything I'd ever felt. Loving him was beyond my control and I knew it. I was in love but it was the worst kind—it was unrequited love. It was the way my dad loved my mom. Her feelings toward him had never come close to his feelings for her. Somehow I'd found myself in the same trap even though I'd vowed I never would.

I was the heroine in the novel who didn't get the guy. Those types of stories were epic and sold millions of copies. It's what romance films were made of. Audiences love a tragic story. I just wished I wasn't the protagonist in this particular plot.

Chapter Seventeen

In light of the new information I'd obtained concerning Reid, I decided to go back to the police station on Sunday afternoon with none other than Tuck Stevenson—my constant shadow. I was torn between really enjoying our time together and feeling like I wanted to punch him in the face for monitoring me like a fragile bird. Dane had gone home earlier that morning and Tuck was waiting with bells on as soon as my front door shut.

But I wasn't as fragile as Tucker seemed to think. I stormed into the NYPD with guns blazing. I was going to make my intentions clear. I didn't want to deal with Officer Danby anymore. I was determined to speak with a female police officer who may be slightly more concerned and sensitive regarding my current plight. Only a woman could truly sympathize with another woman making claims about a potential stalker. Another woman would understand the fear nestled in my heart and the paranoia that accompanied it. A man could in no way relate to the panic that ensued on a day to day basis from having to look over my shoulder and not feeling safe enough to live in my own house. So when I walked up to the front desk and was met with yet another male officer, I squared my shoulders and stuck out my chin. I placed my hands flat on either side of the counter in my best fighting stance.

"I would like to speak to a female officer," I started resolutely, holding the gaze of the officer with steely determination.

The officer leaned forward. "What's your name?"

"Sloane Maxwell. I was here the other day and I spoke with Officer Paul Danby. However, I have new information to report regarding the statement I filed and I'd like to speak to a female officer. And *only* a female officer."

Officer Aiken, as his name tag identified him, shrugged his wide shoulders and stood up. "Stay here. I'll be right back."

I nodded my head with satisfaction.

"Nice job, slugger," Tucker whispered down to me and I smiled.

Before long, an extremely tall officer came to greet us. She was well over six feet tall and her hair was thin and stringy. She had it pulled back and secured at the nape of her long neck and I could see bits of her scalp between the sparse threads of hair. Her eyes were brown, almost black, and she looked intense—like she took her duty as a cop very seriously and I was glad because I could *be* in serious trouble.

"I'm Officer Candy Russell and before you ask, yes, that's my real name. No, it's not short for Candace. No, I was never a stripper. And, yes, my mother meant to do it. Now, how can I help you?"

"You get that a lot, huh?" Tuck asked.

"You have no idea."

I grinned. I liked her already.

"My name is Sloane Maxwell and this is my friend, Tucker Stevenson. I think my ex-boyfriend is after me."

She squinted at me like she was trying to size me up—as if she were trying to assess if I'd be the kind of girl who'd make false claims about an ex-boyfriend because of a bitter breakup or hurt feelings. She wanted to know if I was there for the right reasons. I guess she figured I was because she escorted us to her office and we all sat down.

"Would you like some water?" she offered.

Tuck and I politely refused.

"I have your statement here, but I want to hear it from you. Tell me what's going on," she said pointedly.

I restated everything I'd told Danby and then filled Officer Russell in about my visit to Reid's work and apartment, including the peculiar comment Ronald made. I gave her every fact I had but I noticed she didn't write anything down. She just stared at me with those dark, deep set eyes and I wondered if I was just wasting my time again. When I was finished she didn't speak. The silence was so loud I began to grow uncomfortable and I wriggled in my seat.

"That's not a lot to go on," she finally said and that defeated feeling began to swell in my belly. "But," she continued on, "I think it's worth looking into."

I felt my eyes bulge. "You do?"

"You'll have to file a restraining order first before I can start questioning him. Are you ready to do that?"

Now that the time was here I wasn't sure I was. It sounded so official, so criminal. I didn't want to ruin Reid's life; I just wanted him out of mine. Tuck must have sensed my hesitation because he reached for my hand and gave it an encouraging squeeze. I raised my eyes to his.

"I know it's scary but think of it this way. Someone else has already filed charges against him. He's already on their radar. Let the police look into it."

I knew he was right but if Reid knew the cops were poking around in his personal life, wouldn't that set him off more? Or would it have the opposite effect and scare him off all together? I voiced my concern.

"I don't want to make him angrier."

Officer Russell squinted at me again and I pondered vaguely if she had vision trouble.

"That's a valid concern. But he's already exhibiting frightening behavior if someone else took the time to file harassment charges and from the little bit you told me, I'm concerned."

"Concerned?" Tucker piped up.

Russell raised her long, bony fingers. "I'm not overly concerned. But I've been on the force for fifteen years and most of these cases start off simple enough and then escalate to something far more worrisome. I know the signs."

"And how many of these cases turn out to be nothing at all?"

"About half."

"I don't like those odds." I tried to joke but my heart was in my throat.

"The sooner we can look into this guy's background and find his whereabouts, the better chance you have of beating those odds. In the meantime, you should be extra careful. You ready to get to work?" Russell asked and there was a definite gleam in her eye. She meant business.

I nodded and Tucker squeezed my hand again. We sat there for another half hour while I filled out all the necessary paperwork. When I was done, I didn't feel the relief I thought I would. I was as anxious as I was before—maybe more. I'd been in such a hurry to enlist the help of the police that I didn't stop to think how I'd feel afterward. I should've felt better and instead I felt like I'd lit the match to a stick of dynamite. I knew I'd sealed my fate and Reid's—good, bad, or indifferent.

Work was becoming more of a challenge. The week raced by but I couldn't keep my head in the game. It was exacerbated by Dallas' nitpicky micromanaging and dealing with an entirely new group of suppliers for Winston's. I was buried under mounds of spreadsheets and bogged down with catalogues, proposals, and analyzing market reports. On top of that, Sandra was making travel arrangements for me to fly to Las Vegas in January to attend a trade show to research new summer trends for Winston's, so I was busy trying to establish connections with representatives there. I had more than enough to keep me busy but all I could think about were Sam and Reid. I thought about them both for very different reasons but they were both omnipresent. Sam was a dull ache in my chest that seemed to exist solely to remind me I was barely alive and still alone. Reid was an incessant alarm—like bells going off in my head. They both drained me until I felt like I would implode with the sheer encumbrance of my own existence. I was sinking fast—too fast, and I didn't know how to pull myself out.

Luckily, Sandra seemed to be feeling benevolent because at five o'clock on Tuesday, she sent out a mass email to all the employees letting us know she was giving us the rest of the week off until after the holidays. I wanted nothing more than to be at home without the added effort it took to come to work and make pleasantries with everyone around me. And Tucker was leaving me to my own devices because his mother had called and pleaded with him to come home for Christmas. Well, he wasn't completely leaving me alone. Before he'd even agreed to go, he'd made sure Dane was going to be front and center while he was away. The changing of the guards.

After I'd read Sandra's email I belatedly realized it was Tuesday night—my standing appointment with Sam. Except tonight he wasn't waiting for me and the reality of that hit me hard and made it impossible to breathe. How was I ever going to move on from someone who was so ingrained in my thoughts, meshed with my very being like blood and skin?

I stayed the rest of the week with Tucker. We'd lived a very domestic life together over the past few days. We drove to work together and then came home, where one of us cooked dinner while we discussed work and the day's events. Afterward, we'd sit on the couch and laugh about any and everything over a glass of wine or a board game. Or we'd watch some ridiculous reality show on TV and make fun of celebrities or watch The Property Brothers demolish and renovate homes. It was as close to being married as I'd ever been—and likely ever to get. Although we spent nearly all our waking hours together, when Tuck pulled up in front of my house to drop me off on Christmas Eve, I immediately felt his loss. He'd been my rock. He'd quite literally held my hand through this entire Reid situation and I was wholly indebted to him. Dane must have heard Tuck's car pull up because the front door of my brownstone opened and he gave us both a wave. I turned to Tucker.

"Is it weird that I'm going to miss you while you're gone?" I kidded.

"Nope, because I'll miss you, too. Spending time with you like this has me spoiled."

"I want you to know how much I appreciate you being there for me. I can't even really express—" I broke off.

"I know. I'll only be gone four days and I'm just over the bridge in Jersey. If anything happens or that freak tries to contact you, you call me. Do you understand? And I'll be back here before you can hang up the phone."

I tried to hide a smile. "Got it."

"And until I get back, do not leave without Dane or someone else to go with you. I mean it, Sloane."

"Yes drill sergeant, sir," I barked and straightened to attention.

He chuckled and pulled me to him in a clumsy hug. He kissed

my cheek and I opened the car door.

"Merry Christmas."

"Same to you." He grinned and I felt that familiar pang of desire when I looked at him.

He waited until I'd gone in the house and shut the door before he pulled off into the stream of holiday-congested traffic.

"You seem to be spending a lot of time with Tuck lately. Every time I call you, you're with him. Has Sam taken a back seat to your former flame?" Dane started in as soon as I'd locked the door.

"Not even. It's not like that."

"Then what's with the overnight bag?"

Shit. "I was having some plumbing issues so I stayed at his place for a couple of nights. No biggie."

He seemed satisfied with that. I hated lying to him but I wanted to keep him out of the loop as far as Reid was concerned. It was simpler that way.

"So then your feelings for Sam...?"

"Are as strong as ever. Unfortunately." I sulked.

"His loss. He told me he was leaving for Minnesota to visit his family so you don't have to worry about bumping into him anywhere—at least not over the break."

Somehow knowing he was hundreds of miles away depressed me further. At least when he was in the city I had an off chance of running into him but miles away, I had no hope for an accidental encounter. I already felt the yawning distance between us and now the feeling was magnified by actual miles between us. I didn't know how much longer I could go on feeling this way—living with this pit, this boulder in my stomach constantly weighing me down.

"Are you going to be okay over the break? I mean, with Sam gone for a month you can't have your regular sessions with him." I studied his face.

Dane shuffled to the kitchen and grabbed a cup of leftover cider. "Don't worry about me. I've done enough talking over the past few weeks to last me a lifetime. I'm good with the break. By the time he's back, I'll be ready to go again. And he told me I could call him any time if I needed to."

I dropped my bag to the floor and plopped down on the sofa. "So, it's really helping then?"

"Yeah. I can't believe it. But talking about all that stuff has made me feel better. Who knew bringing up all that shit would actually help?"

"Then I'm glad you have Sam. Really."

He came over and ruffled my hair and then sat beside me, kicking his feet onto the coffee table.

"That's a pretty stellar tree," he remarked.

I looked at the beautifully decorated tree with its sparkling silver and gold ornaments and its twinkling white lights. There was a porcelain angel on top my dad had given me years ago. He said it reminded him of me but I never really understood why because she didn't look anything like me. Her skin was pale and her eyes were wide and blue. I was olive skinned with dark hair and brown eyes. He said there was something behind her eyes that intrigued him. Not long after, he began calling me angel.

"It's a really great tree," I agreed.

"You know this thing with Sam is going to be okay, right? *You're* going to be okay."

"How do you know?"

"Because we've been through too much shit and it's our turn to catch a break. The universe has to right itself in our favor eventually."

I almost smiled at that. I hoped it was true because the universe owed me a great deal.

Dane woke up and jumped on my bed like a kid Christmas morning. We'd spent the last six Christmases alone, just he and I, and every year he woke me up the same way. And every year I was peeved about being startled awake and every year he didn't care. So I rolled out of bed, laughing at his charming face, and tugged on a robe. He barely allowed me time to brush my teeth and run a comb through my hair before he planted himself on the floor in front of the Christmas tree, pulling me down beside him. There were only three wrapped gifts and an envelope under the tree but my little brother acted as if there were an abundance of toys and presents for him. It warmed my heart to see his childlike behavior, to see the playfulness in him. He reminded me of what was good and all I had to be thankful for. Despite everything that had gone on in my life and despite the things that were still going, Dane was my constant. I could depend on him even when I didn't trust myself. At times, he was the only reason I kept putting one foot in front of the other when I felt like crumbling into pieces. He kept me whole.

"Which one's mine?" he asked giddily, interrupting my oversentimental reverie.

I handed him a small rectangular box in green wrapping. He grabbed it excitedly.

"That's from Dad," I explained as I took my identically wrapped box from under the tree.

"Let's see what the old man got us."

We ripped into the gifts, scattering glittery paper all over the floor. I took off the lid and shoved back the tissue. I lifted out a heavy metal frame and inside was a picture of me and Dane. I couldn't have been more than six and he, three, and we were dressed in our pajamas posing by a small, scantly adorned Christmas tree. We were sitting on the floor and I had Dane in my lap, wrapped in my arms tightly. My wide smile revealed a missing front tooth and Dane's overgrown curls nearly covered his bright green eyes.

Dane looked at me as he pulled out the same frame and picture from his box. "I don't remember taking this. Do you?"

"No. In fact I'd question if it was really us except I remember those red footed pajamas I'm wearing."

I peered a little closer at my face, inwardly cringing at my poorly cut, uneven bangs. I could just make out pale shadows of blue and gray underneath my left eye. A memory suddenly rushed before me.

I remembered my mom and dad arguing, as usual, about something insignificant. Mom was enraged, her eyes blazing with a fiery fury and disgust for the man who'd only ever loved her. She reached for a ceramic figurine standing on a nearby table and hurled it at my dad. She missed him and the figurine smashed against the wall. A broken chunk of it hit me underneath the eye, causing it to immediately bruise. I yelped in pain as tears pooled in my eyes. Dad was there in an instant. He looked me over, rubbing his thumb across the puffy welt and he kissed my face. He yelled over his shoulder at my mom but I couldn't recall what he'd said. She disappeared into her room and Dad wrapped ice in a towel and held it to my face to help keep the swelling down. That's what I remembered about that particular Christmas in our house. It wasn't worth sharing with Dane.

He sighed. "Leave it to Dad to send us on a trip down memory lane."

I clenched my jaw and then relaxed it. I wouldn't let that picture ruin the day. "It's a sweet picture," I replied honestly. "I'm glad to remember us like that. And we don't have many pictures from when we were small. I like it."

"I'd rather have gotten a gift card."

I pushed his shoulder. "But look how cute you were. What happened?"

He shoved me back and smiled. "Open mine to you."

Dane pointed toward a present leaning against the wall and I grabbed it. I tore off the paper and was immediately captivated by the beautiful piece of artwork my brother had created. I'd know his work anywhere. Even as an amateur he had a unique style all his own that was instantly recognizable to me. There was a softness in his paintings, an understated beauty and simplicity that always spoke to me. And his present to me was no different. He'd painted a picture of a grand castle. It stood on a hill overlooking a shimmering body of water. Its stone walls seemed to reach the sky and its turrets pushed up from either side, slicing through the dusky clouds. Pale green ivy climbed up its walls and a single yellow light shone from one of the arched windows.

"Remember when we were kids and we wished we lived in a castle? We used to sit for hours dreaming about what it would be like. We talked about it so much I actually started to think we could do it."

I swallowed back tears as my mind flashed to those talks he and I used to have. Even as children we'd dreamt a better life for ourselves.

"We never got the castle, though," I remarked sadly.

"No. But we escaped the dragon. The castle comes next."

I looked at him adoringly. "I love it, Dane. It's perfect. Thank you."

I leaned over and kissed his cheek swiftly, dabbing at my damp face. "Here's yours."

I handed him an envelope and watched him tear into it with the enthusiasm of a four-year-old. He took out a pair of concert tickets.

"Hozier! Are you kidding me? This concert has been sold out for weeks!"

"What can I say? I have connections. I thought you might like to take Hilary."

He high fived me. "This is fucking awesome! Thank you."

"I'm glad you like it." I grinned, standing. "If we plan on eating today I'd better get started."

"I'll put on some holiday tunes."

I trundled off to the kitchen and began taking food from the fridge when my cell phone buzzed on the countertop.

"That's probably Dad calling to see how we liked our gifts," Dane teased as an old Boyz to Men's Christmas song flooded the room.

"You're probably right. I'll be sure to tell him you'd like a gift card instead."

"Don't you dare."

I looked at the phone number and it was a Florida area code but it wasn't my dad. It looked like the same number sex operator Lucy had called me from weeks ago. I grimaced and answered the phone resentfully. Didn't she know it was Christmas Day? Whatever financial questions she had for me could wait until tomorrow.

"Hello?" I sighed, not bothering to hide the irritation in my voice.

"Sloane."

My heart started pounding furiously in my chest and I felt my knees buckle underneath the heft of her voice. I grabbed the counter for support and gripped it forcefully until my knuckles turned white. I saw Dane glance at me and then frown as he neared me. The small, raspy voice on the other end of the line, the voice that made my blood run cold and my breath catch in my chest was none other than Vicky Maxwell. My mother.

CHAPTER EIGHTEEN

"Sloane, are you there?"

She'd knocked the wind from me. I couldn't even form my words; the sound of her disturbingly calm voice disabled me, immobilized my thoughts.

"Sloane. Answer me," she demanded curtly. She didn't raise her voice but there was a sternness that reminded me of my childhood, of her scolding me. I was instantly six-years-old again.

"What do you want?" I whispered and Dane was next to me, glaring at me quizzically.

"Who is it?" he mouthed.

I ignored him. I couldn't focus on anything except my mother and the sound of the blood roaring in my ears.

"I wanted to wish you a Merry Christmas. How are you?"

As if she cared. My eyes begin to cloud over and the room was quickly fading into shades of black. I felt that familiar slide into despair, that fog of darkness I loved and hated.

"Who is it, Slo?" Dane shouted at me.

"What do you want?" I asked her again and I barely recognized my own voice. It was still and small, like the squeaking of a mouse.

"I told you. I wanted to wish you a Merry Christmas and see how you are."

"How did you get this number?"

"You don't think I'd have my own daughter's phone number? I hope it's okay that I called."

175

"It's not."

"Sloane."

I began to shake violently as I grabbed the tie on my robe, twisting it around and around my arm again and again until it chafed my skin. I dropped the phone and I felt myself slithering downward until my bottom hit the cool tile floor. Somewhere in the distance I heard my brother pick up the phone but his voice was muffled and I didn't understand anything he was saying. The house had grown quiet except for the voices in my head and the flickers of memories that were now parading through my mind, invading my thoughts. My mother was everywhere all of a sudden and I couldn't rid myself of her. She assaulted me, reached out with prickly fingers and held on to me. There was no escaping her long reach—she was in my head. Her voice triggered a darkness in me, shoved me into a black cavity, a cavern with no exit. I succumbed to the blackness that was always waiting for me, just on the edges of my sanity it lingered. And I'd let it finally capture me—embrace me, take me and possess me. The reality I knew no longer existed—only this new world I'd created—this place where only she and I lived. I was stuck there, lived there, my new home. I vaguely felt my pulse slow down as I accepted this new earth, this shadowy realm where I was freed from the lies I'd been telling myself. I was free now.

I didn't know what time it was or what day. But it was dark all around me. I wasn't sure where I was but the darkness was pervasive, looming, but it was also comforting as I grew accustomed to its shadowy blackness. My eyes didn't seem to focus properly—I was blinded by my own veil of confusion and torment. I turned my head left and right, trying to see, trying to climb my way out of this gorge I'd fallen into, but I was met with an obstinate haze of ambiguity. I felt a presence next to me and I could just make out a murmuring voice. But I didn't understand. I felt lost and deeply alone. The memories of my mother that had, at first kept me company, had long faded and I was abandoned to suffer in this despondency unaccompanied. She'd done it again. Even in my darkest time she'd disappeared like always.

I felt a heavy hand on my head and then on my cheek. I closed my eyes and pressed into his palm reflexively. And then I heard my name being called softly by a deep, familiar voice. An awareness came over me then, an awakening that offered a glimmer of light to my otherwise darkened dwelling place. Instinctively, I knew it was Sam.

I opened my eyes as he called my name again and I forced my mind to vacate its maze of agony. I followed the sound of his voice out of the web that was enmeshing me and raised my head. My bewildered gaze locked onto his captivating hazel brown eyes and I felt the sentience of him all around me. It was so powerful that I shook with tears and then exploded. I sobbed hard, overcome with a thousand different emotions at once. Sam was here, cradling me against his chest and he smelled just as I remembered him. It awoke something inside, a yearning I had tried to lay to rest. Hot tears streamed down my face and I couldn't control the tremors that shook me. It was a cathartic release I didn't know I needed. I'd missed him so much, ached to be right here in his arms. He numbed my pain and consoled me, my handsome anodyne. His strong hands were gentle as they wiped my falling tears. *Those* hands that I had first loved. He held me so tightly against him I could barely breathe but his soothing embrace brought me back from my bottomless quarry of desolation.

I was exhausted by the time my tears finally subsided. I'd stopped crying but Sam didn't budge. He sat there holding me on the kitchen floor, kissing my hair and rubbing my back. I could've stayed there forever—would've stayed there forever, but embarrassment over my crying fit was settling in and I felt my cheeks blush a deep red. I looked up at him with wet, brown eyes and he smiled softly at me. I felt my heart twinge.

"Do you know where you are?" he asked me but his voice was strained, concerned.

I nodded. "My house."

"Do you know what day it is?"

"No."

"It's Christmas Day."

I glanced toward the living room windows and noted how dark it was outside. "It's nighttime."

"Yes. Christmas is almost over."

"What happened to me?"

Sam took my hand in his. "What do you remember?"

I sighed deeply and drew my knees up under my chin. "I was coming into the kitchen to get ready to cook and I don't remember anything after that."

"Your mother called you and it upset you. Do you remember that?"

I shivered at the mention of her. I didn't remember or I didn't want to. Either way, my answer was no.

"Where's my brother?"

"In the shower. He didn't leave your side until I got here."

Lucidity registered as I gradually began to recall conversations and events. "You were in Minnesota, weren't you? How did you get here?"

Sam chuckled. "By plane."

"On Christmas Day? It must have cost you a fortune. Why are you here?"

"It didn't cost me anything. And I'm here because Dane called me and told me what happened. He was beside himself with worry. I was on the first flight I could get."

I wanted to cry again because I'd unintentionally terrified my brother and because Sam had come back for *me*. It was too much.

"You did that for me? You flew here for me?"

He reached out and touched my face again. "Yes, baby. And I'd do it again if I had to. A thousand more times if you needed me to."

I couldn't help the tear that escaped from the corner of my eye. Sam brushed it away with the pad of his thumb and I bit my lower lip. My head was swimming with unanswered questions and a deluge of emotions.

"B-but what does it mean?" I stuttered.

He held both my cheeks in his hands. "Don't you know by now, Sloane? I'm in love with you."

Before I could respond, he pulled my face to his and his lips sealed mine. I melted instantly as his warmth seeped into me. His lips were supple beneath mine and I surrendered completely to him. He tasted me, shaped and molded my lips to his and I moaned with the sweet exquisiteness of his taste and smell. His tongue frolicked with mine, teased and toyed with it until I thought I would die from the blissful agony of my love for him. I heard a deep rumble in his chest which only fueled my burgeoning desire for him. My insides liquefied as his hands held my face to his and then travelled up and down my back in a mesmerizing rhythm. We were a fury of tangled tongues and lips, a beautiful dance with its own rhythm and sway. When he finally pulled away, I was left off balance, breathless, and desperate for more.

I knew my cheeks were a scorching cerise and I stared down at my knotted fingers. I was overwhelmed—by his blistering hot kiss and his declaration of love. I couldn't believe it was happening to me. We'd left things so definitively over.

"Are you sure you love me? Because a few weeks ago…"

He cut me off. "A few weeks ago I was an idiot and I'll never make that mistake again. I knew I loved you the moment you stepped into my office, probably even before that."

I was steadily growing giddy with excitement. "But you told me you didn't want to see me anymore. That it wouldn't work between us."

"I know. That was the idiot talking. I tried to put some distance between us, tried to convince myself it was best for you and me not to be involved. I really believed it was the right thing. But as soon as Dane called me and told me you were in trouble, I couldn't get here fast enough. The thought of you being scared did something to me, unnerved me."

"I don't know what happened. I guess hearing my mother on the phone made me snap." I tried to explain but I didn't have the answers.

"Has that happened before?"

"Not that I remember."

He grabbed my forearms and gently pulled me up with him as he stood. He sat me down on the couch and settled in next to me, never relaxing his hold on me.

"Your mother is an obvious trigger for you. Like at Dane's art showcase when you saw the picture he painted of her."

"Can we not analyze my behavior now? Not today," I pleaded weakly.

He leaned down and kissed my nose. "Of course. I'm sorry. You've been through enough today. You must be hungry. Let me fix you something to eat."

I grabbed his arm to still him. "Wait. Please. I can't believe you're here. Just sit with me for a minute."

He grinned and my heart took flight. I snuggled underneath the

179

crook of his arm and he rested his chin on the top of my head. We sat there in silence staring at the lit Christmas tree. The previous hours blurred into oblivion. Sam erased my pains. I was in total contentment resting in his embrace, listening to the steady thump of his heart beneath my ear. He squeezed me closer and I dissolved into him, making us one.

I heard the bathroom door close behind us and Dane emerged with damp curls wearing a T-shirt and jeans. He came around the couch and saw me and his face twitched with concealed emotion. I saw the gleam of tears in his eyes and I pushed to my feet, wrapping him tightly in my arms.

"I was scared for you," he admitted quietly against my neck.

"I know. I'm sorry I scared you. I didn't mean to."

He pulled me tighter and then took a step back to look me over. "Are you okay?"

"I think so."

"You didn't talk for like nine hours. I was scared shitless. I didn't know if I should call an ambulance or Dad or what."

I glanced over my shoulder at Sam and then back at Dane. "You did the right thing."

Sam rose to his feet. "I'm going to fix us all some food. I think we need it."

His subtle departure gave Dane the opportunity he was waiting on to grill me further and in private.

"Don't be mad I called Sam. I didn't know what else to do," he begged and the pain in his green eyes broke my heart.

"I'm not mad. I swear."

"He was the only one I could think of to call. I thought he could help."

I reached up to put my hands on his shoulders and made him look at me. "You did the right thing by calling Sam. He brought me back from wherever I was."

Dane's face fell and I was in physical pain from how much hurt I knew I'd caused him.

"I couldn't reach you," he said brokenly. "I tried for hours and you wouldn't respond to me. I was sitting right beside you and it was like I wasn't even there."

"I'm sorry."

"I don't want an apology. I want to know what the hell is going on and I want you to get some help—professional help. I'm sick of both of us pretending nothing is wrong—that it's normal. It's not and we both know it."

My brother had never taken that tone with me before. I'd scared him and I'd hurt him and I would have rather died than do either. But sitting in a therapist's office regaling the horrific tales of my youth to a stranger didn't appeal to me in the slightest. I wasn't strong enough to do it. And more importantly, I didn't want to. I heard him release a sigh and I looked up at him.

"You know I'm not trying to come down hard on you. If anybody gets how fucked up all this is, it's me. But I feel you slipping away from me little by little and I can't take it anymore. I feel like I'm losing you."

His confession and very real fears gave me pause. It broke my heart to know I couldn't protect him from the one thing that was hurting him. Me. But I knew I couldn't do what he was asking. I wasn't ready. I thought I'd been ready to talk to Sam but part of me thought that was because *it was Sam*. I would've done anything to be near him.

"You're not losing me," I argued shakily. "I'm right here."

"But you're not. Part of you is you and the other part is completely unpredictable. I don't know what's going to set you off or when or how bad it's going to be. But this time was bad, Slo. Really bad."

His assessment of me immediately made me think of Reid. I'd thought nearly the same thing about his erratic behavior and now I was being thrown into the same class of crazy. Was I losing my mind?

"You're right and I know you're right. Something's gotta give and I know it. I just can't deal with anything else right now. At least not today."

"I'm not taking any more of your excuses. If I have to throw you over my shoulder and drag you to see someone I will."

I stuck my chin out. "No need for threats. I'll deal with it. I promise."

"Not good enough."

"It'll have to be for now."

"Hey, I've got some food on the counter if anyone's interested," Sam called loudly from the kitchen with the obvious intention of thwarting a full on argument between my brother and me.

I narrowed my eyes at Dane letting him know I was done with this conversation and strolled into the kitchen. I knew I had no right to storm off stomping my feet and having a bad attitude. I'd put Dane through the ringer today and he didn't deserve it. He'd been right by my side in the darkest days of my youth and again today, when I'd tumbled into another black hole. He was there for me in ways no one else had ever been. I sucked on my bottom lip, turned back around, and headed over to him.

"Dane, I love you. So much so that I probably need yet another shrink to assess my very unnatural bond to you. I'm sorry I hurt you and I'm sorry I worried you today."

"I think the worst part was"—he hesitated—"that you couldn't hear me. No matter how hard I tried to reach you, you just sat there in a daze. I thought if anybody could pull you out of it, it'd be me. But I couldn't."

This had to be one of the worst Christmases of my life. My heart had been shredded to pieces today. I didn't know what else to say.

"I can't explain what happened. I can't explain any of it. But one thing I do know is that you have always been there for me. I depend on you and trust you more than anyone else in my life. I will always come back to you. Always."

I saw his chest rise with a deep breath. "How pathetic am I? I'm jealous I couldn't bring my sister out of her catatonic state but her crush could? I need more therapy than I thought."

I laughed at him and it felt good. "We're both severely twisted."

"Understatement."

"I *will* figure out what's wrong with me," I promised again, this time with more resolve.

"And I'll be there every step of the way."

He linked his arm through mine and winked at me. I didn't know, couldn't predict when, wasn't even sure how, but I knew I would be okay. My brother would see to it. I was as sure of that as I was of my complete and utter devotion to him. I'd be okay.

"What time is it?" I asked Sam, well after we'd finished eating and Dane had retired to bed.

He pressed a button on his watch and the face lit up. "11:54. Are you tired?"

I sighed and nuzzled closer to him. His arm wrapped around my back and his fingers moved lazily up and down my forearm.

"Exhausted."

"Do you want to go to bed?"

"No. If I go to bed you'll leave."

He cast me that infamous half smile and ran his fingers through my hair. "I'm not going anywhere. I'll stay the night if you want. On the couch, of course."

"Of course."

"Do you want me to stay?" he asked.

"And never leave again."

"I don't plan on it."

The promise that lingered in his statement filled me with hope. "You said you loved me. I didn't dream that, right?"

His chest reverberated with a chuckle. "No. I said it and I meant it. I love you very much."

I would never tire of hearing that. "Then what does that mean for us? I mean, where do you want to go from here?"

"I want you in my life in whatever way you're comfortable with."

I'd hoped, prayed I'd be living in this very moment, hearing him declare those very words. And here we were, here *I* was lost in his gaze and held in his arms.

"I wanted this all along. It's all I've wanted."

"I'm glad to hear you say it."

I yawned tiredly and tightened my arms around him. I didn't realize just how much the day's events had taxed me. But I was hesitant to leave him. I was scared he'd disappear like a mirage. I glanced up at him through my lashes when I heard him laugh.

As if he'd read my thoughts, he said, "I'll be right here when you wake up. I'm not leaving. I promise."

He put his index finger under my chin and tipped my face up to meet his. I felt his lips brush against mine in an achingly sweet kiss that was too brief and left me wanting more.

"I'm sorry if I ruined Christmas with your family."

"You didn't. I'm right where I want to be. And there's still two minutes until Christmas is officially over."

I smiled softly. "Merry Christmas, Sam."

"Merry Christmas."

He pulled me to him and his lips smothered mine in an ardent kiss. A jolt of electricity charged through me, stirring my senses and sending a shock wave to my system. His mouth slanted back and forth across mine hungrily. I sensed how much he wanted me, how much he was fighting to maintain control. I was battling the same thirst for him. I wanted all of him, wanted his hands all over me. He deepened the kiss and I released a soft, satisfied moan. He cradled my head against his mouth, his tongue licked and savored mine in a riotous, choreographed performance. I felt everything below my waistline clench with need and I reached out to tug on the soft locks of hair at his nape. I was left with a deep sense of loss when Sam abruptly ended our kiss and I stared at him confusingly.

"I've wanted to kiss you for a long time and now that we're together, I have to be very careful not to lose control with you," Sam explained breathlessly.

I was aching with need. "This is the whole abstinence thing, right?"

He nodded. "We have to be very careful."

"Whatever you say, professor. But I can't make any promises."

Reluctantly, I stood, retrieving a pillow and blanket from the hall closet for him. I tossed the pillow down and Sam stretched his long frame down the length of the couch. I covered him with a blanket and leaned down to press a kiss to his mouth.

"Thank you for coming today. For saving me," I whispered.

He leaned up and pecked me. "I didn't save you."

I turned off the lamp over his head. "You have no idea, Sam. You rescued me today—saved me from myself."

"I'd do anything for you."

I smiled down at him. "I love you," I whispered achingly with my heart in my throat. I'd never uttered those words to any man except my dad and Dane and the admission made me feel vulnerable and overly emotional.

He curved his hand around the back of my neck and pulled me down to kiss me again. "I love you, Sloane. Sleep well."

I scampered off to my room and climbed into bed. My head barely hit the pillow before I was fast asleep, dreaming of Sam and his heavenly kisses.

CHAPTER NINETEEN

I woke up feeling extremely groggy and drained, like I'd been run over by a Mack truck. As soon as my eyes popped opened I began to remember yesterday's harrowing episode. I remembered hearing Vicky's voice and how it'd sent me over the edge. I could almost hear the casual conversation between us—as if we'd spoken every day like normal mothers and daughters. My mother was completely delusional and I briefly wondered what Dane had said to her after I'd dropped the phone. It'd been nearly five years since I'd last spoken to her and I was praying it would be another fifty more. I had nothing left to say to her—nothing left to feel or give.

I rolled over and pulled the covers over my head. Then, suddenly I remembered seeing Sam knelt beside me, his face ashen and troubled. I heard his baritone voice softly calling my name and declaring his love for me. It was the single most wonderful and most horrible day of my life. But Sam's acknowledgment of love far eclipsed whatever damage my mother had caused. His love restored everything else, balanced the bad with good. I'd heard his voice and come out of darkness, my hidden places. I came back for him.

What if he'd been a dream? Something I imagined? I wanted him so badly I could have made him materialize, could have made him real and tangible. The thought that he might not have really expressed his love for me depressed me so much, I scrambled out of bed and tiptoed into the living room to see for myself. The house was still quiet and I noticed it was only seven o'clock. I leaned over the couch and let out a relieved sigh as I stared at Sam's beautiful face, so still and peaceful in sleep. I didn't imagine it. He *was* there and he *did* love me.

I reached down to pull the blanket up over his chest. His muscular forearm was draped over his forehead, shielding his eyes from the light of the sun that was beginning to emerge and shine through the living room windows. I could've stood there and watched him for hours but I was still incredibly worn-out, emotionally bruised, and not quite ready to face the day. I opted to return to my bedroom and try and get some more sleep.

After a shower and clean clothes I was beginning to feel more like myself. I made an attempt to look presentable and brushed on some mascara and shoved a black headband on. My eyes still looked tired and dark circles were forming in shadowed patches underneath them. I patted on some concealer, dabbed on pink lip gloss, then stood back and groaned at my look. My mental state was even taking a toll on my appearance. I didn't look like myself. I looked like I'd aged ten years overnight. My youth and innocence were gone long ago but at least I'd never *looked* like it before. And now, in one swift move, one ill-fated conversation later, I had become someone else. No amount of makeup could conceal the lines of pain that creased my forehead or return the light that had gone from my eyes. My mother really had taken everything from me.

I heard laughing coming from the living room and it shook me from my daydream. I tugged my gray cowl-necked sweater down over my hips and walked into the living room. Dane and Sam were sitting on the couch watching a college football game and the sight of them together warmed my heart. There was a playfulness about their interaction that seemed so natural and easy. Watching them, I was racked with guilt as I remembered how my behavior yesterday had scared them both so—enough to make Sam fly back from Minnesota and be by my side. Although I was grateful to him and the end result was that he and I were finally together, it didn't take away from the realization that he'd been concerned enough about me to fly home. How bad off was I and what state was I in when he found me? Had I been completely withdrawn and unresponsive? Had I said things I shouldn't have? Another wave of embarrassment washed over me. I would have to find a way to move past it—now. What was done was done and I couldn't go back and undo it. I was comforted only by the fact that the two of them loved me and I knew they wouldn't turn their back on me. I needed them both. I could at least admit that much.

I sat down on the arm of the couch next to Sam and just the nearness of him made my breath catch. He looked up at me with those eyes and I leaned down to press an affectionate kiss to his lips.

"Good morning," he breathed against my mouth.

"Good morning."

"This is so weird," Dane murmured, rising to his feet.

I laughed and Sam pulled me into his lap lovingly. "Get over yourself."

"You need to go grocery shopping," Dane called from the kitchen as he opened and closed the refrigerator door.

I wrapped my arm around Sam's neck, inhaling the scent of his hair, his skin. I would never get enough of this.

"I have food," I hollered back as Sam's hand moved to my thigh. I linked my fingers through his.

"Not anything I want," he retorted back. "I'm going to run to the store and pick up a few things."

I rolled my eyes and Sam gave my leg a squeeze. "I'll go with him. It'll give me a chance to get to know him a little better personally instead of professionally."

The fact he even wanted to do that, understood how important Dane was to me, moved me. I bit my lower lip to keep from bursting into a silly grin.

"Are you going to be okay here by yourself? We'll only be gone for a bit."

"I'm fine. You don't have to worry about me." Even I recognized how moronic that sounded considering everything that had transpired over the past fourteen hours. Who would ever trust me again?

He winked, grabbing my hand to kiss my knuckles. "If only that were true."

I begrudgingly stood, instantly missing the feel of him beneath me. He and Dane grabbed their coats and headed out. I stooped down to straighten the cushions on the couch and then headed to the kitchen to start on the dishes from last night. I was in the midst of pouring dishwashing liquid in the sink, needing to keep my mind busy and distracted from thoughts of my mother, when the doorbell rang. I jogged over to the door and flung it open.

"What did you forget?" I asked in a rush but was startled to find a young woman standing on my doorstep.

She took a cautious step back and then blinked wildly at me, as if she'd made a mistake by knocking on the wrong door.

"Can I help you?" I asked hesitantly.

"Are you Sloane?"

I tilted my head and narrowed my eyes at her. She was a tall, dark-haired girl with crystal blue eyes. She was quite pretty. Her red, cable knit sweater contrasted sharply against her fair skin and she had a small mole right under her nose. I saw her lips quiver with cold and trepidation and I almost asked her inside but thought better of it.

"Yes. Who are you?"

"I'm Jillian. I believe you know Reid Blackmore?"

The mention of Reid instantly turned my stomach to knots and I nodded warily.

"I thought so. I found your address in his wallet a few months ago and I wondered who you were. I came to warn you."

"Warn me about what?"

"Can I come in and talk to you?"

"No."

Jillian shuffled side to side in her black boots. "Okay, then. I used to date Reid, probably right before you. We were really happy in the beginning but after we broke up, he started acting really strangely. He called constantly for a while and then he started showing up in the same places I was. It freaked me out."

Her story sounded true. It was the same behavior I'd encountered.

"What happened?" I questioned nervously.

"I confronted him one day and of course he denied everything. He's clever, really clever. No one believed me. No one thinks he's capable of doing anything like this."

"Did he hurt you?"

"No. That's not his game. Reid likes to mess with your head. It's like gas lighting. After a while you start to think you're going crazy and you can't prove he's done anything."

That made sense to me on all sorts of levels. "Did you tell the police?"

"Of course. But like I said, it's very hard to prove he's done anything at all. All I had was my word against his."

"Did the police ever talk to him?"

"Sure. And they let him walk right out of the station. They've got nothing to hold him."

I rubbed my hands up and down my arms in a futile attempt to keep warm. This conversation was sending chills right through me.

"Is he still stalking you?"

She glanced over her shoulder as if Reid were standing behind her. "I don't think so. But I can never say for sure. Sometimes I feel like he's still watching me, waiting for me around every corner. I haven't been myself since all this started happening. I feel helpless. I thought if he was doing this to me he might try and do it to some other girl. So I took a chance and came here."

I didn't know whether to be grateful or angry. Jillian had come to warn me of what Reid was capable of but she'd also made me more suspicious and anxious. I didn't know whether to thank her or slam the door in her face.

"I a-appreciate you coming." I stumbled over my words awkwardly.

The corners of her mouth turned up in a soft smile. "We girls have to stick together. I don't know if it'll do any good but I thought you at least deserved to know. Be careful."

I was tired of hearing that—Officer Danby, Tucker, Officer Russell, and now Jillian. "You, too."

I closed the door and leaned my back against it. I was so tired, so extremely tired of the emotions constantly raging through me. I could feel myself getting bogged down in a barrage of feelings—the endless burden of conflicting emotions that were suffocating and paralyzing me. I was desperate for an escape—an escape from Reid, from my mother, from memories and hurts and transgressions and pain. It was impossible to do that when literally behind every door there was someone or something reminding me of the things that haunted me. I felt suppressed, crushed by things I couldn't extricate from—a sticky cobweb of entangled deceits and travails. I was being buried alive by my past and my present.

I didn't know what else to do as far as Reid was concerned. I'd gone to the police and practically moved in with Tucker. And then there was the emotional quagmire that was my mother. I knew I had to get control of my life but I didn't know where to start or if it would even help. I was torn between knowing I needed to make a change and being terrified of doing it. Would I really come out better on the other side or would I break under the weight of my sins and splinter into a million pieces forever? Maybe there was no repairing me. Maybe this was my fate. I'd learned to cope this far and create a good life for myself. If I just stayed away from certain topics I could function as a normal adult. But Reid needed to be handled. *That* I knew for sure.

Suddenly, it was more clear than ever before that I was going to have to take matters into my own hands. I would have to put a stop to Reid. I couldn't leave it to the police department to protect me. Without the aid of people *paid* to protect me, I realized how alone I really was. I couldn't bring Sam into this. In his eyes, I was beautiful and special and I couldn't ruin that. Plus, I was almost positive a complicated head case like myself would be a complete turn-off to him. And if he knew about Reid's recent behavior, he'd run for the hills and who'd blame him? Sam saw me the way I wanted him to—the way I'd presented myself to him. Maybe in part it was a lie. I wasn't sure. But it was working for me for now. Sam had fallen in love with me and in order to be with him, I had to be rid of Reid.

I couldn't tell Dane what I was going to do either because he'd try and stop me. But I needed to figure out my next move. The idea of owning a gun sickened me. That heavy, cold metal in my hands, the ear-deafening sound of a bullet leaving its chamber and tearing through flesh made my skin prickle. Although messy, a knife would do the trick. Silent, precise, deadly. I'd have to get close enough to Reid to use it, but if I managed to get my nerves under control, I knew I could. I didn't want to kill him. I only wanted to send a clear message that I wasn't to be underestimated. I was not his victim or anyone else's. If no one would help me, I would help myself.

In a brief twinge of maniacal poetic justice, I walked into the kitchen and grabbed the same butcher knife Reid had left on my kitchen counter as a threat. A hint of a crude smile tugged on my lips, but I placed the knife back in the block. I didn't want to butcher him, only scare him a bit. The fact that I was even contemplating this scared the shit out of me. But what scared me even more was Reid. It was hard to believe I'd ever dated him for any period of time. I should've seen the signs. Maybe I did. The clinginess, the obsessive behavior, the mood swings. It was all there and I'd chosen not to see it. My behavior was so familiar; I now recognized it so clearly. My willingness to ignore my instincts, to keep trying to make things work, putting on blinders when everything inside me was telling me something was wrong. I enabled his behavior like my father enabled my mother. The difference was, I knew it. It might've taken me six months, but that was a lot less than thirty years.

Still, I didn't want to hurt Reid. But I was terrified he'd get to me first if I didn't act. I had to move quickly before I lost what little nerve I had. Summoning all my courage, I pulled the sharpest knife from the butcher block. I caught my reflection in the metal blade and squeezed my eyes shut against the image. How did I let myself get to this point? With trembling hands, I replaced the knife.

With that decided, I quickly called Officer Russell to let her know about my conversation with Jillian. There wasn't much she could do since I'd been too flustered and absentminded to ask for Jillian's last name or address, but she was thankful that I'd kept her in the know. Every bit of information helped, she'd said. And if Jillian really had filed a report with the police they'd have a record of it. Officer Russell said she'd get back with me as soon as she had anything to report.

"Hey we got some good stuff." Dane burst through the front door holding up two, organic cotton grocery bags.

I shifted my thoughts elsewhere. I'd have to deal with Reid later.

Sam followed in behind him holding another bag and his other hand tucked behind his back. "You miss us?"

"Terribly. I thought you guys were just buying a few things." I joked as they laid the bags down in the kitchen.

"Your brother was hungry when he went in the store so we bought more than we should have."

"I'm growing," Dane jested.

"Yeah, outward. But thanks for stocking my kitchen. Let me fix us all something to eat."

"I'll do it, if you want. I'm a decent chef," Sam offered. "It's the least I can do after everything."

Sam shook his head. "You don't owe us anything."

"He's right," my brother piped up.

"Please let me."

Dane shrugged. "I'm not going to argue with her."

"Me either. I almost forgot." Sam grinned widely as he moved toward me. "I got you an after Christmas present."

My jaw dropped in surprise and delight. "You did?"

Sam took his hand from behind his back and in his palm sat a fluffy, white kitten. It was so small and timid and it licked its paw with its pink, sandpaper tongue. The kitten raised its head and stared at me with curious eyes—one eye was blue and the other green. I was in love.

"I thought he might remind you of me," Sam explained softly and handed me the kitten.

I held him in my hands and he nestled his tiny head against my chest. I petted his soft, downy fur and was instantly taken with his sweet demeanor.

"Thank you. I love him. Where did you get him?"

"A lady outside the grocery store was selling them. They were shivering in the cold and I had to take at least one off her hands. I thought he could keep you company."

"I'll name him Oliver, Ollie for short."

"I like it."

"Thank you," I said again, pushing up on my toes to kiss him. He tasted wonderful. "You babysit Ollie while I start lunch."

"With pleasure." Sam smiled, taking the kitten from me.

I walked to the kitchen and leaned against the kitchen counter, my back toward Sam, while Dane finished unpacking the groceries. I licked my lips nervously.

"What did you say to Mom when she called?" I asked quietly.

He paused for a split second and then took out a bag of fresh peas from the sack. I saw his jaw flex.

"I told her not to fucking call you ever again," he explicated with a forced calm I recognized all too well.

"What did she say?"

"I don't know. I hung up."

"Are you okay? I mean hearing her voice and all?"

UNRAVELED

"I can deal," he said nonchalantly.

"Thank you for doing what I couldn't."

Dane raised his slim shoulders in an indifferent shrug. "She's done enough damage to both of us to last a lifetime. I won't let her do anymore if I can help it."

I abandoned this topic and washed my hands before I started mentally preparing a delicious menu. This was what I needed—normalcy. Cooking, watching TV, laughing, reading, listening to music—these were the things I yearned for; these were the things that would keep me sane. If I just stayed focused on the easy, mundane, everyday routines I would be alright. I was determined to be alright.

CHAPTER TWENTY

Nothing inside of me was prepared for this. I'd waited a couple of days thinking I would change my mind. But the more I thought about Reid, the more I realized what a threat he was to me. If he was willing to follow me around town and break into my home, I could only imagine what else he was capable of. I couldn't wait around and *hope* he'd leave me alone. What would happen when he finally did catch up to me? I would have no peace of mind until I ended this once and for all. I had to tell him to stop. I had to make him listen.

Carefully, I chose what I would wear. I knew the ins and outs of the fashion world like the back of my hand. I knew every trend, every style, and could throw together a kick-ass color palette at a moment's notice. But I didn't know what to wear for stabbing someone. It was a ridiculous notion to even consider. And yet, here I was picking out black jeans and a black turtleneck to stealthily creep to my stalker's place of business. It sounded like a bad crime novel.

I slapped my hand against my forehead. I knew I was being impulsive. Maybe even a bit nonsensical. But when I felt like my back was against the wall, I fought and clawed like an alley cat. Was it ridiculous to try and talk to him? I could very well be putting myself into serious danger. But he claimed to love me once. Maybe he would hear me out. I could no longer recognize if that figurative line was being crossed. If it wasn't, I was dangerously close. I got dressed anyway.

I'd nearly talked myself out of my mission in the seventeen blocks it took to walk to Reid's office. I was a jumble of emotions by the time I circled through the revolving doors and crossed the lobby. I wasn't even sure he'd be there, especially with the Christmas holidays. But he'd said he often worked during holiday breaks so it was worth a shot.

I pulled on the door of his office. I stepped in and casually glanced toward the ceiling. There were no cameras here.

The lobby was empty and I walked past the receptionist's desk and down a corridor. A light was shining from underneath Reid's door and my stomach leapt with a fresh surge of nervous reservations. I turned on my heel, fully prepared to walk out. But my feet wouldn't budge. It was like my psyche was urging me, tempting me to finish the job. I turned again and my feet moved as easily as if they were skating on ice. In a few feet I was at his door. Tucking my hand into my coat sleeve, I turned the knob on his office door as another thought occurred to me. If I didn't kill him, he'd tell the cops I stabbed him and I'd be in a heap of trouble. Maybe I'd *have* to kill him. I'd have to keep him from talking.

I found myself standing in his office before my mental conflict was resolved. I shut the door behind me. I watched Reid glance up from his desk in surprise and then his face hardened, his lips turned up in a scowl.

"What are you doing here?" he bit out.

I hadn't prepared for dialogue. "Are we alone?"

He put his pen down. "Everyone's out until Monday. Why?"

"I want to talk." I felt another twinge of fear. I'd brought a knife to a gun fight. Reid was twice my size. If he wanted to attack me, I wasn't sure I could defend myself. What was I thinking coming here? I'd invited myself into the lion's den.

He leaned back in his chair, regarding me with cool, blue eyes. "You said all you needed to say in the coffee shop. What else is there?"

"I want you to stop following me and mysteriously showing up in places where I happen to be," I blurted out without thinking.

His chair swiveled from side to side. "That's what you came to say? Stop following you? What makes you think I am?"

I clenched my jaw. "Because I saw you walk past my house. And you showed up at the Frenzy opening and at the Spotted Pig."

"So?"

"So, that wasn't coincidence and I know it. If you're angry about our breakup, I'm sorry. I truly am. But it doesn't give you the right to break into my house and try and scare me."

I watched as he stood slowly. I put my hand in my coat pocket, feeling the sturdy handle of the knife. I gripped it tightly. It was only there for protection. *I wasn't going to use it*, I told myself. Unless Reid *made* me use it.

"How did you know I'd left the knife out for you to find?" he snarled.

I felt my knees weaken. "W-who else could it have been?" I stammered. "How did you get in?"

His lips curled into a half smile. "When I stole your purse in October I made a copy of your house key. I thought it would come in handy one day and I was right. I tried to come again, but you'd changed the locks. You're a clever girl, Sloane Maxwell. I didn't think you'd figure that one out."

I swallowed hard. I reported my purse stolen and it had been him all along. I was filled to the brim with unease. "But why? Why are you doing all these things?"

A flash of sincerity crossed his features and for an instant, my grip on the knife relaxed. "I loved you, Sloane. I really did. I was afraid to lose you so I wanted to keep you close. I can admit that. I took our breakup kinda hard. I was acting out—kinda like a spoiled brat."

"Then you'll stop? You'll leave me alone?" I asked hopefully.

Reid sighed heavily. "See, here's the thing. I was prepared to do that until I saw you with that other guy at that restaurant. We'd barely been broken up a week and I see you with someone else already. Do you know how that made me feel?" Before I could reply, he rambled on. "I actually saw you a few minutes before I came to your table. I watched how you were with him. You were looking at him, *really* looking at him. In a way you never looked at me and I didn't like it. So it got me to thinking. Were you seeing this guy while we were dating? Were you in love with him and just buying your time with me? I didn't like the answers I was coming up with."

"I didn't cheat on you. Sam's a friend."

Reid rounded the corner of his desk. "I believe that you didn't cheat on me."

I eased my hold on the knife again. "Then this can be over."

"I wish I could do that. I do. I would've bought the "friend" thing if I hadn't seen you with my own eyes. The way you looked at him was not how friends look at each other. It's the way lovers do. And I'm afraid I can't let that go."

I was beginning to sweat from the heat of my fur-lined coat. "What does that mean?"

"It means I have a real problem knowing you have feelings for someone else so soon after we were together. It makes me feel like what we shared meant nothing to you. Like *I* meant nothing. I don't like the way that feels."

Reid began to advance and I began to lose my nerve. I took a step back.

"That's not true. You know it's not true."

"But I don't know that. And that's a problem for me."

"What are you going to do to me?"

"Do to you?" he repeated disdainfully. "Nothing. It's what you're going to do for me."

I stopped when my back hit the door. Reid was only a foot away from me now. I looked at him—searching for signs of the man I once knew. He wasn't there. No part of him was there.

"What makes you think I would do anything for you?" I spat out in disgust.

"Because I'm not giving you a choice, sweetheart. You're going to take me back."

I let out a nervous, incredulous chuckle. "You're crazy."

"You'll do exactly as I say because you have no choice. To be a little cliché, if I can't have you, no one can."

I opened my mouth to respond, but his hands seized my neck and began to squeeze my windpipe, lodging the words in my throat. I felt the life being taken from me and quickly I began to get lightheaded. With all the strength I could muster, I grabbed the knife securely, reared back, and plunged it into his side with all my might. I felt the knife rip though skin and muscle, tendon and flesh.

Reid gasped and his eyes widened in disbelief. He clutched at his side and I began to cough as air purged from my abdomen and out of my mouth. He pulled the knife from his body and it fell to the floor. He stumbled back and I watched in horror as blood seeped from his wound. It flowed like a slow leak, his crimson blood staining his white shirt like a punctured balloon—slow at first and then expanding with a rush of vibrant color. It was ghastly and I briefly shut my eyes. I opened them in time to see Reid crumble to the floor, his face ashen and pained.

"You little bitch!" he managed to say, the white around his eyes growing red to match his bleeding side.

Tears streamed down my face and I fisted my eyes, smearing his blood across my cheek. I couldn't speak, couldn't move. All I could do was watch as he lay there convulsing on the floor. I stood there emotionless, watching him squirm and writhe like a fish on a hook. He seemed to be sinking in his own pool of blood. I looked on nervously and waited as his breathing became shallow. The only sound in the room was each of his labored breaths, each one softer than the next. He was fighting to take every gasp of air. His head lolled to the side and his eyes closed. Gingerly, I tiptoed next to him, careful not to step in his blood. I checked for a pulse on his neck and his heart beat softly against the tip of my index finger. It was faint but steady. He was unconscious but alive.

I stood there for several more minutes staring at his limp body. Maybe I should've killed him. If he didn't bleed to death on the floor, he'd surely report me to the police once he'd recovered from his injury. Then again, maybe he wouldn't. If he went to the police to report me, he'd have to admit to stalking me. Maybe I'd done enough to get him to leave me alone for good.

I was shaking but forced myself to gather my wits. I grabbed a tissue from his desk and wiped my face and then stooped down to pick up the knife. I wiped it off with the tissue and put the knife and the tissue in my coat pocket. I took a look around the room. Nothing had been disturbed. You wouldn't have even been able to tell that a man had just been stabbed here except for Reid's body and the red-staining blood still spilling from his side. There was no trace of me in the room—nothing to link me to this horrendous crime. I thought about turning the light off, but I left things exactly as I'd found them. I opened the door with my sleeve and peeked into the corridor. It was still empty, still quiet. I assumed the cleaning crew would be coming soon so I left his office and exited the building. I stepped into the frosty air and slipped right into the light stream of pedestrian traffic. I blended in with everyone else—looked like everyone else. Except, I had a bloody knife in my pocket and I felt as if, at any moment, I'd shatter like glass on the streets of the city.

By the time I reached home, I was in survival mode. As soon as I was inside, I shed all my clothes and started a fire in the fireplace. When the blaze began to roar, I tossed in my coat with the tissue in the pocket. After it had burned, I put in my jeans and sweater. I didn't see any blood on them, but I didn't want to take any chances that there were any traces of Reid anywhere.

I thought about calling Officer Russell and telling her what I'd done. I wondered if it could truly be considered self-defense since I sought Reid out. I went to *his* office with a knife. I wasn't sure she'd buy it and I'd just destroyed all the evidence making me look all the more guilty. And what if he bled out in his office? He was alive when I left but maybe he'd died. I couldn't risk calling Officer Russell. I could only pray Reid was still alive.

I sat in front of the flames, naked and reeling from what I'd done. But before I could completely break down, I got up and washed my hands and the knife in the kitchen sink. For good measure, I used bleach instead of soap, nearly scrubbing my skin raw. After the bleach bath, I put the knife in the dishwasher and ran it. When the cycle stopped, I'd put the knife back in the butcher block as if nothing had happened.

I went back to the fireplace and sat on the floor in front of it. I was shivering uncontrollably but I was too dazed to move. I knew I needed to shower and put on clothes, but instead I sat. A million things went through my mind at once. But not one of those feelings was guilt. It was the emotion I assumed would be the strongest but I felt—safe. Reid would've choked me to death if I hadn't of stabbed him. He'd nearly done so. From his own mouth came the admittance that he would never let me alone. Being rid of him made me feel free. When I should've been scared out of my mind, I wasn't. In actuality, my biggest fear was if Sam ever found out. Would he still want me if he'd known what I'd done? The fear of losing him was greater than the fear of doing time in prison. So he could never know. No one could ever know. Not even Dane. Although I was sure Dane would understand, I would never burden him with that type of secret. No, this was mine alone to carry.

As I watched the last of my belongings burn to ash, my secrets burned with it. My fear of Reid went up in smoke with the coat I'd stabbed him in. I don't know how long I sat by the fire. But I eventually fell asleep next to the black cinders of deliverance.

CHAPTER TWENTY-ONE

My cab pulled to a stop outside Sam's apartment building two days later. It was our first official date and I was terribly nervous. It should've been the fact that I'd killed a man that made me nervous but it wasn't. Sam had already seen me at my worst on Christmas but I was nervy nonetheless. I wanted our date to go perfectly; somewhere I realized I needed him to think of me as sane and whole, not damaged and broken. I wanted to be everything he needed. He'd said he accepted me flaws and all, but I knew a part of me wanted to prove I was okay—to myself and to him. I was hell bent on being the epitome of mental health and sanity, even if I had to fake it. And I guess I was faking it. Because two days ago I had a blade stuck inside someone's gut and I'd had a perfect night's sleep ever since. I hadn't heard anything about Reid's death on television or online. I hadn't heard anything from anywhere. Maybe his body hadn't been discovered yet. Maybe I was in the clear. I was ready to move on to what else life had to offer. I just had to keep putting one foot in front of the other. Reid was a thing of the past and I was content to let him stay there.

Tucker would be furious if he knew I'd taken a cab alone without written permission from him and an escort. I knew he'd be back later tonight and would probably stop by my house to whisk me away to his place. Little did he know there was no need for that any more. I'd decide later how to explain that to him. In the meantime, I wanted to enjoy every minute with Sam.

K.D. POLK

I stepped outside into the biting wind and looked up at the brown apartment building in Hudson Square. I'd passed this building numerous times before and it was just around the corner from Sam's office in West Village. All this time he'd been living here and I never knew. How many times could we have possibly crossed paths on the street? Fate had a crazy way of bringing people together.

I opened the heavy, black iron door and walked four flights up to his apartment. I took a second to straighten my plum colored sweater and brush off my black leggings. Suddenly, I didn't like what I was wearing. I rolled my eyes at myself and ran a hand through my hair. I'd put some mousse in it to give it body and my brown curls were thick and full. At least I liked my hair. The sweater and leggings would have to do. I knocked on the door and it resonated in the empty hallway.

Sam opened the door almost instantly and smiled at me right before he rushed forward and grabbed me around the waist. He picked me up and held me close and my arms instinctively curled around his neck in a loving embrace. He smelled faintly of aftershave and cologne; his scent was divine. He put me down and then covered my mouth with his in a passionate kiss. My lips melted underneath his, softened and molded to his. His tongue traced the line of my mouth and my lips parted to allow him entry. His tongue caressed mine, teased me with reckless abandon and I surrendered helplessly. I had completely fallen under his magical spell; he'd hexed me, cast a powerful incantation that offered no release—only sweet, thrilling possession. I felt his hands in my hair, holding my face to his. He held me so tightly I couldn't move and I didn't want to. I was pressed against the full length of his hard body and I clutched his muscular biceps to steady myself. His kisses threw off my equilibrium, unsteadied and shook me. All the weeks we'd known each other had led up to this. It was impossible to fight the chemistry between us— I'd known that from the first moment I saw him. And now it all made sense. There'd been an exquisite buildup, an explosion waiting to detonate and the intensity of our passion was beyond anything I'd imagined. My feelings for him radiated from the deepest place within, coursed through my body, and invaded my veins and bones and blood. He was everywhere, buried inside me, in my marrow; I'd become saturated in him. Somehow he'd managed to coexist with me, become a part of my DNA. Sam was in my heart in the most intimate, most intricate of ways.

His lips were still meshed with mine as he pulled me by the lapels of my coat inside his apartment. I stumbled forward, falling into him and he caught me by the waist, drawing me even closer. I moaned softly in pure exaltation, everything inside me clenching and twisting and unraveling. Without thinking, I blindly reached for the button on his jeans and Sam immediately took a step back, his breath labored and quick. I felt my cheeks turn red.

"I'm sorry," he panted. "We can't. I didn't know it was going to be this hard," he mumbled more to himself than to me.

I bit my bottom lip and shifted on my feet, flushed with heat and embarrassment. He probably thought I had absolutely no self-control. Then again, I wasn't sure I did when it came to him. "I want you," I admitted softly. "In a way I've never wanted anyone."

"Believe me, I feel the same about you, but we can't. Not this way and not yet. It has to be the right time."

He took another step backward and I felt like he was breaking away from me. Instantly my body coveted his, needed his, and it ached at the distance between us. "But we love each other. What better time is there?"

"I told you what I believe and you know I want to wait until marriage. I won't break the promise I made. But we'll have to figure out a better way to deal with—" He paused and pointed his finger back and forth in the space between us. "—*this*."

Already I hated this religion thing. He was making it sound like we were two out of control teenagers. We were grown adults. Why couldn't I just be with him the way I wanted?

"What do you propose we do?" I bit out in frustration.

I knew he'd heard the sharp edge in my voice and he stepped closer to me, gently turning me around to ease my coat off my shoulders. "I don't have the answers yet but we'll figure out something. I want you so badly it hurts, Sloane. I don't know why I thought this would be easy."

His statement softened my touchiness toward him. Perhaps it was the tender look of love in his mismatched eyes or the way his voice dropped to a tantalizingly low rumble. He draped my coat over his arm and stepped close to me again. He reached out and touched my cheek, his knuckles lazily brushing across my face.

"I don't want you to ever think I don't want you because I do. In the worst way. I come undone whenever I'm around you. But I don't want to make any mistakes where you're concerned. I want us to do this the right way."

Knowing he wanted me with the same burning intensity I wanted him was enough to cool my frustration. It wasn't personal; it was a decision he'd made for himself and if I was going to be with him, I'd have to honor it. I vowed to try my best to do that.

I was so distracted by the power of Sam's kiss and its hold on me, that I hadn't taken the time to take in my surroundings. His apartment was tiny and empty, with boxes stacked and shoved out of the way, lining the wall. There were three, tall rectangular windows that brightened the space with beams of natural light but unfortunately overlooked the apartment building next door. A fire was lit and crackled to life in the fireplace and although the space was small, it felt homey. No doubt that had everything to do with Sam. He exuded warmth. There were no doors that I could see except the bathroom door and the entire place was open and inviting. The long galley kitchen wasn't more than a kitchenette but it held all the necessities.

There were several blankets tossed on the knotted, pine floor and at least a dozen brightly colored pillows. Candles flickered on the mantle and cast dancing shadows along the wall as the sky became dusky. A picnic basket sat in the center of the blanket beside plates, wine glasses, and silverware. An exposed brick wall separated the living room from what I presumed was the bedroom. I took a peek behind the wall and an air mattress lay on the ground and more boxes were scattered across the floor. I chuckled.

"No bed, huh?"

"I have a bed. You're looking at it. I don't need much. I'm a very simple man."

But the picture hanging on the brick wall facing his bedroom is what made my heart hammer in my chest like a hummingbird. The massive oil painting nearly covered the entire wall. It was the picture of my mother Dane had painted and displayed at his art showcase. I spun around toward Sam.

Incredulously, I asked, "You bought my brother's picture?"

"Yes."

"Why?"

"Because it reminded me of you. It was my way of being able to see you even when you weren't around. Your face is the last thing I see before I go to sleep every night."

My stomach fluttered with the compliment but I trembled looking at my mother's face again, especially so soon after I'd spoken with her.

"Dane said the sale was anonymous and that it sold for fifteen hundred dollars. That was you?" I repeated even though I was looking right at the evidence.

"Yes." He chuckled. "I wanted it so I bought it. And I'd appreciate it if you didn't tell Dane. I don't want him thinking I bought it because he and I are becoming friends or to boost his ego. It's a beautiful piece of art and I appreciate beautiful things. It's the only thing I've purchased to decorate my apartment. I think it suits the place."

I stared at my mother's solemn, serene face and shuddered. I pulled the sleeves of my sweater down and covered my hands distractedly, toying with the cuffs. I felt Sam's breath on the back of my neck and I shuddered again—this time with pleasure.

"Does it bother you to have it hanging here—that I bought it?" he asked me quietly.

"No. I'm glad you like it and it's your prerogative if you want to hang it there."

"But you're going to be spending a lot of time here, I hope, and I don't want you to be uncomfortable in any way. I'll take it down if it bothers you. Just be honest with me."

I appreciated his concern and truthfully, I wasn't completely sure I could deal with seeing my mother's face every time I came over. But the reason he'd bought it moved me and overshadowed my absurd feelings about how I felt about it. *He'd paid an awful lot for it*, I thought absently. I wondered how he had that kind of money on a teacher's salary. I would've thought he'd want to use the money to furnish his apartment. But the fact that he hadn't and instead, spent his hard earned wages supporting my brother and buying things that reminded him of me, made my heart sing.

I turned to face him and looked up into his dazzling eyes. "As long as you're here, I probably won't notice it anyway." I glanced down. "But I have noticed this picnic feast."

He grabbed my hand and led me back to the living room. "I hope you're hungry."

"Famished."

"Good. Have a seat."

I crouched down on the floor and settled myself amongst the mountain of colorful pillows. Sam stooped down over a crate by the windows and thumbed through stacks of records until he eventually selected an album. He removed it gently from its sleeve and placed it on a small, portable turntable.

"How retro," I teased him as the album crackled to life and the jazzy notes of a saxophone begin to fill the room.

"If you can't hear it live, the next best thing is hearing jazz on a record player. I thought we'd start with a little Coltrane and then move on to some Dizzy for your listening pleasure."

"Sounds great."

Sam came and sat across from me, his long legs stretched out the length of the blankets. He opened the picnic basket and retrieved a corkscrew. The smell of delicious, hot food wafted up from the basket and my stomach flipped with hungry anticipation. Sam reached for a bottle of wine resting in a metal tub of ice and unscrewed the cork, pouring us each a glass of red.

"Can I help?" I offered.

"Nope. Just sit back and relax. Tonight is about you."

He handed me a glass and I sipped the full-bodied, dry wine and sighed. I didn't imagine life getting much better than this.

"How have you been the past couple of days?"

And just like that my euphoria dissolved. I didn't want to spend my time with him discussing my mental health issues and subsequent breakdowns. But his next response floored me. Sam was developing an uncanny ability to seemingly read my thoughts.

"I'm not asking as your counselor. I'm asking as someone who loves you. I'm not trying to conduct a therapy session; I just want to know how you are."

I relaxed some. "I've been okay. Hearing from my mother was a shakeup but I'm getting through it. One day at a time; isn't that what they say in AA?" I joked. It was best I didn't mention Reid. Ever.

He carefully placed a grilled chicken breast on my plate, its skin coated with colorful flakes of seasoning. "I'm glad to hear it."

I took a large gulp of wine as he scooped cheesy mashed potatoes onto my plate. "What made you decide to become a Christian?" I ventured curiously.

Sam's hand stilled over my plate and I thought I glimpsed a moment of unease. But then he reached for another spoon and heaped green beans onto my dish next. When he was done serving me, he paused again and leaned back to look at me.

"I think the initial desire to know more about God came from the same place it comes for most people. I wanted to understand the world around me better and I wanted to know that I had a purpose. My faith gives me those answers. It keeps me focused on what's important."

"Did you not feel like you had a purpose before?"

"No. I was lost and wasting my life away on things that didn't matter. I was consumed with guilt over mistakes I'd made and I couldn't get past it. I needed to know there was more for me in this life. That I wasn't here by mistake or happenstance—that I mattered."

I felt my brow crinkle in interest. "And now you have all the answers you sought?"

He smiled at me and I swore I felt my heart convulse.

"No, I'll never have all the answers and I'm okay with that. But I understand why I'm here and what I'm doing in the time I've been given. Every day I have to ask for guidance to make sure I stay on the right course."

"And you talk to God about these things? And He answers you back?"

"Mostly. Sometimes I hear His voice and other times He puts people in my life to confirm something. He also speaks to me when I read the Bible."

I shook my head in disbelief and cut into my chicken. *I wonder what God would think about me. I'd broken one of his most sacred commandments.* "I don't get it. How can you possibly pray to something you can't even see and aren't sure even exists?"

"But I am sure. I know it as sure as I know I'm sitting across from you now. I believe it in the same way you feel the wind on your face but don't see it. I believe it in the same way you know the earth revolves but don't feel its movements. That's what faith is— believing in what you can't see. It's not always easy but it's the foundation of everything. I've built my life on it."

I took a moment to ponder that. "I guess that's easier to understand if you grew up going to church. You were exposed to all that at an early age."

Sam shook his dark head. "I didn't grow up going to church. My parents took us on Easter and maybe for a Christmas service but not regularly enough that it would make a difference. I had to find God on my own. Or better yet, He found me."

"And you really believe in heaven and hell and all that? An afterlife?"

He laughed. "Yes, and all that. There was a void in me I couldn't fill. Nothing I tried worked until I found God. That's why it's so important to me that you and I go about our relationship the right way. I want us to be the best we can be."

"Have you talked to God about us?" I wondered out loud, as I took a long sip of wine.

"The day after I met you I prayed about you because I couldn't get you off my mind and I didn't know why. And then I saw you again in Chelsea and thought there's no way that can be a coincidence in a city this big. He brought you to me."

"Why would He do that?"

"I don't know yet. But I suspect the answer will reveal itself."

I took a bite of creamy mashed potatoes and the cheesy goodness melted in my mouth. I didn't know if I believed all the religion talk but Sam made it sound feasible. I wondered if God had sent me to Sam. And if so, what was the purpose? On the other side of the same coin, why would God allow Dane and me to suffer such torment at the hands of our parents? Parents are supposed to protect and care for their children. I didn't know if I could believe in a God who'd turned His back on me when I needed Him most—let me suffer in such an unspeakable way. If He did exist, I didn't know if I could ever forgive Him for that. It was easier for me to believe He wasn't real than to believe He was and willingly let Dane and I suffer.

I hadn't gone to church a day in my life. My parents never even mentioned God. Maybe if they had, maybe if I'd had something to believe in, it would've made a real difference in my life. Maybe it would've made a difference in theirs, too.

"What are you thinking about?" Sam interrupted as he began to pile food on his own plate.

I crunched down on a green bean thoughtfully. "New Year's," I lied. "Do you have plans?"

He touched my leg and gave it a gentle squeeze. "All my plans from here on out include you. Did you have something in mind?"

I fisted a pillow tightly to keep myself from lunging at him. Almost everything he said and did affected me in some way physically; I could feel my stomach tighten with unreleased sexual tension. I vaguely questioned if I wanted him more because I couldn't have him. *No*, I decided. It was just *him*—magnetic, sexy, beautiful *him*.

"Not really."

"Why don't you let me plan something?"

I grinned. "I'm in your hands. Are you going to fly back out to see your family since I essentially ruined your Christmas?"

"You didn't ruin anything. And no, I'm staying put for a while."

"Not on my account, I hope."

"Completely on your account. But not because of what happened on Christmas—at least not entirely. I don't want to be away from you right now. Those few days I tried I was miserable."

I understood that more than he knew. "Don't do it again," I warned lightly.

"I don't want to. Now that I have you I'm not letting you go."

I raised a playful brow. "You think you have me, professor?"

He challenged me back. "Don't I?"

"In the worst way."

"Good. Finish your food. We still have dessert."

The hours flew by too quickly. Dinner was long over, followed by a deliciously rich chocolate cake, and the fire consisted of nothing more than faintly sizzling embers. But I was wrapped in Sam's arms amidst a hill of pillows and I didn't know if I'd ever felt that level of contentment. There was a peace surrounding him, something I now realized I gravitated toward. He was warmth and safety and love and comfort—everything I'd ever sought after. I nuzzled closer to him at just the thought and inhaled the scent of his shirt—a potent mix of detergent and cologne and him. The feel of me nestling closer to him triggered his arms to automatically constrict around me and I felt him press a kiss to the top of my head. We were so completely in sync—when I moved he moved; our breaths were even and in rhythm, our heartbeats pounding to the same steady beat with its own time signature and measures and notes. We made our own music while the sultry sound of Billie Holliday floated all around us. I knew I had to go; Tuck would be wondering where I was before long. But I didn't want to move. I wanted to fall asleep right there in his arms. Reluctantly, I sat up.

I pouted. "I have to go."

Sam yanked me back down on his chest. "No, you don't."

I laughed at his silliness. "I do. It's getting late."

He hopped to his feet and reached out a hand to me to pull me up. In one swift, fluid move, I was in his arms again, his nose buried in my hair. My arms encircled him, my hands running up and down the taut firmness of his back.

"I'll walk you downstairs and get you a cab," he said, kissing my temple.

As soon as we were outside, I immediately missed my warm nest back inside Sam's place. Nothing could touch me there—not even my mother's somber portrait. His house was a haven to me. He was my safe place. Already I was thinking of the next time I'd see him.

Sam deposited me safely into a cab but not before kissing me with a fervor that made my knees weak and the cab driver grow impatient. I could still taste him as the cabbie drove off—warm, sweet, and delectable. His taste was imprinted on my lips, his smell ingrained in my mind, the feel of his hands branded onto my skin.

A light scattering of snow began to fall and I asked the cabbie to stop three blocks from my house. I wanted to walk in the freshly fallen snow and enjoy the quiet of the night. I knew Tucker would kill me if he saw me, but I loved this time of year and I wanted to be outside in its enchanted wonder.

I pulled the collar of my coat up around my ears and shoved my gloved hands into my pockets. The streets were relatively empty; families visiting for the holidays were still hibernating inside their warm homes taking refuge from the bitter winter cold. As I neared my brownstone, I saw Tucker parked outside leaning against his car. His eyes locked onto mine and his expressionless face turned into a heated glower.

"What the hell are you doing walking around alone?" he shouted while I was still a block away. "I asked you not to go anywhere by yourself until we solved this Reid situation."

How did I tell him I'd already solved it? I jumped into his arms, hugging him close and hoping to cool off his anger toward me. I kissed his cheek.

"How was your Christmas?" I started.

He hugged me briefly and then uncoiled my arms from around his back. "Don't change the subject. Why are you out alone?"

I hesitated only a moment. "I was taking a chance, I guess, and I'm sorry. But I couldn't stand being on house arrest any longer. I'm not going to let Reid dictate my life."

"I know it sucks, Sloane, but it's for your own good." He paused to look at me. "Why do you have that goofy grin on your face?"

I blushed. "I do not."

"You do. Did you just come from seeing Sam?"

I pushed his shoulder. "How did you know?"

"It had to be Sam. You use to look at me the same way."

I rolled my eyes and laughed. "Get over yourself."

"He should've at least made sure you got home safely."

I began to walk up the steps to the front door. "I'm a big girl, Tuck. I can take care of myself. You coming in for some hot chocolate?"

He followed behind me. "Yes. But I'm still mad at you for disobeying. I want you safe. Until we track down Reid, you have to be careful."

My chest rose on a soft heave. "You're right, of course. From now on, I'll watch my back."

Tucker shook his head at me. "What am I going to do with you?"

I bat my eyes at him, hoping to soften his annoyance with me. "Just keep being my friend."

He smiled, his handsome face morphing into the Tucker I know and love. "You don't have to worry about that. You couldn't get rid of me if you tried."

CHAPTER TWENTY-TWO

I convinced Tucker to let me stay in my own place by throwing an impromptu after Christmas party. I decided I needed more distractions in my life to keep me from driving myself insane with the whole Reid situation and a party was just the thing. As much as I tried to forget, Reid was still there. I was no longer afraid—I had no reason to be—but the gravity of what I'd done haunted me. He'd deserved it, I told myself. But there was no escaping the image of his motionless body on the floor. In order not to completely lose it, I threw everything I had into this party. I still had a few more days off from work and I was going to take full advantage of them. When I returned to work, I knew the Winston's account would keep me too busy to breathe for months on end. Work would take my mind off Reid. It had to.

I invited Sam, Dane and Hilary, Jane, Tucker and Stewart to come hang out at the house for dinner and game night. I was too lazy to cook for everyone so I ordered ten pounds of Mexican food instead. My kitchen counter was littered with trays of fajita meat, tortillas, quesadillas, enchiladas, fish tacos, chips and queso, and all the trimmings. Jane and Hilary were making frozen margaritas in the blender while Stewart set up a game of Taboo in the living room. I'd even made a playlist of saucy Latin music and currently Santana's electric guitar strings were strumming with brilliant expertise. I was surrounded by people I cared for—with the exception of Dane. He'd disappeared into my bedroom half an hour ago and I went to hunt him down.

I found him sitting on my bed talking on his cell phone in hushed tones and wondered who he was speaking with so confidentially. As soon as he saw me, he muttered a hasty goodbye and stood to his feet. My sisterly instincts were immediately on high alert.

"You're missing the party," I started suspiciously, my eyes raking over his awkward posture. I could tell he was nervous.

"I was just coming out."

"Who have you been talking to all this time?"

"Dad."

My eyes widened. "Is he alright?"

"He's fine," he answered shortly.

"Then why have you been hiding out in here?"

"I wasn't hiding. I hadn't talked to Dad in a while and I wanted to catch up. I couldn't hear with all the noise in the living room, so I came in here. Did I commit some sort of crime?"

I balked. "No. I was just wondering where you were."

"Well, you found me."

"Why are you being so short? What's up?"

"Nothing's up. I can't make a phone call in private without you asking twenty questions?" he bit at me.

"Whoa. Chill out." I turned to leave but I couldn't let it go—not when it was so obvious he was upset. "Look, I was just asking. What's wrong, Dane? Talk to me. Did he say something to upset you?"

I saw his slender body heave with a deep inhale and his face softened. "I'm sorry. I didn't mean to bite your head off. Sometimes, it's just hard talking to him. He puts all these ideas in my head and I can't shake him."

"Like what?"

"It doesn't matter. We're missing out on your after Christmas fiesta. Let's go."

He opened the bedroom door and the room was immediately flooded with the vibrant sounds of salsa music, making it impossible to continue a conversation. Dane walked out and I followed, loosely questioning what he was keeping from me.

I took a margarita from Jane to help soothe my hurt feelings. Dane and I shared everything—almost everything—and to know he was keeping information from me hurt. We'd always been open with each other—especially when it came to our parents. No one understood our childhood like the two of us. I sipped on my frozen, strawberry flavored drink and let the refreshing coolness pacify my increasingly sour mood.

I saw Tucker approaching me and plastered a smile on my face. I wouldn't let my brother ruin my party.

"So, you're serious about this Sam guy?" He scowled.

I grinned genuinely as I scanned the room for Sam. He was giving Jane an impromptu salsa lesson. His movements were jerky and quick and I laughed to myself.

"I love him." I sighed, the back of my eyes burning with tears.

"It's really over then between me and you?"

I leaned up on my toes and pressed a kiss to his stubbly cheek. "I will always adore you, Tuck. And I'll treasure what we had. You're my best friend. But Sam is everything to me."

He whistled between his teeth. "That's deep. I've never heard you talk about anyone like that."

"I've never felt like this about anyone before. I wasn't even sure it was possible."

"Well, if you're happy, I'm happy. But if he hurts you in any way, I'll kill him."

"He won't," I assured him and I believed it.

I glanced over my shoulder at Stewart who was in the kitchen tossing Jell-O shots in the air and skillfully catching them in his mouth. "You and Stewart are good together. He cares for you; I can tell."

Tuck wagged his head back and forth indecisively. "I think he does. But he'll never compare to you."

"No argument there," I kidded.

"Please go and save your man from making a complete ass of himself." He pointed. "You could've at least fallen for someone with better dance moves."

"I don't love him for his dancing." I scooted off to save Jane's toes from being further harmed by Sam's awkward missteps.

"Can I steal him away?" I asked Jane, sweat beading on her broad forehead.

"He's all yours. I need another drink." She smiled, heading off toward the kitchen.

Sam took my hand and pulled me over to the couch where we

both sank down into the cushions.

"How much of that did you see?" he asked.

I snickered. "All of it."

"Do you still love me?"

"Completely."

"Good to know. Because I can't sing either."

"Then you're in good company."

"This party was a good idea. You having fun?"

I looked around at people talking and laughing and it made me smile. "I really am. But Dane is acting weird."

"How do you mean?"

"I know my brother and he's keeping something from me."

Sam shifted beside me and his eyes narrowed. "Like what?"

"I don't know. He was in my room talking to our dad and he wouldn't tell me what it was about."

"Does he have to tell you about a conversation he had with his own father?"

When he put it like that, it made me sound ridiculous. "It was the *way* he wouldn't tell me. He was acting all dodgy; I know him."

He shrugged. "I wouldn't worry about it. I'm sure it was nothing. What do you say we get this game of Taboo going?"

I nodded. "Let's do it."

Taboo was a hit. Girls versus guys and we were tied two games apiece and each battling for the win. The groups were extremely competitive and the night had been filled with trash talk and fun. I hadn't thought about Reid all night which was the barometer I used to measure the night's success. The fact that he hadn't crossed my mind once made my after Christmas party a definite win.

However, I'd observed Dane and Sam on more than one occasion whispering amongst themselves. I'd tried not to stare but their hushed conversations were so obvious I had a hard time not noticing. I wanted to know what those two had their heads together about and exactly when had they become such good friends? I was glad they were becoming close, in fact there was nothing I wanted more. But their exchange felt secretive and private and it set me on edge. I wasn't sure why, but every hair on my arms stood on end.

Hilary nudged me. "It's your turn."

I picked a game card from the box when there was an abrupt knock at the door.

Dane hopped to his feet. "I'll get it."

My eyes followed him and I felt my pulse throb in my veins when I saw Officer Russell standing in the doorway. Only a sliver of her appeared in the cracked door but I immediately recognized her blue police officer's uniform and I jumped up with Tucker on my heels. Fear seized my heart as I realized I was getting ready to be arrested—and with everyone I loved watching. Either Reid had died or he'd turned me in.

"How can I help you?" Dane asked guardedly.

"I'm sorry to just drop by. I tried to call first but I couldn't reach Miss Maxwell and I was in the area, so I stopped by," Officer Russell explained and then her gaze jerked to mine.

I grabbed a coat from the coatrack and yanked it on. "It's no problem. We'll talk out here."

I tried to close the door, leaving Dane and Tucker in the house but my brother wasn't having it.

"Not even," he said sternly to me, wedging his foot between the door and the frame. "What's this about?"

I gravely realized there was no point in keeping it from him any longer; he certainly wouldn't back down now. And Tucker was already privy to almost everything, so I let them both stand outside beside me on the narrow porch. I may need them for support when my crimes came to light. I closed the door and Officer Russell took a step down, her dark eyes level with mine. She had come alone, I noticed. I expected at least another officer with her to make the arrest.

"Are you sure you wouldn't like to discuss this alone?" Russell asked, squinting at me in that way of hers.

"She's sure," Dane answered for me and I shot him a perturbed look.

"It's okay," I mumbled. Did I really have a choice with the Goof Troop beside me?

"I spoke with Mr. Blackmore," she started.

I blinked at her in confusion. I had no clue what she was talking about. I remained silent, staring at her with curious eyes. When I didn't reply, she carried on.

"He's been on vacation in Mexico and he came back yesterday.

That's the reason he's been out of his office."

I briefly wondered if this was some sort of trick to get me to confess. She was trying to make me believe that she'd spoken to Reid. My best bet was to play along for as long as I could.

"No, he left for disciplinary reasons," I corrected her. "What about the temp? Did you talk to Jessica? She said the prior receptionist filed sexual harassment charges."

Officer Russell swayed back and forth on the heels of her feet, teetering on the edge of the step. "I verified all his travel arrangements. I checked with the airline, the hotel, I even tracked down the taxi driver he rode with from his apartment to the airport. It all checked out. And…" She paused. "There was no temp."

I leaned forward because I knew I hadn't heard her correctly. "No temp? I spoke to Jessica, the temporary receptionist at Reid's office. She told me the regular receptionist filed sexual harassment charges. Talk to her again. Maybe she was scared of losing her job and didn't want to say anything to you."

"Miss Maxwell, there was no temp. The receptionist, Sarah, is the same receptionist that's worked for Mr. Blackmore for the past three years and she didn't file any charges against him. There's no record of any allegations. In fact, she was recently named Employee of the Month."

I couldn't believe what I was hearing. I felt like I'd been punched in the gut. I stood there in the freezing cold with my mouth gaping wide in blatant disbelief. If she was playing games, she was playing them to the hilt.

"What about Jillian?" I argued. "She came by my house and told me Reid was stalking her. She was scared. I could see it in her eyes. She said she filed a report. There has to be a record of some sort."

"Except no one saw her but you, right? And I checked the system. There is no record of any Jillian filing a report against Mr. Blackmore."

I closed my mouth, tightening my jaw in frustration. "So what? I'm making the whole thing up? Why would I do that?"

"Mr. Blackmore moved apartments and his new one is located just a few blocks from his old residence. He didn't break his lease; it was time to renew and he chose not to. I spoke with all of the management and no one's ever seen or heard of you before."

"How can that be?" I shouted frantically. "I spoke with Ronald at the front desk! I spoke with Jessica and Jillian! And what about the night Reid followed me home? He threatened me at the Frenzy opening! And what about the butcher knife in my kitchen?"

Officer Russell pulled her hat down over her thinning hair, partially shielding her eyes. "Did anyone else hear him threaten you? And is it possible *you* left the knife out by mistake and don't remember?"

"You did say you weren't sure," Tucker chimed in and I wanted to kick him in the shin.

"I didn't make it up! I know Reid is after me. I saw him walk right past my window! I didn't make it up. Tucker was there the night at Frenzy. He heard him threaten me."

Russell's dark eyes blazed as she turned her attention toward Tucker. "Did you?"

"Not exactly. I knew Sloane was visibly upset about him and she *said* Reid threatened her. But I didn't actually hear him myself," he confessed quietly.

Russell cocked her head to the side and her bony features softened. "Miss Maxwell, I looked into everything you told me thoroughly. I double checked everything. I wanted to make sure I wasn't missing anything before I came and spoke to you. Reid Blackmore was out of town when you were making these claims. It's impossible for him to be in two places at once."

"*Claims?*" I snapped. "I know what I saw and what I heard. I'm not an idiot."

"I don't think you are. But I do think something else is going on. It's not my area of expertise but I think it's something you should see a doctor about. Think about it; nothing you've said about Mr. Blackmore can be proven. Everything you've said happened to you while you were alone. I don't believe there was ever a Jessica or a Jillian or that Mr. Blackmore was ever after you."

A strange relief and an equal amount of worry made me weak in the knees. Did I stab Reid or didn't I? I didn't know how I could've imagined the entire thing, but I was pretty sure Officer Russell wouldn't have taken this so far. If she'd found Reid and spoken to him, that meant I hadn't stabbed him. And if I didn't stab him, what exactly did happen to me that night?

"Are we done here?" I bit out through gritted teeth. Contempt was the only emotion I could give her. I was confused beyond belief, my mind reeling with thoughts I couldn't quiet.

"I know this is not what you expected to hear. But if you ever need anything else," she began.

"I won't."

"Take care of yourself, Miss Maxwell."

Tucker walked Officer Russell to the curb and I turned on my heel furiously. I couldn't believe the incompetence of the NYPD. I guess I'd have to be maimed or dead before they believed me and took Reid's threats against me seriously. If he was alive, that meant he was still after me and I was back where I started. I was swirling in emotions, the dominant feeling now being a growing rage and deep confusion. I couldn't even look at Dane. I knew he was glaring down at me; I could feel the icy shards of green emanating from his eyes.

"Slo," he started with such a tender achiness in his voice that my head popped up in surprise. "Why didn't you tell me Reid was after you?"

I promptly noted he hadn't discounted my reports regarding Reid. "You believe me?" I asked shakily. If he didn't trust me, didn't have faith in me, I knew I'd break in two right there.

Dane pulled me to him roughly and I felt his lanky body tremble with cold. "Of course I do. I'm on your side, Slo. I'm always on your side."

I felt tears prickle the back of my throat as I hugged my brother. He really was my rock.

I sniffed. "You're shivering. Let's go inside."

The living room held an odd quiet, a palpable stillness as the three of us entered the house. Sam was waiting by the door and I gave a quick, reassuring nod and I saw him exhale a sigh of relief.

Almost instantaneously, I was bombarded with polite excuses and words of thanks for hosting a great party as Hilary, Jane, and Stewart grabbed their coats and left. I was embarrassed and angry and I had entirely too much food left over. Even worse than that, I knew I was getting ready to face the firing squad: Sam, Dane, and Tucker. I sat down on the couch and mentally prepared for the attack.

"What were the police doing here?" Sam started as soon as the front door was shut.

I couldn't even bring myself to start the conversation and I was grateful for Tuck's intercession on my behalf.

"After Reid and Sloane broke up he started exhibiting some strange behavior. We thought he was stalking her."

"He was. He is," I said, feeling defensive, but even I wasn't sure any more.

"He popped up in a couple of places where she happened to be and then we had a hard time tracking him down so we went to the cops. Officer Russell stopped by to give us an update."

"I can't believe you didn't tell me this," Sam exclaimed crossly. "Was that the guy in the restaurant?"

I nodded. "I wanted to keep you out of it—you and Dane. I was trying to handle it on my own. I didn't want either of you to worry."

"So you told Tucker instead?" Dane probed delicately.

"He was there when I found the butcher knife in the kitchen. He was as suspicious of Reid as I was."

"Butcher knife?" Sam spat out, his hazel eye turning dark brown to match his other eye.

I was going to have to start at the beginning.

When I was done reliving and retelling every detail from the past few weeks, (conveniently leaving out the stabbing),I was again met with a deadly silence. All eyes were on me—scrutinizing me, raking over me, doubting me. I felt the familiar slide into darkness, that welcoming obscurity that didn't allow anything else to exist. I was shaken from it abruptly when Sam and Tucker stood to leave. Feeling a swirl of uncertainty inside my chest, I looked up at them.

"I think it'd be better if we left," Tuck said, reaching for his coat and scarf.

Dane rose to his feet. "I agree."

Sam crouched down at my feet, his amazing eyes blazing up at me. But they were so filled with concern it masked the usual light that shone there, concealed the hope that helped keep me sane. He took my hand in his.

"I'll check in on you tomorrow?"

I nodded. I couldn't trust my voice not to reveal my disappointment and hurt. He was looking at me as if I were a tiny, wounded creature that needed to be coddled and managed. As if I were a fragile, breakable thing. I wasn't that. I would never be that.

"I love you," he said, placing a chaste kiss on my forehead.

"Me too."

"Whatever comes, we'll get through it together. I promise you that."

The door shut and it was just me and my brother. I heard him in the kitchen fiddling around and then the clinking of glasses. He joined me on the couch with two shots of tequila and handed me one.

"I thought we could use something stronger than margaritas."

I drank my shot in a single gulp, the fiery liquid burning the lining of my throat and stomach. I felt its warmth travel down into my belly and begin to numb my humiliation.

"I didn't want to say this while everyone was here."

Oh boy. I felt my stomach twist into knots. "What?"

"I think you know. Your behavior over the past few weeks is very familiar to me—to both of us and you know why."

He was waiting for me to say it—for me to admit it out loud. I wasn't going to do it. I wasn't *capable* of doing it.

"Slo?"

"Go to hell," I whispered angrily as hot tears began to stream down my cheeks.

"If you won't say it, I will. You show the same symptoms Mom showed in the beginning. I think you're schizophrenic like her, Sloane, and we have to deal with it."

And there it was. He'd said it. The word schizophrenia circled around the room, bounced off the walls, permeated the air until it choked me.

"I'm nothing like her," I breathed, my lungs tight with emotion.

"But you will be if we don't get you some help. I know you see the signs."

The thought that I was anything like her made me sick deep down in the core of me. My brother was wrong. She was a madwoman; she was crazy and selfish and uncontrollable. I was nothing like her and I resented him saying so.

"I know it's not what you want to hear but we have to face facts. Your breakdown in Florida, my art show, Christmas. Now your paranoia over this Reid thing. You can't deny any longer something's really wrong. I want to help you fix it, Slo. I'm with you every step of the way. Whatever you need. All of us are—Sam, Dad, Tucker…"

I'd stopped listening. I bit down hard on the inside of my cheek until I felt the soft tissue began to loosen. I wasn't anything like her and I refused to believe I ever would be. Sure, I'd had some frightening moments where I let my past sneak in and wreak havoc for a bit, but I'd come out of it. I was a survivor. There was no way I was going to turn into the raving lunatic my mother was. She was an unholy mess and I was… I was just me. I was mixed up at times, confused, maybe even a little paranoid, but I wasn't my mother and I definitely wasn't a schizophrenic. I was lucky to function semi-normally at all considering the hand life had dealt me. I was so much stronger than anyone gave me credit for. Why couldn't anyone see that?

To add to the pain, I now realized Dane didn't really believe what I'd told him about Reid and his doubt crippled me. He'd lied in order to pacify me, appease me.

Dane's voice began to sound muted in my ears and the blackness began to tiptoe in, surrounding and consoling me. This time I invited it in, welcomed it with open arms.

CHAPTER TWENTY-THREE

Sam met me on the curb when my cab slid to a stop in front of his apartment building. It was New Year's Eve—the night when the promise of a new, more promising year was on the horizon. It was just what I needed. I needed to hit the reset button, needed a fresh perspective and a clean slate. New Year's Eve held all these things for me, held a new future and a new outcome, an opportunity for second chances. I was more determined than ever to carve out a fresh, unmarred path for myself—one that didn't include painful recollections or talk of my mother. I'd made a vow to myself to forget the things of my past and focus only on my future. At the stroke of midnight I would leave this old life behind—the sufferings and offences and lies would be far behind me—buried forever. I'd told my brother that very thing. I'd promised him my disturbed adolescence was behind me and I'd never frighten him or myself ever again. He believed me—he wanted to. My healing was as much for me as it was for him. Things were going to be okay for me and him. The new year was the new beginning of it all.

I had too much to be thankful for to let my shaky past jeopardize my future. I had a fantastic job, great friends, and a handsome man I loved. I was especially reminded of this last fact when Sam grabbed me in his arms and kissed me madly in the street, effectively quieting my inner monologue and stifling any lingering fears or anxieties. I was so easily lost in him.

"I didn't think you'd ever get here," he breathed against my lips.

"Traffic is a nightmare. It took me forty-five minutes to get a cab."

He grinned, rubbing his nose across mine. "I'm glad you're here now."

"Me too."

The party had already started in the city and it was only nine-thirty. Car horns blared and people shouted in the street, lively and full of alcohol. Music could be heard from all directions and the sidewalk was crowded with people wearing plastic bead necklaces, party hats, and blowing noisemakers. The energy was contagious. Strangers greeted one another with a friendly smile and a cheerful "Happy New Year." The promise of good things to come seemed to be felt by everyone and it made me giddy for what the future held. Snuggled safely under Sam's arm I was already feeling like the new year had begun for me. I was optimistic and bright.

Sam and I hadn't discussed Reid any further or my meltdown at Christmas. I think we were both content to let sleeping dogs lie. I knew I was. A part of me was grateful Reid was alive. The guilt of being a murderess was too much—even for me. But the fact that he was still out there was unsettling. I didn't know how to solve the problem and I was tired of thinking about it. Tonight, just for tonight, I wanted to forget.

Sam and I went inside the gate and when we bypassed Sam's floor, I glanced at him quizzically. He laughed at my expression and gave me a wink.

"It's a surprise."

I followed him another five floors up and then through a door that read "Roof Access Only." When Sam threw open the heavy metal door I was stunned into silence as my eyes took in the view. Strands of clear light bulbs were tethered and crisscrossed in the air above our heads lighting the night sky. A large, stone fire pit, easily five feet long and three feet deep, roared in the center of the patio, its hot, blazing flames seemingly moving to the rhythm in the street. Wicker chairs and tables were dotted around the large rooftop and a daybed, with turquoise colored pillows and two large blankets, sat next to the fire. A bottle of champagne, chilling in an ice bucket, sat on a metal stand and on the ledge of the fire pit, a bamboo tray held a tall thermos and two mugs, bowls of assorted fruits and cheeses, and ingredients for s'mores.

"What's the thermos for?" I asked, a delighted smile aching my cheeks.

"It's hot water to make hot chocolate in case you get too cold. There are marshmallows, too. Do you like it?"

I looked out over the rooftop wall at the twinkling lights of the city in the distance and I couldn't think of a place I'd rather be.

I exhaled in awe. "It's incredible." The cityscape took my breath away. So did Sam's thoughtfulness and kindness and love for me.

"I wasn't sold on this place until the landlord showed me this rooftop patio. Then I knew I had to move in. In August, when it was warm, I'd come up here and just sit. I'd spend hours reading or thinking or praying. When spring comes, we'll have a barbeque and invite everyone over."

The thought of being with him in the spring or the fall or the next winter made me tingle all over. This man was in my life for the foreseeable future and he was making it very clear he wanted me as much as I wanted him. I'd hit the jackpot and I'd done nothing to deserve him—nothing to deserve his love. We'd met under the most unusual of circumstances, he'd seen some of the darkest parts of me, and yet he loved me anyway. But there were still more secrets I held. Would he love me even then? Would he love me knowing the deepest, blackest parts of my life? I didn't want to know. I suddenly realized a part of me was terrified of losing him. I was scared to death my past would destroy us—destroy the one thing I wanted most in the world. I'd already avowed to bury my secrets. Now I was more determined than ever to do so. Sam could never know my truths. My relationship hinged on it and I wouldn't risk what I had with him for anything.

I felt his arms encircle my waist from behind and his chin rested on top of my head. I placed my hands on his; the heat of his body thawed me from the inside out.

"Does the idea of being with me a year from now scare you?"

I turned in his arms and lifted my eyes to his. "On the contrary. I can't think of anything I'd like more."

I felt that familiar crackle of electricity spark between us. I watched Sam lean in close to me and then hesitate. I could feel him fighting me. He chewed on his lower lip in frustration.

"You have no idea how hard it is to resist you," he breathed against my cheek.

"Oh, I think I do."

"It's a fight every day. A fight I am slowly losing," he confessed softly.

I leaned back in his arms and caressed his smooth face. "Even with everything you've learned about me you still want me?"

"Baby, I don't think I've learned half of everything I need to know about you. But there's nothing you could ever say or do that would change the way I feel. Don't you know how much I love you?"

His lips touched mine before I could answer and any response I had evaporated like mist. His kiss transported me somewhere else—a place where anything was possible. I seemed to be floating—every molecule in my body quaked and vibrated and came alive. His mouth slanted across mine, his lips achingly soft and gentle. I pushed up on my toes and pressed myself against him, feeling the rock solid length of him pushing back against me. His hands tangled in my hair and his sweet kiss turned insistent and frenetic. It was a spine-tingling juxtaposition of tender reverence and dark desire. I heard a low groan in his chest as his tongue twisted around mine, thrashed and savored me. I saw fireworks before my eyes—mini explosions with each move of his heated lips. I melted into him—I no longer knew where he ended and I began. My stomach clenched tightly and I felt a dampness between my thighs—evidence of my arousal and unquenched desire for him. He awakened everything inside of me; every nerve ending tingled and popped and sizzled. I was on fire. Very quickly, I had on too many clothes and my forehead was perspiring with pent up sexual frustration. I was overheated. Sam's body heat and the intensity of his kiss was literally making me sweat with yearning. But I couldn't stop. I didn't want to stop. My hands were on the nape of his neck tugging at the dark, silken threads of hair. His mouth continued to ravish mine until I felt my lips gently bruise from his passionate, wild kiss. It was all I could do to not rip his clothes off. He must have sensed the same longing because he broke away from me abruptly, his eyes dark as they searched my face, his hands twisted in my hair. Breathlessly, I gazed at him. He'd taken the words from my mouth.

"Like I was saying," he panted, "it's becoming increasingly difficult to be strong around you."

"Let's make some hot chocolate," I managed to say, my voice

barely above a whisper. I needed a breather, too. The inferno churning inside of me needed a desperate cooling down.

"Good idea."

Sam went to the fire pit and poured steaming water into two mugs and then added a packet of hot chocolate to each. He stuck two marshmallows on an uncoiled hanger and handed it to me. I sat on the ledge of the pit and stuck the fluffy marshmallows into the fire. The heat from the flames did nothing to cool down my body temperature, but fortunately the crisp air did. I watched the fire begin to melt the white, pillowy marshmallows, their edges turning brown then black. I removed them from the fire and Sam was waiting with a square of chocolate and a graham cracker. He slid off a marshmallow with the cracker and set it on a plate and then slid off the other one.

My mouth watered as the chocolate began to melt and drip down onto the plate. "Chocolate is the perfect way to bring in the new year."

"I couldn't agree more."

"I feel on top of the world up here. Like nothing can touch us."

"Nothing can. At least not tonight."

"What do you mean at least not tonight?"

He handed me a mug. "I just meant tonight will be perfect. Tomorrow we have to return to the real world. Back to jobs and families and commitments."

"Not for you. You still have like three weeks off from work, professor."

"A good deal of that will be spent gearing up for the new semester."

I sipped my hot chocolate slowly. "I should come visit you in class one day. I'll be the naughty TA," I teased, licking my lips at the thought of a little dirty role play.

"How do you expect me to teach a class knowing you're sitting five feet behind me? I'd never make it through the lesson."

To know I affected him in such a powerful way made my toes curl. He'd captivated me in much the same way.

"I'd still like to see you in action. I loved English Lit when I was in school."

"Really? What did you enjoy reading the most?"

"Shakespeare. Hands down."

"Why?"

"The language is so beautiful. The sonnets he wrote are poetic perfection. I don't know of another writer who could turn a phrase like him and make the words come alive the way Will did. His works are true examples of exquisite literature."

"Will?" He laughed. "Like you know him?"

I shrugged and reached for my s'more. "We go way back."

"I wasn't aware you had a personal relationship with the great William Shakespeare."

"Live and learn, buddy. I've read almost everything he's ever written."

I bit into my s'more and moaned in pleasure as the crunchy, gooey dessert fell apart in my mouth.

"Good?"

I sighed. "Divine."

"Why didn't you tell me about Reid?" he asked abruptly.

I nearly choked on my s'more. I thought he'd let that go. Obviously not. "Where did that come from?"

"I was taken completely by surprise when that officer showed up at your house and I didn't particularly care for the feeling. Why didn't you tell me about him? That you thought you were in danger?"

"When did I have the time to tell you? We'd just gotten together and the holidays were a whirlwind for both of us. Besides, I didn't want you to worry and I was dealing with it."

"Sloane, if you and I are going to work as a couple, we have to be honest with each other. We can't keep secrets. Especially ones that endanger you."

"But I was never really in any danger, was I? According to everyone, I was making the whole thing up."

"I don't believe you were."

I cocked my head to the side. "You don't? Even though there's absolutely no hard evidence to corroborate *anything* I've said?"

"Even so."

"Why?"

"Because I choose to believe you. And I know *you* believe it."

I didn't know how to take his last remark. Did he really believe me or did he only believe that *I* believed it?

"I haven't seen or heard from him since Officer Russell stopped by so maybe he got scared and decided to leave me alone," I fibbed.

Did I see him or didn't I?

"I hope so. But you do understand what I mean about keeping secrets from me, right? We can't have that in our future. I don't need to be protected. I can handle anything as long as you're up front about it."

Future. The one I so desperately wanted with him. Everything else in my life was over and done with. I could delve into my life with Sam unencumbered and free to love him wholly. And I did.

"I understand, professor."

"So, before we ring in the new year, is there anything else you want to tell me?"

I got the sinking suspicion he was hunting for something specific—waiting for me to say or admit to something. Fat chance in hell.

"No," I lied.

Sam and I laid on the daybed together next to the fire pit, cuddled underneath two heavy blankets, warm and content. We talked and laughed and made a futile attempt to count stars through the haze of city lights. It was nice just being next to him, although my wanton body craved more—needed more. His chest pressed up against my back and his hand rested on my hip as we spooned and kissed and joked and planned a life together. It was heavenly. I almost forgot we weren't the only ones in the world until I heard the blare of a siren or a shout from nine stories below. Every ounce of me belonged to him. I could be like this with him forever.

I linked my fingers through his and stared down at our hands intertwined as one. I raised his hand to my lips and pressed a kiss to his knuckles. I heard his breath catch and I smiled inwardly; the simplest touch from me unsteadied him. He unknotted his fingers from mine and glanced at his watch before he sat up brusquely.

"We have to go," he announced and effortlessly hopped over me to the champagne bucket.

I sat up startled and glanced down at my own watch. "It's 11:50. Where are we going to go?"

I heard the cork pop and fizz spurted over the top of Sam's hands as he filled two champagne flutes with the bubbly, amber liquid.

"We're having an early toast," he explained, handing me a glass. He sat back down beside me.

"Cheers to the rest of our lives together," he toasted affectionately.

My heart was in my throat and tears threatened to overflow. There was a mysticism glinting in his colorful eyes that held me captive in my seat. His feelings for me were so evident—his expressive face beautifully conveyed everything he felt. Before, when I was getting to know him, he was impossible to read. And now the vulnerability he displayed—the strength it took *to be* vulnerable—overwhelmed me.

I sniffled, trying hard to stifle the sobs in my throat. "Cheers."

We sipped the pear flavored champagne and the bubbles tickled my nose. I laughed at myself and Sam cast me one of his infamous, lazy half grins.

"Come on. Bring your glass with you," he said, grabbing my hand and tugging me toward the roof door.

"Can we come back up here tonight?"

"If you'd like. But I have to take care of something first."

I obediently followed behind him. I'd go anywhere with him—to the moon and back. I was nearly out of breath at the pace he was dragging me downstairs and by the time we reached his apartment and stepped in, I was winded.

"What's the rush?" I huffed.

Sam flipped on the lights and glanced at his watch again. "11:55."

"So?"

He took another sip of his champagne and then took both of our glasses and set them down on the mantle. "I want to show you something."

He grabbed my hand again and we rounded the corner of the brick room divider into his bedroom. Woodchips littered the bare floors and the room was heavily scented of maple wood. Crumpled sandpaper lay in abandoned sheets on the ground and there, in the center of the room, was a bed frame carved of vanilla colored maple. The headboard was wide and skillfully etched with delicate scrolls that started from the middle and flowed outward. In the center of the headboard, between the scrolls, was carved the letter S and another S intertwined within it until the two letters together formed a heart. It was so beautiful, so elegant, and I glanced up at Sam in bewilderment.

"It's 11:58," he started. "Before this year ends and a new one begins, I wanted you to know how much I love you and how thankful I am that you're in my life. I had no idea loving you could feel like this. You're more than I ever could have prayed for. I built this bed for two. And it's one I hope we can share together."

I felt my heart begin to pound madly in my chest and my eyes shimmered with tears. Sam clasped my face in his hands—those hands that I loved so. Those hands that had built us a bed. His eyes bore into mine, riveting me to the spot.

"Marry me, Sloane."

THE END

MORE BY THIS AUTHOR

COMING SOON

The Candle Wick Series Book 2: Untangled

Independent, but troubled, Sloane Maxwell is back—ready to confront her hurtful past and a new relationship head on. But before her budding relationship with Sam Brody has a chance to blossom, an unexpected turn of events keeps them separated for months. When they're finally reunited, will Sloane be able to forgive Sam's betrayal and move past the hurt caused by the ones she loves? Will she even get the chance for happiness before her buried secrets are unearthed and puts everyone she knows at risk?

Join Sloane and Sam as their journey to rediscover love, trust, and forgiveness continues.

UNRAVELED

Thank you for
your support, Vicki!
I hope you enjoy.

K.S. Polk